Catch

Toni Kenyon

Published by:
Apeople Publishing

ISBN 978-0-9922518-1-9

First published in ebook

ISBN 978-0-9922518-0-2

Learn about other works by Toni Kenyon at www.tonikenyon.com

Catch is a work of fiction. Names, characters, places, and incidents are the products of the author's imagination or are used fictitiously. Any resemblance to actual events, locales, or persons, living or dead, is entirely coincidental.

A Personal Message from Toni Kenyon:

I love writing books! But even more than that I love hearing from my readers. If you've enjoyed this book, or any other of my books, please take a moment to email me and introduce yourself - I always respond personally to my readers.

I would also love you to join my book club so you receive notifications about future books, updates and contests. I promise you won't be inundated!

Please visit http://www.tonikenyon.com/contact and introduce yourself so I can personally thank you for trying my books.

Romance from Toni Kenyon - a fresh look at the world

For Mum

- I know Dad would have been proud of us both

CHAPTER ONE

"I wouldn't give a damn if she was the Virgin-bloody-Mary. I told you I wasn't available and yet you put her through." Matthew Solomon's voice echoed ominously through the marble foyer of Harding & Kilpatrick, Barristers & Solicitors.

"Poor man. Do you think he's having a bad day?" Tamsen Parsons spoke directly to the Golden Comet held captive in the small plastic bag in her hand and about to be introduced to the display aquarium she tended. She was beginning to have second thoughts about leaving one of her babies in this volatile environment. No wonder she struggled with the mortality rate here. Fish were sensitive creatures: if things didn't rapidly improve, she'd have to consider removing the aquarium, regardless of the cost to her and her business.

Tamsen's closest friend, Gina the recipient of his verbal barrage looked ready to burst into tears. "I'm really sorry, Matthew, but I was distracted and I-"

"There's no excuse, Gina, it's been happening too often. You're just going to have to get your mind back on the job - I won't stand for this kind of unprofessional behavior. Do you understand?"

Mr Wonderful-but-grumpy - who now stalked his way back down the hallway toward the rear of the building - did, Tamsen had to admit, have one tidy backside despite attempts to camouflage it in an Armani suit.

She turned her attention back to the Comet captured in his carrier bag. "Hey, baby, calm down." Her voice was gentle and soothing, while the poor frightened fish continued to try and find a way out through the clear plastic. Tamsen lowered its wriggling form into the aquarium that had pride of place in the firm's reception area.

Gina sidled up, having escaped the confines of the ostentatious reception desk. "You don't think you could whisper sweet nothings into that bastard's ear so he'd get off my case, do you?" Her tone was terse.

"Unruffle those fine feathers, sister. His other half probably just didn't give him one this morning and he's taking it out on all and sundry."

Gina giggled. "Tams, there isn't another half and I think it disturbs him his bits just don't appeal to me."

Tamsen smiled at her friend. "So he makes Orlando Bloom look like the boy next door and he's got a body to die for. The man is spiritually bereft. Ghandi, he is not."

Gina laughed again. "Are you sure you can't spend more time here? Calling in once a fortnight to check your babies over just isn't enough."

Tamsen turned her attention back to the aquarium. "Sorry, sweetness and light. The babies only need to see me twice a month for a pep-talk and if the rest of the bods you work with are as charming as your friend back there - " she cast a hand in the direction Matthew had disappeared " - I'd die a thousand deaths if I came more often."

She took another worried look at her charges who were nosing around their new tank-mate in the plastic bag. "Actually, I'm wondering if that might be why I'm losing so many of my babies here."

They were interrupted by the shrill ringing of a phone.

"Ah, filthy commerce calling" Gina scurried back behind the marble façade that served as a desk.

"Better not let anyone else through or your friend-"

"He's not my friend. He's my boss."

"Well, your boss will string you up by the beautiful pearls that adorn your throat."

"You attend to your fish, girlfriend, and leave the corporate heavyweights to me."

Tamsen set to untying the plastic bag and scooping a good amount of the water from the aquarium into her newcomer's transparent environment. "There you go," she whispered. "Trauma reduction's my specialty. Don't want you dying of shock in the first hour or so, now do we?"

"If I were a fish would I get that kind of TLC?" Matt asked.

Tamsen looked up and found herself gazing straight into a pair of intense brown eyes. They were so dark she struggled with where the pupil ended and the iris began. She felt her stomach plummet, her hands became slick with sweat and she could barely think for a head full of cotton wool.

"I...I'm sorry?" she stuttered.

"The fish. I was wondering if you whispered sweet nothings into all their ears?"

"Well..." Her brain had gone on strike.

The man before her reeked of elegance. She noted fine features almost to the point of beauty, but in a masculine and testosterone-loaded manner. She could even find it in her heart to forgive him for his lousy outburst at Gina. In that moment she probably could forgive him for anything.

"I suppose you're going to tell me that fish don't have ears, hmm?" He laughed quietly at his own joke. His laugh like liquid velvet running down her body, a perfect match for his lilting speech.

"Well, technically fish don't have ears, but they do react to sound." She pointed at one of the Comets, a globular orange-and-black cutie with bulbous eyes that hung like two small orange grapes from the side of its head. "You see the thin line that runs along the side from the head to the tail?"

Matt studied the fish. "Looks a bit like a shift in the scales?"

"That's it. It measures vibration."

"So I couldn't sneak up on them then?"

Tamsen poured another scoop of water into the Comet's bag. "No. In fact, they get to know the rhythmical footsteps of the person who feeds them."

There was no automatic feeder on this aquarium; it encouraged a member of the staff to feed the fish every day, building a valuable emotional bond between the weaving fish and the staff on site. It was also a great way to start the day.

"I wondered why they rush up to the glass when I walk out here."

"You feed them?" She was astounded.

Matt whispered. "At night. When no one's looking." He threw her a grin, so disarming she let go of the plastic bag and her new charge escaped into the aquarium. "Promise you won't tell anyone - it'd ruin my reputation.

Office ogre and all."

"Er, no. Not at all. You can trust me."

"I thought I could. I haven't seen you around here before. I'm Matthew Solomon."

He offered his hand. Tamsen's were wet and she searched frantically for something to dry them on. Nothing appeared like magic, so she hurried to wipe her hand on her jeans before proffering it. His felt strong and warm and he shook hers with authority and command.

He smiled again, exposing perfect white teeth and a certain twinkle in those dark eyes. Another chill ran across her body.

"No, I'm new. I took over the business a month or so ago, so this is only the third - or is it the fourth? - time I've been here."

"Great, so we'll be seeing a lot more of you then. Hopefully you can keep a few more of our tank friends here - " he waved at the aquarium " - alive, yes?"

Tamsen felt a moment of irritation. "The army have tanks, we have display aquariums."

"Forgive me." Could that be a tinge of red on his cheeks, she wondered?

Unsure of what to say, she continued busying herself with aquarium maintenance and hoped Mr Phantom-fish-lover would go away.

He remained. Watching her work.

Tamsen wasn't usually concerned about being watched. She visited a number of sites and there would always be someone on the staff lurking, either making snide remarks about the Goldfish Girl or asking her inane questions about fish. Almost everyone needed to share a childhood story about their favorite fish who died and the irreparable damage they suffered when parents replaced the offending fish with an impostor. The stories were part of the job she'd grown to love.

She'd actually prefer it if he would tell her some story. But he continued to just stand there. Tamsen could sense him - or could she smell him? She didn't want to turn around, or further acknowledge his presence. She just wanted him to go away.

The escalating tension seemed unbearable. All her nerve endings were strained and her body felt as if it were on alert for him, for any movement. The small reflection on the far side of the aquarium wasn't enough to confirm whether he still stood behind her. Torn between acknowledging his presence by turning around and asking him what he wanted, or pretending he wasn't there, Tamsen opted for continuing to feel stalked.

Routine maintenance complete, the sense of uneasiness that had crept up on her like the resident fish sneaking up on their new companion began to ease.

The little Comet seemed happy, and a small area where the weed had been eaten away by the other fish had been replanted. With nothing left to do, she'd have to turn around and ignore the fact he might have been standing there just watching her, or try and pretend he didn't exist - a ridiculous notion, since they'd struck up a conversation.

As she stepped down from the ladder that allowed her access to the top of the aquarium, she took in her own reflection wondering what he might be thinking. Did he see a crimson-haired woman, struggling to keep unruly curls pulled back in a business-like fashion, the odd tendril making a dash for escape around her almond shaped eyes? Or nothing more than a young, inexperienced girl?

Allowing herself to dream a moment, Tamsen saw a Wiccan woman wearing earthy, vibrant, lacy layers who wouldn't be moved on her opinions, a fatalist weaving around on impossibly high heels. Not a girl in jeans and sporting a work shirt.

He had been there and now he came closer. No more time to wonder what he might be thinking; getting lost in her own thoughts sometimes wasn't a good idea.

"I'd like to discuss the current contract with you. Is there any chance we could do it over a cup of coffee sometime?"

Turning to face him, a familiar feeling came over her, a sense of mystery that caused a small rush of adrenaline. "I don't see why not."

Where was this going? Not in the habit of accepting invitations for coffee from men who made her feel this uneasy, albeit an exciting type of unease, she couldn't be sure if this was good or bad. Save for something. Something she didn't quite understand pushing her to give this man a chance. Having learned a long time ago to ignore these kinds of feelings at her peril, she let her soul have its say.

He looked quite delighted. His eyes lit up and a small smile erupted on his face. Tamsen decided that she quite liked the way his face changed when he smiled.

"Great." He shuffled around in his pants pocket and took out his wallet. "Here's my card. It's got all my numbers on it. But what say we head to the coffee bar downstairs now? You look like you've finished here and I could help you with all your bits and pieces."

Oh, he could help her with her bits and pieces all right. Mentally slapping herself, Tamsen dragged her thoughts back from the depths, where they were swimming with bottom-dwelling catfish. He was offering a cup of coffee and already she had mentally stripped him and was damn near trying him for size.

"Actually there are a couple of things I have to do first." She was loath to let the invitation slide and that amused her. "But how about I meet you downstairs in, say, half an hour?"

He looked at his watch; she couldn't help noticing it was Gucci.

"Sounds fine, I'll see you then." With that, he turned on his heels and she was left gaping like one of her fish.

Gina rushed over. "Have you just made a date or something with that jerk?"

Tamsen was still stunned. "Yes, it appears I have. But it's just business."

"*Business*!" Gina looked furious.

"I know." Tamsen's voice sounded dreamy. Her eyes drifted from Gina to follow him up the corridor, his rhythmic movement adding to his allure.

"Tammy. Look at me." Gina's abrupt tone brought Tamsen back to the here and now.

"Sorry, what were you saying?"

"I was saying, you saw him being the anti-Christ not less than twenty minutes ago. So what's up?"

"Don't know. It just felt right." Tamsen shrugged. As far as she was concerned, the spirits knew something she and Gina did not and she wouldn't risk crossing them. "Look, Gina, don't sweat the small stuff."

"You can leave the clichés out of this conversation. He's heavy-duty shit and you just don't want to go there."

Tamsen packed the last of her equipment back into the small carrycase she'd brought with her and cast an eye around quickly to make sure nothing had been overlooked. "Relax, it's a just cup of coffee. How much trouble can I get into?"

Gina cocked an eyebrow. "How much do you want?"

"Give me a break. How long is it since I've been anywhere near a man, never mind one as mind-blowingly sexy as..." She fished around for the business card she'd put in her pocket. "Matthew Solomon, Partner, Harding & Kilpatrick, Barristers & Solicitors?" Tamsen giggled. "I mean, how much trouble can a little old anti-Christ be?"

Gina sighed. "I don't think you want to know."

"Maybe it's time I found out." Tamsen turned in the direction of the lifts. "I'll see you at home tonight and fill you in on the whole thing." She blew Gina a kiss and headed out into the lobby.

Matthew was baffled. Not the usual state for a successful corporate lawyer who prided himself on being skilled at logical thinking. He'd spent years being paid well to avoid trouble and confrontation, so why the hell had he just asked that enticing bundle of trouble at the fish tank out for coffee?

Like he didn't have enough women problems. An ex on his back like a limpet. A mother who refused to keep her nose out of his life and constantly demanded progress reports on the chances of her getting grandchildren in the near future. Russell Crowe he wasn't, so why head back into the arena?

Yet something about her had "clicked" and that disturbed him. He'd never followed anything remotely like gut instinct before, but for some reason - one he was unable to explain - he didn't want to override his internal compass on this one.

He seated himself at the large oak desk in his spartanly furnished office. His secretary, Danielle, often complained about the lack of anything personal surrounding him, but it gave him a sense of calm and control.

Casting his eye across the desk, he noticed a new proposal had appeared in his absence. Another franchise agreement for one of his major clients - his area of expertise, but it seemed less exciting these days.

"Danni!" He hated using the internal phone system and insisted on yelling through the office for his secretary, a constant irritation to his partners and the other staff.

Danielle appeared at his door, looking as tempting as ever, a short white miniskirt exposing the length of her long brown legs. Her Spanish descent showed in her deep blue eyes and olive skin, and the thick, jet-black hair that hung to her shoulders. Her looks were one of the reasons he'd hired her: he'd figured if he was going to have to spend eight hours a day with this woman, she might as well be easy on the eye.

"Yes, Matthew?"

"When did this arrive?" He held the offending contract aloft; the sheer weight of the paper was enough to give him carpel syndrome.

"It's been on your desk since this morning. I don't know how you could've missed it. Tim's been on the phone already wanting to know if you've looked it over and when he can come in and discuss it."

Matt sighed heavily. "What's my day look like tomorrow?"

"You've got a conference call booked at 9.30 with Sheldon that is likely to take at least an hour. The rest of the day's free, but Tim was hoping to come in this afternoon."

"There's no urgency and I haven't even looked at the damn thing."

"You want me to tell reception to hold your calls so you can look it over now?"

Matt checked his watch. He was supposed to be meeting Miss Fish in twenty minutes. "No, I'm not getting to it today. Put him off until tomorrow afternoon, and if he complains tell him I've got so much on I've circumnavigated myself and ended back up my own ass."

Danni laughed. "Right. You don't mind if I paraphrase, do you?"

He smiled back. She was a great girl. Pity she was married, and happily at that. "You tell him what you think is appropriate, Danni. You always do."

The coffee bar turned out to be one of those trendy places that were springing up around this part of town. Filled with women who had nothing to do in their day except sip lattés and discuss their husbands' career paths and what private school they were sending their children too. Tamsen felt distinctly underdressed and as if she should be looking for the tradesmen's entrance.

Beginning to regret agreeing to the coffee idea, it felt bad enough sharing a home with the receptionist, but Tamsen wondered if this overstepped some sort of professional boundary agreeing to coffee with a partner. Too late to back out now, she spotted Matthew walking out of the lift lobby. He moved with a sureness and grace that melted her insides. Probably lust, she decided, although it had been so long since she'd found any man remotely attractive her body's response to the sight of him surprised her.

The fact she should find this supposed bundle of trouble enticing worried her no end. What had Gina mentioned about working with a Greek-God-woman-magnet? She must have described this man.

When he spotted her across the busy lobby, a smile lit his features. She half expected to find that somebody he knew was standing behind her.

He covered the distance between them quickly, running the gauntlet of afternoon office workers and a horde of privately schooled kids who were moving in the usual adolescent pack, oblivious to passers-by and cell phones in need of surgical removal from their heads.

"Great, you made it." He smiled again and she had an instant desire to touch the small dimple that appeared on his cheek. "I was concerned you might find some more fish to talk to and stand me up."

"No, the Comet I put in your aquarium was my last live drop for the day, so I'm all yours."

"Sounds promising." He cast her a glance that spoke of potential pleasures to come, throwing her insides into complete turmoil. "So, what'll you have?" His gaze didn't falter and she felt exposed, her mind in a whirl and the urgent need to sit down taking hold, even though they had yet to secure a table.

"Chamomile tea." That should settle her nerves. She reached for her purse.

"No, my treat. You can buy next time."

He was already planning a next time? "Thank you. Why don't we sit outside?" The effect he was having on her, she needed the extra air.

"I hate the traffic fumes. There's a great courtyard out the back, it's reasonably quiet and they've got your sort of people back there."

They headed out through the kitchen into a small-enclosed space while she wondered what sort of people he could mean. It was lush and green; she was struck by the stillness and the complete feeling of harmony. He pulled up a couple of wooden seats for them by a small walled fountain that trickled into a beautiful, clear pool. There were half a dozen goldfish swimming in the pristine water and all became clear. Tamsen couldn't help smiling.

"See, I knew you'd feel at home here."

"It's lovely. How come more people don't sit back here?" "Ah, you know the beautiful people; they dress up to be seen. I'm sure the Celestials and Veiltails here - " he cast his hand toward the pond, "would be happy to see them, but alas, only the staff and I spend much time out here."

She was stunned. He knew goldfish.

She sat back in her seat and looked at him in a new light. "You asked me down here to pick my brains about fish, huh? Most people wouldn't know a Fantail from a Comet, so what was with the dumb blonde imitation back at the office?"

"Well, I wouldn't want just anyone to know I had a soft spot for fish now, would I?"

She giggled. "I presume you must have been the one who got the company to consent to the installation then?"

"Maybe," he said.

"Hey, Matt, here's your double shot to keep you going for the afternoon." A young lanky man who looked no more than seventeen delivered a short black and Tamsen's tea.

"Thanks, Steve."

"No probs." The look he exchanged with Matt spoke of a shared history. "Hope you enjoy the tea as much as the company."

Matt's expressive eyes screamed scram. Steve duly turned on his sandaled heel and headed back into the undergrowth.

"The café owner's son, paying off some repair bills. Got drunk a couple of months ago and nearly wrote off the old man's latest BMW Coupe."

"Ooh, nasty."

"Yeah, he's back to a 10-speed until he pays off the bill and gets his license back."

"Remind me never to have children. Though I don't suppose I'd have to worry about a coupe being smashed up."

He smiled and her stomach did a flip-flop again.

"Come on, there's money in fish, especially if you look at franchising the business."

"Yeah, well..." She took a sip of the tea; it was tart on her tongue, but warming and soothing. "It's early days yet."

"What a good job you met me, because I'm just the man to be steering you in the right direction."

She nearly choked on her next mouthful. The right direction for what, she wondered?

He downed his coffee in one mouthful, put the small white china cup back in the saucer and turned a look on her that could have knocked her off her feet if she hadn't been seated. Was the sparkle in his eyes passion, or just the caffeine hit? She suspected the latter, but secretly hoped for the former.

"So tell me, how do you know the brain-dead bimbo on reception? I saw you two talking."

"She's my best friend. We share an apartment."

He went as pale as the teapot Tamsen had just topped up her tea with.

"If it's any consolation, since the day she started at Harding & Kilpatrick she's been moaning about some arrogant prick she works with. I figure that's you."

"So we're even then?" He was regaining some of his color.

"I suppose you could say that. Though she does want a full report when I get home tonight. Should I give her your regards?"

He loosened the tie around his reddening neck and quickly undid the top button. "For someone who works with living creatures you've got quite a cruel streak."

CHAPTER TWO

Awash in soothing chamomile tea, Tamsen couldn't help studying him over the rim of her cup. He gazed studiously into the pond as the fish frolicked near the surface. Small, dark chest hairs escaping from the open neck of his shirt brought on a flush of lust that made her blush.

"It really is beautiful here." A vain attempt to change the subject and distract herself from mentally undressing him. "Do the kitchen staff use the herbs growing in the garden or are they just for show?"

His body slumped in relief. "What herbs?"

"Those ones over there." A small herb garden had been planted in the corner opposite where they sat. Tamsen presumed, though it seemed some distance from the kitchen door, it had been placed for the best of the sunlight.

"What, the patch of weeds under that privet?"

She couldn't help laughing. "You may know your fish, but you don't know your shrubbery, do you?"

"And you do?"

"I do."

"And how am I to know this?"

"Well, to begin your horticultural lesson, the tree is not privet, it's a bay tree."

"As in the brown dried leaves that come in packets from the supermarket?"

"Absolutely."

Matthew moved his chair backwards, thrust his long legs out in front of him and settled his hands across his solar-plexus - the classic "I'm totally relaxed and am about to interrogate the life out of you" lawyer pose, she thought.

"So, Miss Fish, tell me how you came about this knowledge on weeds?" He cocked his head a little to the left. It doesn't have much to do with goldfish."

Great. This was usually where she told some unsuspecting interested male that she'd been practicing witchcraft for years and they looked for the nearest cross and ran for the hills. "I'm interested in natural healing."

"Weeds. For healing?" He sounded skeptical.

"They're not weeds - well, strictly speaking they are, but those ones over there are really just your usual selection of classic culinary herbs." Her mouth began to run away with her and she was powerless to stem the flow. "Having said that, most people don't realize a lot of culinary herbs can be used medicinally."

"Medicinally?" He cocked an eyebrow at her as if she'd just suggested he lick the back of a frog to cure warts.

"Yes, like the parsley growing under the bay tree. You know what parsley looks like, don't you?"

"Yeah. Real curly and green, but I don't see any over there."

"The plant in the corner, the one with the leaves that look like the tops of celery?"

He nodded.

"That's parsley, Italian parsley, the best one for cooking - it has the best flavor. The other one, the one used for garnish..." She waved her hand in a dismissive fashion. "That's merely a plastic imitation in my view. No culinary qualities whatsoever. I don't even bother growing it."

"A gardener as well. My, my, a woman of many talents."

"I try." She couldn't help holding his gaze.

"Oh, I bet you do." His tone set off alarm bells in her head. "So tell me, Miss Fish, how would you use parsley for healing?"

"It's a diuretic."

He looked puzzled.

"A tonic for the urinary tract. It was historically used for the treatment of kidney stones and fluid retention. Legend has it that sprigs put in the water with ill fish will make them well."

"So it makes you pee heaps?"

"A crude analogy – but yes."

"Maybe you should put some in the tank back at the office. Pardon me, *display aquarium*. Then the fish might not shuffle off their mortal coils quite so quickly."

She giggled. "It might be worth a try."

"So what do you do, just grow it in your garden and put it in tea?"

He was humoring her, she felt certain. "You don't have to pretend to be interested."

Matthew leaned forward in his chair, his gorgeous bulk moving in a fluid motion toward her. "I'm not pretending. I find both you and the subject matter fascinating."

Tamsen cleared her throat. "Well, you could just drink the tea. If your system was balanced and you only needed to nourish your body. It could be argued that most of the food we put into our mouths has some kind of medicinal value, or it should have. The problem we have these days is that we process the life out of our foods and we're basically left with bulk. Next to no vitamins and minerals. If I was going to use parsley medicinally though I'd use the root, which has to be harvested in the autumn of the second year of the plant's life -"

"Whoa there, this is getting complicated."

"It's not really, it's just a matter of knowing what part of the plant you want to use and making sure you collect it at the optimum time, when it's constituents are at their highest and you can benefit most from the minerals and nutrients it's mined from the earth."

"And you have to wait for a quarter moon, have your black cat pass twice across your path and kiss your sister's pet turtle, right?"

She kept a straight face. "Not quite, but you're pretty close to the mark."

He looked mortified. "You don't really believe in all that mumbo-jumbo, do you? I mean, isn't it faster to just visit the doctor and get a pill for what ails you?"

"If that's what you're into, but sometimes I think that's using a sledgehammer to crack a peanut. You know, you can do an awful lot of damage to your body just firing a quick-fix pill into it. Sometimes it can be beneficial to look at the problem holistically and try to treat it that way."

"You're a modern hippy, aren't you?"

"No, I don't think so."

"I'll bet you hug trees and talk to pot plants too."

If only he knew, she thought. How would a solicitor who spent his days knee deep in slices of dead tree cope with an unabashed tree hugger?

"It's been really great talking to you, you know - furthering your herbal education and all - but I've a couple of things that need tidying up this afternoon."

"So you need to get on your way, right?"

"Yes. What part of the contract did you want to go over?" She should have stuck to business instead of getting sidetracked and lecturing him on food and herbs.

"Contract?" He looked confused.

"The reason we came for coffee."

"Oh, right. The contract."

The words hung in the air, like the delicate purple blooms on the heads of the chive plants. She suddenly realized there was nothing to discuss in the contract.

"Look..." He fidgeted with his tie, those chest hairs enticing her again; it took all her self-will to look him in the eyes. "I'd really like to see you again. Is there any chance we could, say, meet here for lunch tomorrow?"

Joy, he wanted to see her. "Yeah, sure." She tried not to sound too enthusiastic even if her soul was somersaulting. "Would one o'clock suit you?"

He smiled. She melted.

"That'd be great," he said. "Come on, I'll walk you at least as far as the lobby."

"I can't believe you've agreed to see him again." Gina's voice rang from the kitchen of their beachside apartment.

"Believe it." Tamsen continued to harvest chives and Italian parsley from the small garden she lovingly tended on the terrace.

One day she was determined to have a proper kitchen garden, twice the size of the one she'd secretly lusted over at Armadillo's this afternoon with Matthew. But first she knew she had to get her aquarium business off the ground; then she'd be able to look at her plans to create her perfect retreat.

"Have you got those herbs yet, or are you still apologizing for our desperate need to eat them?"

"Don't listen to her," Tamsen whispered to the parsley plant. "Thank you for your contribution - it's much appreciated."

Traversing the loft-like room that serviced their immediate living and dining needs and heading for the galley kitchen beyond, Tamsen carried a sense of gratitude for her day.

"Great. Can you chop them up and throw them in the marinara?" Gina, busy draining pasta, spoke through the clouds of steam that billowed out the picture window overlooking the communal courtyard and swimming pool below.

Tamsen tossed the chopped herbs through the seafood sauce. She'd stopped on her way home at the fish market to pick up fresh mussels, shrimps and fish for their Tuesday night feast. It was the only night of the week she and Gina ate together and they always liked to have seafood of some description. It was a ritual they'd enjoyed for almost three years now. Men came and went, but Tuesday night was a commitment to their relationship.

"So, does he know you're a regular Dr Dolittle, talking to the animals and the plants?"

"No, and I'll thank you not to tell him, Miss You-think-you-know-what's-good-for-me."

"I keep telling you I'm good for you." Gina cupped her friend's face, placing a full, tender kiss on her lips. "But you will have your fancy men."

They seated themselves at the ornate wrought-iron table-and-chair set that served as a dining table, a legacy of one of Gina's past passionate flings. For a few months it had looked like it could be serious enough to set up house, but no agreement could be reached on the simple things, such as which dining room suite to acquire, so they'd purchased one each - the beginning of the ugly end.

"Aw, come on, Tams, it's not like you two have got anything in common. I mean, he's a corporate lawyer and you're a free spirit who babysits goldfish for a living."

"It's a viable business opportunity." Tamsen scooped a steaming spoonful of the marinara mix onto her plate.

"Balderdash. We've been through this a thousand times. It might be a viable business opportunity but it's just not you. When will you accept that your dream is building that retreat up north that you've been warbling on about for years and you're only doing this because your mad mother and father insisted that no daughter of theirs is going to be head of some hippy outfit in the sticks?"

"Gina-"

"Don't give me that look. I know they've financed you into fish, but why in hell couldn't you have put a business plan together and gone and found some other backer for the thing you're really passionate about?"

Tamsen sighed. It was utterly useless trying to have a discussion with Gina when she was in this kind of mood. "Is it that time of the month by any chance?"

Gina threw a despairing look at her. "That's always your comeback when you know I've got you on the ropes."

"True." Tamsen smiled sweetly at her friend. At least she'd forgotten about Matthew - that had to be a good sign, she thought.

"But you still haven't answered my question."

Thought too soon. "What question?"

"Why you think there's any good reason you should start seeing Matthew Solomon."

"You're jealous."

"You're a sick woman. He's a prick, I told you. Argumentative, stroppy, pedantic, meticulous, demanding-"

"Stunningly good looking, rich, successful in his field, body to die for, sense of humor, warm nature, articulate, intelligent, thoughtful, director of a number of investment companies that have small holdings all over the city. Did I mention he's as sexy as hell?"

Gina looked appalled. "He told you all this over a coffee? Arrogant bastard."

"No, he told me he likes goldfish."

"Anyone can say that - you're too trusting."

"He knows his species, Gina."

"What about the rest? I've worked with the man for nearly twelve months and I didn't know any of that other stuff."

"Well, maybe you should do some research, dear." Tamsen helped herself to seconds; marinara was one of her favorites.

"Have you been cyber-sleuthing again?"

"Who me, would I?"

"You bloody would. You've got it bad for him, haven't you?"

"Let's just say, I'm simmering."

"Potentially stalking more like."

Tamsen giggled, "Careful, I could always have one of your bosses sue you for libel."

Gina poured herself a glass of iced tea. "Oh, Tam, what have you put in here tonight? It looks like I'm drinking the floral arrangement."

"Just a couple of marigold petals and some heartsease. Don't you love the way the purple and orange set each other off?"

Gina pulled an orange petal off her bottom lip. "I just worry that one of these days I'm going to drop dead as a result of some of the weeds you feed me."

"Trust me, Gina. It's the only thing that keeps your liver going, the amount you drink."

"Hey, steady sister, it's your bad habits we're discussing here. Leave mine out of it."

Tamsen poured herself a glass of tea and realized she'd eaten far too much. "Actually, I don't think he's a bad habit. In fact, he's not even a habit yet. But if you must know I'm meeting him for lunch tomorrow, so it does look promising."

Gina flung her hand across her forehead and swooned dramatically. "I can see my wisdom and experience of dating the worst possible bastards on earth is wasted on you. But at least know that I'll be here to pick up the pieces after he's done the dirty on you."

Matthew's honest attempts at wading through the lease and franchise agreements strewn across his desk seemed fruitless. Strange, he mused, he hadn't been in the mood for a lot of things about the practice lately; it was all rather disturbing and out of character. He'd spent years working his way through the system, from top graduate through wet-behind-the-ears associate to attaining partnership at 31.

Maybe he'd achieved everything too quickly. The firm had taken a gamble on him, but he'd been pretty clear he'd have moved on to greener pastures if they hadn't supplied a sufficient carrot to keep him.

Matthew looked out the seventh-story window. The moon hung in the evening sky though he couldn't remember the sun setting. The remnants of the sushi he grabbed for a quick bite in his office lay amongst the offending paperwork. To make matters worse, he must have walked out to the aquarium in the foyer at least half a dozen times in the last two hours. It drew him like some kind of liquid magnet. Sod it, he thought, he needed to check once again how the newbie was doing - at least that was his excuse to walk away from tedious paperwork.

He made his way down the long corridor. At this late hour he knew he would be the only idiot still in the office, but that wasn't unusual; workaholism ran in the family.

Passing the thin office partitions, he felt the need to scurry. They always reminded him of those awful mazes he built for rats in Psychology One when he'd spent months torturing the poor beasts. Unlock the puzzle pathway for a reward of food. He shuddered.

The aquarium looked beautiful. He marveled at how Tamsen had rearranged it. It wasn't just an aquarium with fish and plants in it; she'd created a complete environment - a moving, magical work of art. The entire structure stood a little taller than him, which must make it quite difficult for a petite woman like Tamsen to manage. He measured in at just under six feet, so he picked her at about five foot four. It hadn't occurred to him before now, but that would have been why she carried a small stepladder with her. A minor miracle she didn't kill herself wearing those lethal heels.

Three panels of clear glass and three panels of black, a tall pentagram, made up the unusual aquarium. Tamsen had filled the structure with long aquatic grasses that swayed gently in the currents from the filter. Fish idled in and around the weed - playing hide and seek, he imagined, with each other. There were nine residents in all, including one unusual black suckerfish that seemed to spend most of its time vacuuming the glass. The tiny bright Comet Tamsen had delivered that afternoon nosed the glass at Matt's nostril level. Every time he came out here to look it had been the same; the pint-sized fish would rush out from wherever he hid to greet him.

"Hey there, little fella." Matt placed his finger against the glass, careful not to tap and scare any of the occupants. "How's your new home? Have you settled in okay?"

He almost imagined the little guy was making an effort to connect with him, frantically wiggling in the water to catch his attention. Matthew ran his fingers through his hair. He must be tired; he really needed to go home to bed - standing here talking to fish. If anyone in the office saw this, he'd be a laughing stock.

A random thought struck him - he wouldn't mind if Tamsen caught him. Matthew exhaled through his teeth. Oh boy, this was all about her; it had nothing to do with the fish. He was trying to find some way to connect with her again and this water vertebrate with gills was the nearest he could get.

Matthew realized he wanted to get to know her, discover what made her laugh. Tamsen was charming and witty and off-center in the most intriguing way. Areas of life he knew nothing about fascinated her, and he wanted her tell him more. She sparked something inside him - something decadent and dangerous and terribly alive.

CHAPTER THREE

Tamsen lay listening to the crashing of the waves on the beach, the symphony of the ocean competing with the orchestral maneuvers of the first birds singing in the dawn. She especially loved the pre-dawn chorus, the birds and waves battling it out for her attention.

Little illumination came from the terrace windows, though a light covering of muslin barely hindering the breaking light of dawn. It was enough, however, to make out the shape of the Victorian bedstead, a gift from her grandmother.

She had, one uneventful Saturday afternoon, voiced a request that Mary Ellen leave it to her in her will and was more than a little surprised when the woman who loved her so unconditionally arranged a week or so later for the entire bedroom suite to be delivered to her apartment. Any attempt to return such a gift given in love would be useless and so she graciously accepted the goods.

Tamsen stretched, overwhelmed by an immense sense of gratitude, lying there in her grandmother's bed, listening to the birds beginning their day and contemplating the start of her own.

How simple their lives were; not for them the worry of where the next worm came from, or where they would find the right building material for their nests. Did sparrows get migraines fretting about whether or not they'd have somewhere safe to sleep at night, she wondered. No, they just opened their eyes and trusted - singing, she imagined, for the pure joy of being alive another day. Knowing all their needs would be taken care of.

This kind of faith Tamsen carried with her often, but some days she found it elusive.

Stretching again and reveling in the feel of the cool cotton sheets on her naked body, she noticed the sensation of slightly rough weave from the top sheet across her nipples. Still present was the faint scent of chamomile oil she'd dripped on the edge of her pillowslip to help her sleep the night before - it always reminded her of Juicy fruit chewing gum.

Tamsen ran her fingernails up the length of her stomach and goose bumps prickled her flesh in their wake. A sudden vision of Matthew came to her; she relaxed and played the mental game of undressing him in the cinema of her mind, fingers exploring intimate parts of her flesh as she surrendered herself.

Tamsen sighed. Nothing so perfect as the fantasy of vicarious lovemaking.

Matthew's day began with an aching sensation in his groin, almost like lover's balls. A ridiculous notion since he'd been nowhere near a woman in months. Angie had seen to that, thank you very much. He'd rather be in an arena with a Rottweiler than take on another woman at the moment - so why had Miss Fish caught his attention?

He opened his eyes gingerly, hoping it was still the middle of the night, but no such luck; the luminous digits on his alarm clock glared 5:45, a full half-hour before the alarm usually woke him. What the hell was going on? He must have had some sort of nightmare.

Matt rolled onto his back and groaned out loud; pain wasn't a welcome visitor at this hour. Trying to ignore the discomfort, he turned his mind to drifting back into unconsciousness for another half hour, then was jolted from his stupor by the sudden vision of Tamsen.

No wonder he'd woken up feeling as if he were trying to sleep on a baseball bat. He must have been having some sort of teenage dirty dream about her. How bizarre.

True, he found her attractive. Matthew snorted - who was he kidding? He hadn't been able to stop thinking about her since coffee yesterday. It was frightening, a little obsessive even, and he didn't like that. Being out of control didn't suit him, especially over a woman – he'd been burned too many times before.

Another attempt to settle back under the covers thwarted, he decided there was little hope of getting any more sleep. With a huge and heavy sigh he threw the crimson duvet cover back from his futon and drove himself to the adjoining bathroom. May as well get the morning ablutions underway, he thought miserably. The day ahead loomed long and large, the only respite another meeting with Miss Fish.

He hated conference calls at the best of times – and old man Sheldon would likely try and drag him through the hoops. Then there was Tim's contract and lease, which he'd spent the better part of last night digesting and now had to go over with him. As usual Tim had managed to persuade Danielle to give him an appointment just before lunch; always a pushover for Tim was his Danni. A lot to do with the fact he often arrived at the office with a box of chocolates under his wing.

Flushing the toilet, Matthew lowered the seat and headed for the shower, then stopped dead in his tracks. In a sudden moment of defiance he returned to the lavatory and lifted the seat back up.

Matthew spoke directly to the seat itself. "Ha, no one here to demand that you be put down now, is there?" The pleasure of victory surged through him, marking his moment of conquest.

Tamsen repeated the mantra to herself, wishing with all her might she could believe the three simple sentences. "We are the greatest thing that will ever happen to us. Believe it. It makes life much easier."

Sitting on the terrace, she took in the sight and sounds of the ocean, the remnants of her carrot, celery and parsley juice hanging like fluorescent porridge on the inside of her glass. The first spoonful of muesli, fruit and yoghurt had scarcely passed her lips when Gina breezed out, black coffee in hand and doughnut hanging out of her mouth.

She removed the offending pasty. "You know that healthy shit's going to be the death of you, don't you?" Gina said.

"Good morning, G. Did you sleep well?" Tamsen chose to ignore the taunt; it was the same every morning.

"Ah, not bad. You know me, couldn't get to sleep but now I don't want to get up - nothing changes."

"Well, you could-"

"Yeah, right." Gina cut her off mid-sentence. "Save your breath for the brethren you'll convert when you get your retreat up and running." She smiled sweetly. "So you still having lunch with His Poxiness then?"

"I know you're just jealous and yes I am."

Gina shoveled the balance of her doughnut into her mouth and sluiced it down with half the coffee. "Don't come running to me heartbroken 'cos he's treating you just like the last poor bitch."

Tamsen could feel the indigestion coming on watching her friend eat. "I won't."

"Gotta go." On the run didn't come close to describing Gina's morning ritual. "Will I see you at lunchtime or is he meeting you somewhere?"

"Meeting me somewhere."

Gina rolled her eyes. "Well, don't say I didn't try to warn you off."

"I won't. Have yourself a great day."

"Yeah. Whatever." And she was gone as fast as she'd arrived.

Finishing the last of her dandelion tea, Tamsen spotted Gina's sunflower yellow VW maneuvering out the secure gates of the apartment complex. On her way to fight the rush-hour traffic into town, clouds of blue cigarette smoke billowing from the driver's window. Tamsen despaired. Her best friend ran on anxiety, adrenaline, coffee and cigarettes, probably the very reason she looked stick-insect thin. "Can never be too thin or too rich," Gina always joked.

Tamsen was neither. She had to constantly reassure herself that it couldn't be much fun making love to a table leg, although a number of Gina's girlfriends didn't seem to have a problem with the concept.

Grateful that working for herself meant she could duck the morning crawl over the harbor bridge into the city, Tamsen picked up her journal and began to write. Something she did every morning, allowing the nonsense that accumulated in her brain a chance to discharge itself onto the page. She could never be sure whether the words would be rants or thanks until pen hit paper. Either way, it was cathartic.

Some mornings she just wrote, 'nothing to write, nothing to write,' until she found her truth point, usually midway down the second page. A point where she was unable to hide from herself any longer. Written truth serum. Who needed drugs?

Matt backed the Audi out of the tea-tree lined driveway, careful to avoid the ponga logs that were blocking half the entrance.

He would have to talk to the gardening contractors, he thought. It was bad enough he couldn't turn the car around by the garage for their bark, topsoil and plant supplies, but having to play dodge-the-log in the driveway was more than he could cope with at this early hour.

Not for the first time this week he was running late and he'd promised to pick Danni up on the way. Throwing the Audi into a right-hand bend, he was nonplussed at meeting banked-up traffic for what seemed like miles into the distance. Anxiety rising in his stomach, he speed-dialed Danni.

"Hey, it's me."

"Morning, boss. You sound as if you're talking from inside a rubbish bin."

He cast his eyes around the inside of the car; she had no clue how close to the truth she was. A valet service wouldn't go amiss, he thought. "The traffic's hellish. Didn't want you to worry I'd forgotten you."

"Not a problem, Matthew. The radio said there'd been some sort of pileup on the motorway. I'll just wait for you at the top of the driveway. You know where Mum's is?"

"Presumably the same place it was the last time I picked you up." Teasing Danni had become an occupational hazard.

"Right. So I'll see you in about five?"

"Hours maybe. It could be faster to walk in, you know. Then you could have a nice long black waiting for me on my desk."

"Ha-de-ha."

This was no way to be starting the day, Matt thought as he disconnected. He needed everything to go smoothly this morning - for some reason he felt riddled with anxiety about lunch with Tamsen.

A sudden surge came in the traffic, brake lights parting like the Red Sea. It seemed a good omen. Saying a quiet thank you to God, Matt sped through the divided vehicles, grateful that for some reason everyone else seemed to be going in a different direction than his own.

Why so many problems with the road today? The weather was beautiful, one of those clear antipodean spring mornings. The sort of morning he used to miss so much when he was working in London.

The big OE hadn't been at all to his liking. Living in close quarters - damn near squatting in damp and dreary concrete apartments - and supposedly having the greatest time. He couldn't get back to good old clean and green Aotearoa fast enough.

Danni waved from the pavement. Pulling the Audi over, Matthew was immediately assailed by an irate motorist's horn blast. Rush-hour traffic turned perfectly sane people into raging lunatics, he decided.

"Moron." Danni slammed the door and rearranged a beige pencil skirt around her shapely legs.

It was going to be one of those days; he alternated between loathing and loving that skirt. It had an impossibly long split up the back, tempting his eyes all day to follow the curve of Danni's legs to areas off limits.

"I see you're in fine spirits this morning."

"Pardon?" Danni looked puzzled.

Matt took a moment to wave thanks to a kind woman for allowing him to rejoin the crawling mass of traffic. "Good morning, Matt, would have been preferable. But if you think I'm a moron..."

"I was talking to the dick in the land cruiser who seemed to think just because he was driving a three-ton truck on a residential road we should all get out of his way."

"Ah, four-wheel-drive issues then?" Matt wasn't fond of them either.

"Something like that. My brain-dead brother-in-law's just bought one. I mean, he lives in Ponsonby, for God's sake. You can hardly swing a cat down those streets."

"Not much call for off-roading either, is there?"

"I suppose parking on the sidewalk doesn't count?"

Matthew laughed. He'd grown to love Danni's quirky sense of humor.

"How's your mum holding up?"

"Not too bad - the doctor says she'll be right as rain in a couple of weeks. It's amazing how quickly she's recovered from a hip op. I thought it'd be months."

"So you'll be back home with Glen before he knows where he is?"

"At the weekend, actually. My seven days are up and my sister, bless her little cotton socks, is coming up from the South Island to have a couple of weeks with Mum, so I'm off the hook."

They turned onto the motorway, the traffic still crawling. "Great, so I've only got another two days of the diversion from hell to deal with."

Danni looked perturbed. "Honestly, Matt, I really can take the bus into work if you want to get in earlier - or later...I mean, I know how much you hate this."

He smiled. "It's not really been a problem, and it's woken me up to how the other half lives. I'd forgotten just how lousy it was trying to get in and out of town at peak times. The privilege," he teased, "of being the boss and able to work a 60-hour week in your own time."

"So who is she then?"

Startled, he asked, "I'm sorry?"

"The woman you're having lunch with?"

"What makes you think I'm having lunch with a woman?" How could she know?

"Your diary."

He hadn't put anyone's name in his diary for lunch. "It just says lunch."

"Exactly." Now Danni sounded smug.

"Why would that make you think I'm having lunch with a woman?"

"It's a man? You're coming out?"

"No, you brat."

"Sorry, sir. Punching the homophobic buttons?"

"Not at all. I've nothing against man on man."

"Just as long as it's not man on you, huh?"

"Correct."

Danni continued her line of investigation. "If it was anyone other than a woman you'd have put a name, not just the word lunch."

Snapped. "You ever thought of changing vocation? I hear private eye jobs pay treble what lowly solicitors pay."

"Wouldn't be as much fun, I'm sure."

"Playing Peeping Tom all day instead of holding my hand? I'm flattered." The traffic began to speed up as they reached the extra lanes on the approach to the city.

"You should be. So, who is she?"

"You don't give up do you?"

"No. I thought you'd been too burned by Angie to go anywhere near another woman."

"So did I."

"So spill. Who is she?"

"Not telling."

Danni's voice took on a playful tone. "Why not?"

"Because gentlemen don't tell."

"And she's someone in the office?"

Technically not, he thought. "No." He felt happy running with that little half-truth; he didn't need any more of his love life doing the rounds at the water-cooler.

Though the hostile beast who manned reception lived with Tamsen and could be a problem. Matthew made a mental note to try to be nicer to Gina in future.

Danni punched him playfully on the arm. "Don't worry, boss, I'll find out who she is - there's not a lot happening in your life I don't know about."

"Isn't that the sorry truth."

A red light made him pull up at the intersection by their building. Danni gathered her purse and unbuckled her seatbelt. "I'll get out here, Matt. It's likely to take you another ten minutes to negotiate your way into your park, and I can have your coffee on your desk and the mail sorted by then."

He smiled at her. "How would I ever cope without you?"

"I'm sure you'd find some demonstrative female to beat you into line. You usually do." With that, she slammed the door on him and was gone.

CHAPTER FOUR

Tamsen stood naked, five assorted outfits littering her bed, and mentally chastised herself. Only lunch. Why the hell had it necessitated a complete search-and-destroy mission in her wardrobe? She'd not been this nervous about what to wear for a very, very long time.

The morning had gone without a hitch and the new set-up at the health club across town had been a breeze. If she hadn't been so nervous about the impending lunch she might have taken her time. Nothing more delicious in life than admiring gorgeous men working out. All that taut muscle, tanned skin and body heat.

Visual delight equals primal lust.

It didn't matter that half the men working out were most likely gay; Tamsen knew gay men took pride in their bodies and their health. Just because she looked didn't mean she needed to touch.

Besides, she was having lunch with one sexy hetero creature who also took pride in his appearance and she looked forward to maybe playing touch soon.

But what to wear? Tan muslin dress with stretch lace sleeves? No, too gypsy. Chanel deep-blue suit? No, she looked like she'd been dressed by her mother. Sparkling cherry halter-neck dress? No - it was lunch, not a club. Beige miniskirt with black off-the-shoulder top? No, she looked too eager. This was getting worse; another four outfits joined the five on the bed. Closing her eyes, Tamsen prayed and decided to wear whatever came out next.

"Thanks, Goddess." She breathed a sigh of relief, pulling out a figure-hugging, forest-green, paisley print dress that finished just above her knee. It had a neckline that didn't mean an eyeful for him all lunchtime, but would let him know she had breasts worth pursuing.

Bundling the reject pile together and thrusting them back in the wardrobe, she ignored the nagging thought that she must get it organized properly one day. Today she didn't have time and she slammed the door on the mess before anything had a chance to fall out.

Checking herself out in front of the full-length mirror, Tamsen thought she could still lose a couple of pounds. Maybe she should put in a few more hours at the gym. She mentally flagellated herself. This was lunch; being naked shouldn't even be on the menu.

However, to be on the safe side she selected a nice matching set of underwear. Even if Matt wouldn't be seeing her silk-and-lace ensemble, this meeting felt important enough for her to need to be lovingly put together.

She shimmied into the tight-fitting dress, applied the lightest touch of makeup, her lips carefully outlined in lip pencil, then glossed over to make them shine. The tawny brown pencil, one of her preferred choices, added to the earthy tone of her complexion. Finishing with a dab of her favorite perfume on her pulse points, Tamsen checked the overall package and smiled; she looked gorgeous. Now if the tide of anxious butterflies trying to escape her stomach would settle she'd be fine.

Matt sat in the garden watching the fish swim idly in the pond. He wished he could be that calm - he hadn't felt this on edge in years. Every time he took a sip of his soda water he thought the glass might rattle against his teeth. An inclination to order a scotch to calm his frazzled nerves made him laugh out loud; it was testament to his frame of mind that he even entertained the thought.

He sensed her before she arrived, a shift inside himself he couldn't explain - the same feeling he'd had upon waking this morning. Casting his gaze across the courtyard, he saw her, a stunning figure in green, and his immediate thoughts were of a lush rainforest.

Standing to pull the chair out for her as she approached, he knocked his glass of soda across the table. The small river ran toward her chair and pooled on the seat.

"Shit." He looked up. "Sorry, I can be such a clumsy fool."

Tamsen smiled. A dazzling warm smile that immediately set him at ease. "Not to worry. Why don't we just move? I know you like the fish, but I look at them all day and I'd much rather be by the herb garden over there."

"Okay, fine." He'd forgotten about the garden. Matthew made a mental note to look up a few facts about herbs.

Carrying his glass and half bottle of soda, Matt realized he no longer had a hand free to pull the new chair out for her. He told himself to relax and enjoy her company; otherwise he'd be looking like a complete prat by the end of the afternoon and Matt certainly didn't want that.

"So, having poured my water all over your chair, all that remains is for me to trip up and pour the balance down your back and we'll have gotten off to the perfect start, don't you think?"

At least she giggled at his lame joke, seating herself as close to the garden as she could manage. "Well, I spend most of the day with my hands in water, so what's a bit down the back between friends?"

"Ah, so you think we're going to be friends then?"

"I'm reserving judgment. But from all accounts, my friend Gina hates you."

"I'm doomed." He'd been right to worry about that little rat at reception.

She laughed again. "No, actually that's quite good. Gina's taste in men is absolutely awful."

"So I don't have to worry about the water-cooler gossip she brings home about me?"

"Gossip? Do tell." Tamsen leaned forward, her elbow on the table, her chin resting between her thumb and forefinger.

His eyes were drawn in an instant to the texture of her lips; he had an intense desire to taste them. "Honestly, nothing you really need to know about. The story of my life will bore you to tears." He needed food. Needed to get his mind back on track. "I'll just grab the menus from the table we've abandoned so we can order, and then you can tell me all about yourself."

She'd only just arrived and his desire to shag her senseless gnawed at him, extreme and intense, almost as if he'd already tasted her - some illogical sense of knowing he couldn't fathom. If he didn't find something to distract himself with soon he'd be in big trouble.

Back at their table, he watched her open her menu. "So, what do you fancy for lunch?" He hoped like hell she fancied him.

"You eat here all the time." She gave him back the menu. "Surprise me." She looked him square in the eye. "I love surprises."

The words rolled off her tongue and his mouth went dry. Half of him screamed he should run in the opposite direction, but the other half demanded he stay.

Knowing the menu inside out did not help; he was having trouble thinking coherently. "Er, is there anything you don't eat?"

"Meat," she teased mercilessly.

"You don't have a problem with fish, do you?"

He noticed a blush appearing at the base of her lovely earlobes. "No, I mind them all day, but fish is fine."

"Good." He felt in charge again. "We'll have the smoked salmon and scallop linguine then."

"You didn't ask me about shellfish."

"You said the only thing you don't eat is meat."

"Well, not on the first date anyway." He nearly inhaled the soda he'd been about to drink and she giggled. "Am I upsetting you?"

"No, not upsetting me, driving me to distraction."

"I'm sorry. I'll try to behave myself."

He smiled. She was the most provocative and endearing woman he'd met in a very long time. "Please don't, not on my account. I'm quite enjoying myself."

Steve arrived to take their orders. "Hey, Matt, how's it goin'?"

"Great, thanks, Steve. Can we both have the linguine and I'll have another water. What about you, Tamsen?"

"A water will be fine, thanks."

"Be back shortly."

"Does he do anything quickly?" Tamsen watched Steve saunter away, clearly in no hurry to get back to the kitchen.

"Drive vehicles I think is about the only thing. I feel sorry for him being stuck here. He likes it when I come in - he can drop the pretense of being a uni student on speed. It's the look they like out front."

Steve returned with their water, poured Tamsen a glass and removed Matt's empty bottle.

"Hey, sorry mate," Matt said, "but I poured most of that over the table and chair by the pond. You might want to clean it up."

"No problemo. If that's the worst thing that happens to me today I'll be sweet."

Matt raised his glass. "Here's to getting to know you, Miss Fish."

Tamsen joined him in the toast. "And to getting to know you too. May I call you Matt?"

He was touched she'd asked his permission. "I'd like that."

"Here's to getting to know you too, Matt."

She took a sip of the water and he was drawn to her mouth again. In an irrational moment of jealousy he wanted to be the glass.

"So, tell me," she asked, "how does someone who obviously doesn't like the city and has a hankering for the outdoors and fish end up being a corporate lawyer?"

"What makes you think I don't like the city?"

"You spend your lunchtimes hiding out in an inner city garden talking to the fish."

"I don't just talk to the fish."

"You talk to the plants too." He blushed. "It's okay, I won't tell Gina - she can think you're the bastard from hell. It'll be our little secret." Tamsen tapped the side of her nose.

"You'd better not," he warned.

"Or what?"

He couldn't help himself; she was playing with him and he liked it. "Or I'll have to punish you."

"Really?" A smile creased the edge of those engaging lips.

He leaned back in his chair, taking pleasure in playing back. "Yes. Really."

"I might enjoy that."

"Then we might both be in real trouble."

Steve made a timely appearance with their lunch.

Matt said, "You're looking a little harried, mate. Lunchtime rush getting to you?"

"I'm over it." Steve mopped his brow, and shuffled off at twice the speed he he'd moved last time.

Matt watched Tamsen delicately pick a scallop out of the tomato-and-caper sauce, allowing the fork to linger far too long in her mouth for his liking. He decided to attack his own lunch before the temptation to attack her overcame his appetite for food.

"So you still haven't told me what a potential tree hugger's doing in corporate law."

"My mother told me I was going to law school."

"That was it?"

"You haven't met my mother; she's not a woman to be crossed."

"Sounds like she could have taken lessons from mine."

"Oh, great, more things we have in common - tortured, dysfunctional childhoods."

She smiled. A drop of tomato sauce hung to the side of her lip; he wanted to lick it off. She said, "I don't really remember mine being too tortured, but then I did spend a lot of time in fantasy land, playing with fairies and elfin folk."

"Interesting. I'd never have gotten away with that."

"Why not?" She looked puzzled.

"Fairy folk are all a bit too pagan for my family. Staunch Roman Catholics and all."

"Hellfire and brimstone, huh?"

"Absolutely - I spent most Friday nights sitting with my mother saying decades of the Rosary. I could never understand why the other kids never had to do that."

"On your own?" She asked.

"I'm an only child." He laughed. "Mom said she'd never go through that again after I arrived." He'd always had guilt about the pain he caused his mother, she'd never let him forget it, either.

"Do you think it taught you anything, the Rosary stuff? You know, helped you with life?"

"I haven't ever really thought about it." He pondered the question for a couple of moments. It intrigued him that he'd forgotten those countless Friday nights. "I suppose it taught me discipline and that you didn't have to go to church to have some sort of contact with God - you could talk to Him anywhere."

"But you still did the Sunday church deal?"

"You betcha, the whole damn nine yards. We'd traipse off to church on a Sunday – Mom and me."

"What about your dad?"

"I don't know. He always seemed to get out of it for some reason that escaped me. He used to drop us off and then pick us up, but we were never told why he didn't have to go."

"You didn't ask him?"

"Er, no."

"Enough said."

They sat in comfortable silence for a while, enjoying the garden and their meals.

As driven as he was by a lustful desire to tear the clothing off her, Matt found himself happy to just sit and watch this beautiful woman consume her food. She had an incredible sensuality and grace about her, savoring every mouthful. He found it unimaginably erotic watching her.

Tamsen glanced up at him. "Why are you watching me eat?"

"Because I can."

"Do you always invite people to lunch so you can stare at them?"

"No, only beautiful, intriguing, intelligent people."

"Sheesh, you're forward." Tamsen put her eating utensils down.

"I haven't even started with you yet." He steepled his fingers, appraising her from over the top of his manicured fingernails.

"What do you mean?"

"You're still wearing your dress, aren't you?"

"I was the last time I looked." Her eyes never left his.

"Why don't you come to my place for dinner tonight and we'll see if we can't fix that small problem?"

"There's a bit of a food theme going on here, don't you think?"

"I was hoping for a bit of a sex theme, actually, but having you right here would get us both locked up."

"What for?"

"Indecent exposure, doing an indecent act, offensive behavior - you want me to carry on?"

She laughed. He liked the sound when she laughed and the look on her face. "No, I get the point."

"That's what I was hoping." He couldn't help winking. "At home, later on, maybe over the dining room table."

"You're awful."

He read mischief on her face and hoped she'd accept his outrageous proposition. "So that's a yes?"

"Why not? You only live once, right?"

"Absolutely." He couldn't believe what he'd just done. Insanity. But he couldn't get enough of her.

"I suppose I'd best get back to the salt mine if I'm going to get finished in time to prepare some gastronomic delight for dinner."

"You cook too?"

"I'm a man of many talents."

"Sounds promising." Tamsen got up from the table. "If you're getting dinner, then I'll get lunch."

"No way."

"You bought coffee yesterday, so it's my turn and no arguments, or I'll renege on the dinner date."

"Jeez, you drive a hard bargain."

"I do. So no arguments."

Matt followed her out of the garden, discomfort mounting at the prospect of not picking up the tab. Steve cast a quizzical look in his direction, as Tamsen paid for lunch.

"Where do you live?" She tucked her credit card back into her purse. "I don't think your address was on the card you gave me yesterday."

"You mean you haven't looked me up in the phonebook yet?"

She blushed. "No."

His legal instincts told him she was lying. He scribbled it down on the back of another business card and handed it to her. Their hands lingered on the small piece of card. Excitement bubbled inside him; he could barely wait for this evening.

It seemed ridiculous to shake her hand, so he made a fuss of pecking her on the cheek. She smelled of lunch and something earthy, something he craved. "Now, don't you dare change that dress - I have dibs on it."

"I'll try to remember." She smiled in a wicked way. "What time do you want me at your place tonight?"

"How does seven suit you?"

"Seven it is. I'll see you then."

"I'll look forward to it."

She turned and strode away with purpose and he was left gazing at her sensual, swaying derriere.

"Shit, Tams, this just gets worse." Gina was on her high horse again, yelling from the kitchen. "I was floored that you went to lunch with him, but this -

his place for dinner? Why don't you just tattoo across your forehead 'I shag on first dates'?"

"It's not a first date - technically it's our third."

"He's even got you talking like a lawyer. This is scary." Gina arrived on the terrace with an open bottle of chardonnay and two glasses.

"I don't want a drink - I'm driving."

"Well, on the strength of this news I need one and I'm not drinking alone."

"It's never stopped you before."

"Don't start that again, Tams. You can at least have a glass."

Tamsen sighed. "Pour me half then." If Gina needed to pretend she didn't drink alone that was her problem. Anyway the wine would take the edge off her anxiety about what she was getting herself into.

"I just don't know what you see in him, Tams. He's a prick."

"You believe what you want to believe, but I don't see that and what I see is all that matters."

"And it sounds like you might be seeing a hell of a lot more of it tonight."

They both giggled. "It does, doesn't it?"

Gina softened. "I suppose I have to admit he is rather gorgeous looking."

"Tell me about it."

"But you get over that when the bastard's yelled at you a few hundred times."

Tamsen nodded. "You would."

The wine left the tang of apples and pears in her mouth and, even if she only admitted it to herself, was helping settle her nerves. Unable to take her dress off because she kept fantasizing about Matt taking it off for her, Tamsen had been wound like coil all afternoon. She knew she was being a total fruit-loop and Gina was, in fact, a welcome distraction, but Tamsen wasn't going to let her best friend know that.

"You never did tell me what he was yelling at you about yesterday."

"His ex called. I was distracted and put her through."

Tamsen nodded. "I heard that part."

Gina continued, "She's been a daily stalker for about three months now - been thrown off the premises twice."

Gina refilled her wineglass, settling in to tell what had the makings of a sordid tale. Tamsen wasn't sure if she wanted to hear any more, but it didn't look like she had a choice.

"Rumor has it they were getting married. She's the society sweetheart his family want, but he called it off. They'd been living together for a while, but apparently he got tired of the society crawl - couldn't stand some of the people they had to spend a lot of time with. She works with charities, organizing those huge balls and hoopla events that you see in the local gossip mags and he just wasn't up to the whole deal. Told her it was all off, chucked her out and she's been trying to get back in ever since. I think she must have his mother on her side, 'cos she's constantly on his case about it too."

Gina took another swig of her wine and cast Tamsen an evil glance. "I've met his mother, so if you've got any ideas already that he might be the one just bear in mind she's a scary looking creature. Even worse than your mother, and that's saying something."

Tamsen felt queasy and it wasn't the wine. Maybe she should just give the whole evening the bum's rush and go to bed. She giggled to herself. Problem was she wanted to go to bed all right - with Matthew Solomon.

"What the hell," she told Gina. "I'm not looking for marriage. I want a half-decent shag and he's the first man in a very long time who's done anything for me."

"You horny tart."

Gina slipped off her chair, and brushed a hand across Tamsen's breast as she planted a kiss on her wine-soaked lips.

"I'm always available for you, honey - you should have let me know you were in need."

"With your schedule? Excuse me, who's had...let me see, was it three or four different women through the checkout on her bedroom door in the last month?"

"It was three."

"That's right; Carey made a comeback after...who was the blonde surfie chick with the eyebrow ring?"

"Don't remind me. I was drunk and out of my mind."

"You're always drunk and out of your mind."

"Below the belt."

"Serves you right for calling me a horny tart."

Gina looked at her watch, then drained her second glass of wine.

"Shouldn't you be on your way? Didn't you say you had to get to Titirangi?"

"I did. But hopefully I'll miss most of the traffic."

"Take the Dub - you can hardly turn up on Mr Wonderful's doorstep in your fish-mobile."

"And pray tell what's wrong with the fish-mobile?"

"Nothing, but if you take the Dubby you'll have to get it back for me in the morning."

Tamsen laughed. "You crafty cow."

"Ah well, just looking after my sister. Can't have us both getting lousy reputations, now can we?"

"And since when has a reputation worried you before?"

"It hasn't, but I wouldn't like a lovely girl like you getting one."

Tamsen gave her a hug; Gina really was the sweetest girl sometimes. "So I don't have to worry about you spreading gossip around the office then?"

"Absolutely not. My mouth is sealed." Gina ran through the universal monkey, no-see, no-hear, no-speak routine. "But I do expect a full report, preferably with intimate details plus explicit descriptions of every carnal act of pleasure he performs - okay?"

"Pervert." Tamsen headed out to her room to check her makeup.

"Well, at least put in a good word for me so he stops yelling at work, would you?"

"Done."

"Thanks, sis. Go make a pig of yourself."

Tamsen laughed. "Shut up." Some days Gina was a gift from the heavens.

Tamsen had worked out which off-ramp she wanted from the motorway before leaving home. But now came the moment she hated, winding her way through unfamiliar parts of town trying to keep a handle on which direction she was going – always a problem with the way Auckland's satellite cities circled the central business district and their orbiting suburbs.

Tamsen was a North Shore girl born and bred and, like so many of her friends, after she came back from the big OE had settled back in the suburb she knew and had missed while she was away.

West Auckland was another world. As for heading out west to meet a Central City lawyer, this was even more ass about face. No wonder the socialite in his life had trouble; he should have been living by the waterfront in Herne Bay, or at least on some beautiful tree-lined street in Remuera.

Traffic hadn't been too bad. She pulled over on the side of the road. The well-thumbed map of Auckland, her constant traveling companion, stared bleakly at her from the passenger seat. She still had a huge mistrust of electronic navigation systems. Gina swore by her nav system, but Tamsen hadn't even turned it on.

Pulling Matt's card out of her purse, Tamsen checked the address for the umpteenth time. Map reading wasn't her forte and Tamsen resorted to turning the map upside down, so at least the streets on the right were coming up on the right. Every little thing helped.

Tamsen put the Dubby into gear, released the handbrake and set out again. Negotiating street names with the map upside down was a challenge, and the soothing effect of the wine with Gina had long worn off - her resident butterflies were back.

Hell, she was going to be at least ten minutes early. What to do? Sit at the top of his driveway or knock on the door? Tamsen resigned herself to sitting in the car like a nutter waiting for the digital readout to get to at least 6:58 before she'd allow herself the luxury of getting out.

There was no sign of a house, just a long private roadway. The clock read 6:47. Perhaps she should just get on her way, she had no idea how far it was down the driveway and she'd rather be early than late.

Dense native bush surrounded her and the whole atmosphere was incredibly lush. To her surprise, Tamsen felt a sense of ease and peacefulness. She hadn't expected to feel the same connected calm in the bush that she felt from her ocean.

She climbed the front steps of an eco-friendly building, carefully avoiding the replanting material strewn all around, and stopped in front of a dark blue door, complete with ornate brass door knocker. Tamsen smoothed down her dress, the one she hoped Matt would be removing later as promised, the memory making her skin tingle with anticipation. Checking her watch, she noted with amusement she was now only about seven minutes early.

CHAPTER FIVE

Matthew had had the worst day. He really should've just stayed in bed this morning, he thought ruefully. The only highlight had been lunch with Tamsen, and thankfully she was due any minute, a welcome relief from the dire and unmanageable circumstance his life had become.

If things hadn't been bad enough his mad ex Angie had got through to him on the phone, and then the dragon who would have become his mother-in-law had snatched the phone from her and given him a burst just for good measure. He stopped what he was doing, crossed himself, and took a moment to thank God for saving him from that mistake.

Their receptionist really was just a waste of space. How could someone as intelligent and likable as Tamsen live with her? He'd spent an embarrassing half an hour on the phone to the mother-in-law-from-hell explaining why he wasn't going to be getting back with her daughter, even if she turned out to be the last surviving female on the planet. The relationship with Angie left a nasty taste in his mouth and he was glad to be rid of the whole family.

Matt tucked the last of the dirty washing in the hamper in the laundry room and checked again that the bedroom was spotless. He laughed at himself for changing the sheets, but it didn't hurt to be prepared.

Moving the last of the pizza boxes out of the kitchen into the recycling, he realized there also was a pile of banana skins that should have gone out into the worm bin.

A resounding and unmistakable banging on the front door announced Tamsen's arrival and all thoughts of worms went out the window.

His mouth went dry, guilt washing over him: he'd set the scene for seduction. Too late to back out now, he thought. He'd best temper his behavior and behave like a gentleman.

He opened the door and all thoughts of gentlemanly behavior went straight out of his head.

"Hi." He struggled to get the simple word out of his mouth.

She looked utterly beautiful, the light of the setting sun turning highlights in her hair to spun gold, creating an almost halo-like effect.

"Hey, I'm early."

He looked at his watch. "Only a couple minutes, but if the place isn't up to your expectations then I've got an excuse, right?"

"Right."

He couldn't stop staring; it was as if an angel had appeared on his doorstep. "You'd better come on in then." He stood aside and allowed her to enter the roomy foyer.

Her heels clicked on the parquet flooring; its dark-stain gave an impression of age to the reasonably young establishment. Tamsen hesitated at the stairs, appearing unsure whether she should go up or down.

"Sorry, we're going upstairs. I'll show you round later, but down there's fairly grubby." Matt pointed to a closed door sat at the bottom of the second set of stairs. "It's where I work out, where the car's stored and where I do all those blokey things with power tools you probably don't want to know about."

"I don't know - you shouldn't underestimate me. I'm pretty versatile with hand tools." She winked at him and Matt's temperature skyrocketed.

As they both emerged at the top of the stairs, Matt took Tamsen by the elbow and guided her into the kitchen. It was a large affair, sitting neatly between the lounge and dining room, with access from all three rooms to a huge deck that ran the length of the house.

"What can I get you to drink?" He hadn't forgotten how to be a good host, despite the increase in his internal thermometer.

"Have you got a mineral water?"

"A mineral water? I'm not exactly going to get your knickers off with a bottle of mineral water, am I?"

She laughed out loud. "No, you might have to do some work. Now that'd be a challenge, wouldn't it?"

He hunted through the fridge; he knew he had a bottle of Perrier in there somewhere. "Ah, there it is. Tell me, water doesn't go off living in the fridge, right?"

"Don't think so."

He poured her a glass and plucked a beer for himself out of the fridge. "You don't mind if I imbibe?"

"Absolutely not."

"Come on, let's enjoy the last of the evening. I've dusted the old barbie off and I thought I'd toss a few prawns and some chicken on and throw a bit of a salad together. How's that sound for dinner?"

"Really great. Thanks."

He pulled a heavy wooden folding chair out for her, set it on the deck and seated himself just to her right. He wanted to be close enough to engender intimacy, but far enough away that Tamsen didn't feel overpowered by him.

"So, you don't drink." It was a statement, not really a question.

"Oh, I do." She took a sip of the mineral water and wrinkled her nose, her obvious distaste for the bubbles making him smile. "I just don't like to overindulge. Gina opened a bottle before I came out, so I had a glass with her." She smiled at him, a look of mischief in her emerald eyes. "And I wanted to make sure I had a clear head to deal with you."

"And here's little me thinking it might be because you had to drive from one side of our fair city to the other."

"How do you know I live on the other side of the city? I don't remember telling you where I live."

He could feel the heat crawling up over his collar. He'd sprung her out at lunchtime and now he'd been stupid enough to get caught in the same trap. "You live with Gina and I know she's on the Shore."

Tamsen leaned forward, snaring him in her steely gaze. "Strange you'd know where your receptionist lives, especially one you can't stand."

He held his hands up in mock surrender. "Okay, you got me, I'll come clean. I looked your address up in the phone book, so sue me."

"I'm sure I can think of things I'd much rather do than sue you."

The words went straight to his groin. She idly ran her index finger up and down the stem of the crystal flute holding her water while Matt had lewd visions of where he'd like her hands to be.

"Maybe I should get the chicken on the barbecue?" Anything to get his mind out of her knickers. Food to the rescue for the second time today.

"Is there something I can do?"

"How'd you go with making salad?" Matt headed into the kitchen to get the chicken and prawns out of the fridge. She followed him.

Tamsen had come in after him. "My speciality. With or without unique accompaniments?"

"Er, with?" He wondered what the hell she was talking about, but decided to go with it. This going with gut feelings seemed to be opening all sorts of interesting doors.

"So can I use whatever I find in the fridge?" Tamsen's question followed him back out onto the terrace.

"Yeah, go for it - use whatever you want." He popped his head back in through the bifold windows over the sink, "There's a crystal bowl in the cupboard next to the fridge and the salad servers are in the drawer underneath the bench."

"No probs, chef. You cook and I'll chop."

He'd always appreciated the ease with which the house lent itself to alfresco dining. He was also quite enjoying having Tamsen in the kitchen; the physical distance between them eased the tension in his groin.

There was a continual knot in his stomach. That bubbly feeling of anticipation - it had been present since the first moment he'd set eyes on her and he was unable to shake it.

Throwing the chicken on the hot steel, he took a swig of his beer, grateful that Tamsen didn't seem to have any objections to his drinking straight from the bottle; he'd so had enough of airs and graces.

The sizzling chicken sealed quickly and he expertly turned the kebabs, careful to avoid being spattered by hot fat. As much as he loved barbecued food, he hated wearing the scent of cooking and went to extraordinary lengths to make sure he created as little smoldering smoke as possible.

He could hear Tamsen singing softly to herself in the kitchen. He couldn't make out the words or the tune, but was taken with the gentle harmony.

"Matt?" She was leaning out the window. "Those flowers round the front door - you don't spray them or anything, do you?"

He laughed. "You're kidding, right? I live in the country's leading eco-city - what do you think?"

"That'd be a no, then?"

"Correct." What the hell could she want with flowers when she was making a salad?

After throwing the prawns on the barbecue, he headed back into the kitchen to pick up his new favorite serving platter - a huge oval fish Danni had painted in ceramics class and given him last Christmas.

The kitchen looked as if a bomb had exploded in it and he couldn't help wondering what sort of chaos she'd have created if she'd cooked the entire meal. There were lettuce leaves from one edge of the bench to the other, water all over the draining board, and a pool on the tiled floor where some of it had run down the cupboard doors. One little person – one large mess.

"Oy, you, out of here - I'm creating." Tamsen returned with a small bunch of flowers in her hand.

"I can see that."

"Oh, right, the carnage." He saw the start of a blush as she dropped her eyes from his and looked at her feet. "Gina doesn't like me cooking. She says it's not worth the effort of having to clean up after me. I'm afraid I'm not the tidiest of people."

He shrugged. "Hey, no big deal. So you're creative - create away. I can clean up later."

Matt walked outside, adding to his list of mental notes. Passionate. Tick. Sensual and creative. Tick. It made for a heady mix. His mind wandered again to the promise of the pleasures of her flesh and he experienced another hot and sweaty moment that had nothing to do with the heat coming from the barbecue.

Tamsen arrived outside with the salad - a work of art contained in a simple white bowl.

"Wow!" He was impressed. "I'd never have thought of putting flowers in a salad. Are you sure it's okay to eat them?"

"Absolutely." She beamed at him and he was touched she received so much pleasure from his affirmations.

"It's a great idea to eat the centerpiece."

"Keep up the compliments and there's a damned good chance you'll get me between the sheets tonight."

Tamsen vacillated between angelic, virginal schoolgirl and sultry temptress. Matt had trouble keeping up, although parts of him seemed to be in no doubt as to where the evening was heading.

"I told you, I'm having you across a table," he said. "How does this one look, or would you prefer the one inside?"

"Oh, I get a choice. That's kind."

"I always aim to please." He pushed the platter of chicken and prawns toward her, "Now, you'd better get some of these down you - you're going to need all the help you can get to keep up with me later."

Eyeing him with a suspicious look, Tamsen picked up a couple of prawns and some chicken. "Is that so?"

He turned his attention to the salad. It really was a work of art and Matt had a pang of guilt at the prospect of destroying the display by dropping some of it on his plate.

He said, "You'd best explain to me what it is I'm eating. I had no idea there was anything even remotely edible in my garden."

"You've got plenty." Tamsen dug into the salad herself, small petals falling onto her plate like confetti. "The purple petals are heartsease - those small violas that you've got growing under the roses at the front door. The orange skinny ones are calendula petals. They're often referred to as pot marigold. There're nasturtium petals - they were growing on the bank down the driveway, the orange and yellow petals - and if you look there's some baby nasturtium leaves too. They're the little hexagonal ones."

He was impressed. "What's this one?" He was holding a small, five-petaled cream flower.

"Try it."

"You do know you have to marry me before you can pick up the life insurance?" He must be relaxed - he never joked about marriage, with anyone.

"It won't kill you." She urged him on, "Promise."

"It's a potent aphrodisiac, right?"

She laughed. "I don't know, I'd have to check my book at home for its constituents."

"It tastes like peanut butter." He was amazed. "What is it?"

"It's rocket. There're leaves here too from the packet greens you had in the fridge, but you've got flowers down the driveway."

"I never thought I'd be eating flowers from my own garden." He wondered what other interesting surprises she had lined up for him.

Matt's astonishing receptiveness to new experiences added to the man's enigma. Other men in her past - not that there'd been many – had run a mile whenever she suggested anything new. She wondered, not for the first time, what drove this man.

His home wasn't at all what she'd expected. It had been clear the moment she set foot down the driveway that extreme garden renovations were underway, and she'd had to clamber over piles of bark, mulch and topsoil to get to the flowers she'd collected for the salad.

She hoped he wasn't too upset over the mess in the kitchen; she just got so involved in creating, she was completely oblivious to the disorder around her.

It was lovely having someone to share her knowledge about the plants with too; he seemed to have a genuine interest, although she couldn't at this stage discount that as mere lip-service to his undisguised attempts to get her undressed.

Watching him eat, his sensual lips covered with a fine oily sheen from the chicken, she imagined them traversing the length of her body. He slowly licked his lips, aware she was inspecting him. Teasing.

Warmth flooded her body and her nipples reacted in an instant, anticipating his tongue. He was gorgeous and she wanted him. Tamsen sat there, torn between her lustful desire to experience him and the conventional school-ma'am voice lecturing her in her head.

"It's beautiful watching the dusk turn to night from here, don't you think?" Matthew leaned back in his chair, surveying the rapid descent of night.

Tamsen had to agree. It had been magical watching the sunset colors cross the horizon as they ate their meal. The sky ran now like watercolors, from deep black down through dark blue, with the lighter sky blue merging into pale grey as the last sliver of red danced on the horizon behind the black silhouette where trees met sky.

She sighed, feeling replete and satisfied with life. "I wouldn't want to be anywhere else."

"That makes two of us." He stood, collecting up dirty plates and cutlery and made movements toward the kitchen with the crockery and the remainder of the food.

"Here, let me help you." She picked up the fish platter and his two empty beer bottles.

"No need, really, I'm an expert. I was a waiter in former life."

"Cool, a Catholic who believes in reincarnation."

He laughed. "I meant when I was a struggling law student."

"A man of many talents."

"We've had this discussion before." The look in his eye spoke of pleasures yet to be unearthed. Did she have the courage to dig, she wondered?

"You keep threatening. I'm beginning to think you're all mouth and trousers." What a thing to say, she could have slapped herself. Maybe it was time to just call it a night and head home.

His desire registered in his eyes and her world came to a grinding halt. All thought of walking out the door left her head. His pupils dilated and she felt something inside of her ping. Her brain screamed a warning, but her soul held her rooted to the spot, caught in his gaze.

"Mouth and trousers, hmm?" He moved toward her, invading her aura, close enough she could feel his breath on her face. He didn't touch her, but still his energy infiltrated its way into her every cell. Her temperature rose. Her heart beat erratically. She had an acute awareness of the lack of distance between them – she was hypersensitive to him, warmed by a passion that flared within him.

He reached out to touch her face, running the back of his hand from the top of her cheekbone down, the tips of his fingers lingering at the base of her throat.

An erotic touch that sparked a response inside her. She held her breath, not daring to move, waiting to see what he would do next.

An immediate desire to reach out and touch him consumed her and she ran her hand up his bare arm, the hairs tickling her palm. She trembled, the tension building between them.

His eyes never left hers, unblinking pools of dark brown, the pupils - smaller pools of black. Matt let his fingers slide under her chin, tracing the outline of her jaw, all the way to her silver earring, then swinging on the metal hoop. The intimate action sparked a sudden flush of vulnerability and Tamsen swallowed involuntarily.

"Am I disturbing you?" His voice was thick with desire.

"You've been disturbing me from the moment I first set eyes on you." It was the truth, though she'd been afraid to admit it even to herself. It seemed strange vocalizing it for him.

"Do you want me to stop?" The gleam in his eye spoke of wicked things to come.

"No."

Tamsen moved closer to him, reaching out and mirroring his actions with her hand. His skin was warm, and she decided he must have shaved before she arrived - there was absolutely no hint of regrowth. She was touched that he'd made such an effort for her.

He dragged his finger along her cheek, down to her mouth, pausing just below her bottom lip. She reflected the action and he smiled. She stroked her finger across his bottom lip, waiting to see if he would pick up on her lead. He did. She suckled his finger, drawing it deep into her mouth. Tasting him, enjoying the intimate contact, allowing him to explore her mouth, rubbing her tongue up and down and around him.

She teased his mouth with her index finger, not quite allowing him to suckle hers, toying with his lips, making him reach out with his tongue, the tip hunting for the tip of her finger, letting him lick her, then spreading his own spittle around his lips, coating them, rubbing her finger along his teeth, feeling the hard sharpness, permitting him to clamp tenderly on her while his tongue flicked up and over her manicured nail.

A powerful need to kiss him overtook her, to taste with her own the lips she was so enjoying. The anticipation of his flavor crippling her, she trembled in the most exquisite way.

He moved closer to her, slipped his arm around her slim waist and pulled her toward him. Parted her legs with his thigh so that she leaned astride him, the weight of her body sitting on her pubic bone, further inflaming the heat and need his nearness was creating.

She could smell him now, his scent hot and vibrant, a touch of musk hidden under layers of cinnamon and deep citrus. His body was solid when she ran her hands over his chest, the silk of his shirt smooth and seductive.

She lingered over his erect nipples, rubbing them with the open palms of her hands through the sheer material. Her desire was building and still she had yet to taste him.

"Do you have any idea what you're doing to me?" The words were spoken quietly.

He'd leaned forward, was rimming the outside of her ear with his tongue, his breath coming in ragged, shallow gasps, hot on her neck like the humid air of a balmy summer's night. She tipped her head to the side, giving him full access to the length of her neck; she wanted to feel his tongue and his teeth on that most sensitive part of her body.

He was bringing her ever so slowly to the boil and she, in no rush, was enjoying the sensations, all the while sedately riding his upper thigh.

She slid her hands through his hair, massaging his scalp with her fingertips and fingernails, and he moaned in response. The sound struck at her core, ran musically down her spine and she felt the beginnings of wetness. Her knees went weak and she leaned more heavily into him. He found his way past her neck, stringing butterfly kisses across her cheek until his lips rested tenderly against hers.

A bubble of emotion escaped her heart, some sort of physical recognition she couldn't begin to describe. She was incredibly turned on and aroused by this man, but here was a moment of tenderness and purity she didn't understand that evoked deeply buried emotional responses beyond anything she'd sensed before.

For a moment she breathed his breath, touched by his soul, a potpourri of emotions somersaulting through her body. Then she relaxed and allowed him to bring his lips to hers in a joining that was like coming home.

Everything felt incredibly right - his touch, his lips, his probing tongue. He tasted clean and special and real. As he held her tighter she wrapped her arms around the back of his neck. His hands cupped her buttocks and tiny explosions went off inside her head. She felt alive and vibrant, moved by powerful energy and emotion.

Feverishly she began exploring his body and mouth with her own, unwilling to disengage from the contact and touch, such feelings he was evoking. She wanted the kiss to go on forever. Wanted to bask in the heat of their desire, be scorched by the flames of passion, to hold onto this moment forever, it felt so vital and right.

He pulled away, breaking the spell, gasping for air, his cheeks flushed, his neck clammy, his scent strong. Softly he whispered, "That was some kiss."

She rested her forehead on his. "It was, wasn't it?"

Neither was willing to give up complete connection, rubbing noses slowly backwards and forwards, claiming the intimacy of the moment.

Matthew wanted her. Wanted her desperately and with a passion born of a desire he'd seldom experienced before. He'd planned to seduce her slowly, build a scalding passion, bring her to the edge and not let her fall. Leave her longing, leave her in need of him. But things hadn't gone as he planned.

Gazing into her green eyes, their foreheads touching, he stroked down the muscles of her back to those beautiful buttocks. She was still rubbing herself gently against his upper thigh; it was driving him insane with lust and desire.

He didn't want to move from the kitchen, so anxious to ensure they didn't defile the moment. The immediate emotion of the kiss had evaporated, but it was replaced with a burning hunger for her that felt insatiable.

He wanted her. He wanted her now, and he wasn't prepared to risk losing momentum. She disengaged herself from his forehead, started running gentle kisses - interspersed with nips of her teeth - down his neck.

His instant response was in his groin. The pressure in his jeans intense, he needed some relief and release. He reached down and unbuttoned the first three buttons, groaning as she continued to nibble his neck. Her hand followed down his arm, pushing his aside and cupping him through the silk of his boxers. Another shot to his groin and his cock pulsed under the warmth of her touch.

"Excited?" Her voice was husky and all he could do was moan in response.

"Would you like me to lick you - take you in my mouth like I did with your finger?" She continued mercilessly licking behind his ear.

He was mad with desire. She was a vixen, yet she'd masqueraded as some sort of innocent. His mind was confused. He should be resisting her, taking the lead, taking control, but his body was betraying him, reacting to her every touch. He was completely powerless in her hands.

Licking then kissing the hollow in his throat, she started to unbutton his shirt, blazing a trail down his chest, a lick then a kiss where each button sat. He had a white-knuckled grip on the granite bench as she undid the last of the buttons and knelt between his legs.

She looked up, hovering seductively over the ache beneath his boxers, threatening to release him into her warm and inviting mouth. She licked her lips, that carnal mouth making promises he couldn't possibly resist. "You haven't answered me."

She rubbed her chin up his aching shaft, the sensation through the silk excruciating, and he let out a sharp gasp. "Yes."

"Yes what?" Her thumb raked over the tip of his cock, milking him through the blue silk.

"Yes, please. You're killing me."

She smiled. "Look how wet I'm making you and I haven't even started yet."

His grip on the granite tightened.

Deftly she released the other buttons on his jeans, slipped the blue denim together with his boxers down his legs, then prodded his thighs, as you would a horse, inviting him to step out of the clothing. When she kissed her way back up the insides of his thighs his excitement continued to mount.

"I'm so glad you don't wear shoes – it's so un-erotic removing shoes and socks, don't you think?"

Matt was unable to think. She was hovering menacingly over his genitals again and he was desperate for her to take him in her mouth.

"Suck me, please." The words were almost a growl.

Reaching up his body, she dragged her long manicured fingernails the length of his torso, drawing all sensation down to the concentrated area of his groin, bringing his focus to the center of himself. His cock bobbed and dribbled in front of her lips. She blew softly across his tip and he shuddered in response. Gripping him with her hands, she ever so slowly lowered that carnal mouth over him. The sensation was electric, the heat of her mouth heaven. He threw his head back and closed his eyes, moaning long and loud.

"Take me all the way in, as deep as you can." The words were dredged from someone else. He felt whiny and needy but he didn't care; all he cared about were the superb sensations of her suckling.

She mouthed him in slow and luxurious strokes. He was out of his mind with desire; the sensations were incredible. He held her head, ran his fingers through her hair, allowed her beautiful lips and tongue to milk him, caress him. She cupped his balls with one hand, the other grasping his cock, creating a funnel to the warm, sweet, wetness of her mouth. Over and over she took him, long, steady stroking. He wanted to come in her mouth, wanted her to feel the full force of him, wanted her to devour him.

A small voice of reason struggled through the pleasurable cloud. He also wanted this to last, wanted to give her pleasure, show her what he could do for her - make her come.

He reached down again, interrupted Tamsen and lifted her up toward him. Her mouth was red and puffy, her lips savaged from her savaging of him. He kissed her - hungrily, powerfully and desperately. Her tongue danced with his, delving into his mouth; she tasted salty, and her heat aroused him even more.

He found the zipper at the back of her neck, tugging at the material, frustrated when it wouldn't co-operate. He quickly turned her around so he could look at what he was doing. The sea of green material parted for him, exposing the pale plane of her back. Leveling a kiss in the middle of her shoulder blades, he disposed of the fastening of her bra, pushing the straps down in the sweep of her dress.

Flesh dancing in front of his eyes, her hair cascading down her shoulders, he pulled her to him, snuggling her bare back to his chest, luscious skin on skin contact.

Cupping her full, heavy breasts in his palms, the rosebud nipples begging for the attention of his mouth, he squeezed each hard and she shuddered against him, a small moan escaping her lips.

"Nice?"

She nodded. "Squeeze harder - I like it when it hurts."

More than happy to oblige, he felt a throbbing sensation shoot to his cock. The thought of her appreciation of a little pain turned him on more than he cared to admit.

"Oh, God, that's so good." She arched back against him, grinding her backside into his rock-hard cock. "Lick inside my ear - it turns me on."

He was grateful for instructions. As he ran his tongue inside her ear an urgent moan was rapidly followed by a gyrating backside. His immediate thought was to get some space between his cock and her backside or he was going to explode all over her and the kitchen.

CHAPTER SIX

Matt released his grip on Tamsen's tortured nipples and turned her round to face him, taking in the canvas of her body. Her face was flushed with passion and her eyes glazed with desire and yearning; he'd almost overlooked how beautiful she was, with her curves in all the right places.

"You're gorgeous," he moaned.

Matt hooked his thumbs in the minuscule green G-string she wore, removing it in a single downward motion. Tamsen held his shoulders and stepped gingerly out of the scrap of material. He made no attempt to remove her shoes, liking the naughtiness of her wearing nothing but high heels.

He turned around and pushed her up against the bench-top he'd vacated. Capturing one of her nipples in his hungry mouth, he allowed his hands the luxury of exploring the uncharted territory of her stomach and thighs. He could smell the heat of her body, the hot sweet scent emanating from her pores, as he continued suckling and caressing, alternating from nipple to nipple, her hands running through his hair, then raking his back in long, agonizingly slow strokes.

The harder he suckled, the harder she scratched. Each time he increased the suction it felt as if she took another layer of skin off his back. He wanted to keep going until she drew blood - scraped her way through flesh to muscle and bone.

Sucking harder, he felt her arch under his mouth. "Oh, God...no more...enough," she panted.

He released the tormented nipple, shades of purple and red appearing where his mouth had been. His back was on fire.

"I want you to lick me." She ran her fingernail down her stomach, past the golden barbell in her navel; he noticed that the stone in the ball matched the emerald she wore at her throat. "Taste me."

He didn't need asking twice, helping her onto the bench top with the dirty dishes, bottles and glasses pushed swiftly to one side. She'd shaved, except for a small strip of cropped red hair leading to her swollen lips. He ran his tongue down the prickly line until his tongue reached her sweet juice.

Matt tasted her and she wriggled and moaned in response, thrusting herself at his face, perched atop the bench amongst the leftovers. He found himself torn between the desire to have her explode on his face, or to stop what they were doing so he could get inside her. Never good at delaying gratification, with her trembling beneath his mouth he knew she was close. Shit, he was close to coming too. A decision was in order.

He pulled himself away; she groaned in frustration and looked at him as if he'd gone completely mad. He kissed her and she lapped at him, devouring her own juices from his face.

"I want you," he gasped between kisses, "but we need a condom."

"No, don't stop." Her strangled cry was more ammunition than his tortured body needed; he couldn't deny her, couldn't leave her hanging. Working his way back down her sweaty body, he parted her with his thumbs. At the touch of his tongue her trembling began anew. Matt peered up as best he could and she moaned incoherently, grasped his head with one hand and ground him into her.

As she bucked and writhed he felt his own orgasm rumbling deep inside, felt the familiar stirrings in his balls, that aching need for release. If he didn't stop this he'd come all over the floor. There was no way of stopping any of it. He resigned himself and waited for the rush of her orgasm.

Letting go of his head, Tamsen gripped the counter top, caught her breath, arched back and he felt the sudden gush of her climax. Her satisfied growl coupled with the sweet taste of her sent him over the edge. Grasping her thighs and exhaling into her groin, he exploded in a rush all over the kitchen cupboards.

Collapsing to his knees, he heard quiet giggling - not hysterical, but a little loopy sounding. He cast a glance skywards and she was smiling down at him, her face flushed, her eyes shining. She was even more beautiful and he was even more taken with her.

"I've made another mess in your kitchen, haven't I?"

He smiled, lifting himself so he could kiss her just under her navel. "No, I don't believe this was all your doing - I think I have to take responsibility for some of it."

Tamsen's post-coital bubble broke and she had a sudden flash of what she must look like, perched on the countertop in amongst the used plates and cutlery, wearing nothing but her shoes. Color rushed to her cheeks and she knew it had nothing to do with delayed orgasm. The man had a mighty way with his mouth.

Matt backed away, almost awkward, putting some distance between them, globules of come dripping from his rapidly diminishing cock.

"This is typical of me," he stammered. "Not thinking through the consequences of my well-thought-out - *not* - actions."

The emphasis on the word made her laugh. "Come here." She motioned to the space between her legs, all modesty gone; it really was way too late to be shy.

She wrapped her legs around his waist and placed her index finger over his bruised looking lips and then down to his chin, still sticky with her juices. "Has anyone ever told you you've got an amazing mouth and you know how to use it?"

A light touch of red kissed his cheeks. "And that was only a warm-up. Come shower with me and I'll show you what I can really do."

She shuddered, but what the hell? The night was young, and how much more trouble could she get into, really? "Lead the way, I'm still all yours."

"So, you brazen trollop, what time did you get in last night?"

Gina's assault broke Tamsen's train of thought. She should have been writing her morning sheet, but she sat there, gazing out to sea and thinking of Matt. The touch of his hands and mouth on her skin. "Hmm, what'd ya say?"

"I wanted to know what time you dragged that sorry, and by the look on your face, well-shagged ass home last night?"

Tamsen giggled. "I think it was about quarter to three when I eventually fell into bed. And it wasn't my ass that got shagged." She took a sip of her dandelion tea. "Not that it's any of your business."

"Girlfriend - " Gina lit a cigarette and took a long drag " - if anyone's getting any action around here it's definitely my business." She swigged her coffee and took a bite of the ritual breakfast doughnut. "So spill. From the grin pasted on your face he's built like a horse and you were at it like rabbits all night."

Tamsen smiled. "Ladies don't tell."

"That good? Damn, I was hoping he'd be pencil-prick material and you hated every minute of it."

"Sorry, he's a keeper."

"Come on, let's not get past tag and release at this stage. You've only known him two days."

"Okay, then - " Tamsen chewed thoughtfully on the end of her pen " - a prospective keeper."

"Better." Gina swallowed the last of her coffee. "Well, I'd best be off to the pit-face, see what time yonder Prince Charming stumbles in."

"Hey, Gina."

"Yep?" She stopped at the door.

"Thanks for lending me the Dubby."

"Ah, no probs." Gina waved her hand dismissively. "And if you feel the need to bring lover boy back here I won't be in tonight - I'm off to stay at Cassie's."

"Ooh, sleepover."

"Don't get your hopes up. She's having a few friends around for dinner and I'll be too pissed to drive home, so there won't be any of that, I can assure you."

"Don't drink so much and you never know what'll happen."

"Whatever." Gina headed for the doors. "See ya tomorrow. Don't do anything I wouldn't do."

Tamsen turned her mind to her journal again.

I've mixed feelings about where last night went and where it's taken me. I sit here, the sun's shining off the sea, the dog walkers are doing their usual round of the sand and the gulls do what gulls do. Nothing's changed in the scene before me, but I feel as if I'm looking through different eyes. How can an encounter with someone you barely know touch you in such a deep and personal way?

Tamsen sighed and closed her journal. Her one true friend in life.

These pages were the closest she'd ever come to unconditional love.

Matt hadn't made any mention of when he wanted to see her again. Tamsen could already sense needy and obsessive tendencies trying to surface. Gina wasn't going to be home tonight. An opportunity to return the favor and prepare a meal for him, perhaps. Who was she kidding? She was a disaster in the kitchen. She could cook, but it took three days and a water blaster to clean up afterward.

Besides, it wasn't eating she was interested in. Last night had whetted her appetite for the man. She couldn't get enough - just thinking about what his mouth was capable of made her wet.

She shivered. Best be off to work, take her tiny mind off the man before she decided to have herself on the terrace, in full view of the dog-walking brigade.

Matt was besotted. It was the only way he could describe his feelings. He'd slept log-like for a couple of hours after Tamsen left and woken raring and ready to go. Even her bratty receptionist roommate wasn't able to put him off his stride this morning. Gina's smile had been smug, as if she knew some dirty little secret and might hold it over him, but he didn't care. Nothing would get in the way of him having a great day.

Danni had other ideas.

"Morning boss." She dropped what looked like a seventy-five-page agreement on his desk. "Tim thought you needed a little bit of reading material to keep you going."

"Shit, Danni, don't suppose there's any chance of saving a few trillion trees by sending these things by email, is there?"

"You know these guys as well as I do. Dragging them kicking and screaming into the 21st century's a mission impossible. Most of them still think a mouse is something we need pest control for."

"No, honestly, I'm serious. Can't we find some way of persuading them to use the technology we spend thousands on?"

She shrugged. "I could try to organize some in-house seminars for the secretaries, but really it's a matter of you working on the fossils at your end. Someone like Tim just doesn't trust the technology. No matter how much I tell him it's okay, he can't believe if he isn't holding the pages in his hand then it's likely to disappear or be changed, and he'll never be any the wiser."

Matt dropped his head in his hands. "It's like pushing the proverbial uphill with my nose."

"That's lawyers for you - not big on change."

Danni busied herself filing correspondence on the relevant client files while Matt contemplated the huge document on his desk. He was already way behind on a couple of jobs; he just couldn't seem to find any enthusiasm for the work these days. Even after the night he'd just had with Tamsen.

"So was she good?" Danni cut into his wandering thoughts.

"Sorry?"

"The mystery woman you took out for lunch yesterday. You've got one of those I've-been-up-shagging-all-night looks on your face."

He felt his cheeks redden.

"Ha, I knew it."

She pulled up the seat opposite his desk, a vision in black crushed silk with a white lacy camisole under her suit jacket. She had a way of looking feminine and business-like. "So, spill. Who is she?"

"Not telling."

"Matt..." Danni leaned forward and eyed him over the desk.

He knew he was in deep trouble. A woman on a mission, and him clean in her sights. What kind of hell must her husband have gone through when she made the decision he was going to marry her?

"You can tell me now, or we can sit here all day until you do. What's it going to be?"

"I don't have to tell you." A feeble come-back and he knew it, but at least the verbal battle might distract him from obsessing about Tamsen.

"I'm your personal assistant, I need to know what's going on in your life - and besides, I'm not going to tell anyone."

"And you're not going to leave me alone until I tell you."

"Correct, so spill."

"Tamsen."

"Tamsen Parsons. The fishy girl. Gina's friend. That Tamsen?"

He nodded.

"She's not exactly your type."

"What do you mean, my type?"

"Well, she seems a bit hippyish- one of those girls who'd set a metal detector off in the airport. You never know what's lurking under her clothing." She looked at him slyly. "Though you probably do now, don't you?"

Matt felt a sudden, inexplicable need to defend her. "Steady on. You can't judge someone by how they look."

"You've tried telling that to your mother, have you?"

"Leave my mother out of this. And you're not to breathe a word to anyone. It's bad enough the creature on reception knows."

Danni made the universal motion for zipping her lips and went back to her filing. Matt couldn't miss the smug look on her face.

Why did she have to bring his mother up? Danni was right, his mother would not approve. She approved of the vile and poisonous Angie though Matt couldn't wait to get her out of his life - it had been like living with a pit-bull in twinset and pearls. He shivered at the memory. There were days when he couldn't even smile right. It hadn't even occurred to him until he booked into a hotel in a furious rage that he'd walked out of his own home. That's how twisted and distorted his outlook on life had become. He'd vowed never to go there again, and if that meant he had to run a little against the conventional grain, then so be it.

Sod it, he thought. He picked up the phone and dialed Tamsen's cellphone.

"Danni, can you close the door on your way out." His PA knew when he wanted to be alone and obediently closed the door behind her as she vacated his office.

"Hello?"

"Tamsen?"

"Yes."

"Hi, it's Matt." She probably thought he was a complete idiot but it was too late now.

"Hey, I was just thinking about you."

His mood lifted. "Clean thoughts, I hope."

"Utterly filthy. You want to come over to my place tonight and I'll share them with you?"

"I'd like that." More than he cared to admit. "You could give me a hint though."

She giggled. "If I told you what I'd been thinking about you'd never be able to keep your mind on your job."

"I'm having enough trouble after last night, so you can't do any more damage."

"I was just putting a fish in a new aquarium and it occurred to me you might be fun in water. I've got a rather large sunken spa bath at home and - "

"Stoppit." His mind ran a million miles ahead of the rest of him. "What time do you want me? And I'm warning you now, I'm not bringing trunks."

"Damn and I was planning to take them off with my teeth."

The vision dancing in his head was causing undue straining in his pants. "You don't play fair."

"But you're so much fun."

"How about 7.30 and I'll show you exactly how much fun I really can be."

"Sounds great. I'll look forward to it."

"Oh, so will I." She had no idea how much. A thought crossed his mind. "What about Gina?"

"She's out for the night, so you don't have to worry about the entire office knowing where you are. We've talked and she's going to keep her mouth shut as long as you're nice to her."

"Sounds like bribery to me."

"Yup. You have a problem with that?"

"Suppose not."

"Good. Hey, I'd better go. I'll look forward to seeing all of you later."

Oh, how she turned him on.

Tamsen hung up and found to her horror and surprise she was trembling. She'd spent ages hoping he'd ring while tormenting herself with should-I-shouldn't-I arguments as to whether she should ring him and now they'd spoken she couldn't control the shaking. It was ridiculous. She was breaking all of her own rules. Sex practically on the first date though she'd told Gina it was their third. She'd only just met the man - who was she trying to kid?

Tamsen checked the small charge she'd just released into the aquarium at her local doctor's surgery. "Some days I think it would be nice just to come back as a fish, you know, little fella. Swimming round all day, not a care in the world, being fed on time, everything you could possibly need on tap."

She traced her finger along the glass, reassured when the fish followed it. She loved playing games with her fish. She'd sat for hours like this as a child, escaping into a fantasy world, being the little mermaid swimming with her fish friends. They'd been easier to get along with than the people in her life at the time. She still spent more time talking to animals, plants and trees than she did real people.

After stripping the office battledress and changing into his workout gear, Matt stretched in anticipation of the endorphin rush from the workout to come. Life improved in staggering bounds when you let it, he mused. Work was as bleak as ever, but light had entered the dim darkness of his world in the form of the effervescent Tamsen. How he'd overlooked such a beautiful creature was beyond him. A sparkling gem cast upon the sands of his analytical life, a gift of unprecedented proportions from the gods themselves.

A surprising knock on the front door interrupted his decadent rumination.

"Mother! What are you doing here?"

"I've come to sort you and Angie out. Now hurry up and get my bags from the taxi. I've paid the poor man, but he couldn't get down your dreadful driveway for all that soil and rubbish. It's no wonder Angie up and walked out. What are you up to this time?"

"She didn't walk out, Mother - I asked her to leave, remember?" Why did his mother have to choose now to arrive? "And I don't need sorting out," he added as an afterthought.

Matt ran his hands through his hair; it was no use trying to argue anything out with Marguerite when she was in this frame of mind. Like the dutiful son, he headed out to relieve the poor taxi driver. One look at his face confirmed the man's suffering. It was a long drive from the airport.

Two huge suitcases, testament to his mother's inability to travel light, perched precariously on a pile of ponga logs. He so did not need this; he wanted to have a workout and then get to Tamsen.

He hauled the suitcases down the drive and up the stairs, wondering if the guest room was fit for guests. He knew from bitter experience that any suggestion she go to a hotel would fall on deaf ears. He was stuck with her for the duration.

"Okay, Mother, so what have I done to deserve the honor of your company?"

She threw him a look that would have served Medusa well. "You know exactly what you've done, Matthew. You've called off an engagement to possibly the most eligible young lady in the country and I want to know what happened."

In a foul mood, Matt stowed the suitcases in the barely passable guest room and trudged off to the lounge. It was apparent his workout wasn't going to happen; now he fixed his intentions on saving the evening with Tamsen. He sat down heavily on the couch and waited for his mother to join him.

Marguerite was old-school society. Having spent her life supporting his father in his business dealings, all she knew were cocktail parties, dinner parties, and being seen at the right places with the right people. It was a life he had been brought up to emulate and one he saw as devoid of soul. Since his father passed away, Matt felt increasingly responsible for Marguerite. But he drew the line at Angie. As far as he was concerned, he'd narrowly missed marrying his own mother and no way was he going to reconsider, no matter how much pressure was brought to bear.

Taking a look at his mother perched on the window seat in his living room, not a single hair out of place, turned out in the latest Dior fashion for the season, he had a surge of gratitude at the thought of fleeing into the arms of Tamsen.

"I'm sorry, Mother, but I've got a dinner engagement and I'm due there in just under an hour." He was reduced to lying and that disturbed him. "I don't have time to talk about Angie, and to be perfectly frank I don't think it’s any of your business. As far as I'm concerned I've had a lucky escape and that's the end of it."

"Well, Matthew, that's where I think you're wrong. You've never made a single responsible decision in your life without help from your father and me."

"That's bollocks and you know it!" Her words stung his skin. "You wasted your time coming over. I don't need you to run my life. You should be in Sydney with your charity cronies, where you're needed." He stood up to leave; the conversation was on a fast track to nowhere.

"Don't think you can just walk away without discussing this with me, young man." His mother's tone was terse and he had a familiar feeling in his gut. The one he used to get as a child, when he knew he'd let his mother down.

It took all his strength and will to head for the shower. "I told you, I'm going out for dinner, and I suggest you don't wait up because it'll be late when I get back."

"And what am I going to do for dinner?"

"Mother, you got yourself all the way here from Sydney without an invitation. I'm sure you can organize yourself a little dinner."

With that he bolted for his bedroom, out of earshot, so he could pretend she wasn't there.

CHAPTER SEVEN

Standing under the stinging hot water of the shower, feeling insignificant and unloved, barely aware of the pounding water, Matt tried to remind himself he was a thirty-year-old man not a sixteen-year-old boy. What his mother thought about the way he wanted to live his life was his mother's problem, not his. Yet Marguerite's cold, harsh words sucked the warmth and heat of the entire universe from his body and left him again longing to escape from his own home.

Marguerite couldn't keep her sticky fingers out of his life. Whatever possessed him to think taking a job with a firm back in New Zealand would put enough space between him and his family? Clearly the Tasman Sea wasn't a large enough body of water to keep his meddling mother out. He'd also had a naïve belief that being in another country would mean his father's influence would go unnoticed and he could make his own way in the world. But even after death, the old boy network still ground into action. It appalled him sometimes, the way business worked.

Toweling off, Matt located his most worn and comfortable jeans in the dresser. Gratitude that he could go and spend the evening with someone who seemed not to care about who he was, or where he came from, or what he did for a living gave him some comfort.

Then it hit him, with the thunderous power of a punch, something his mother said about the decisions he'd made in his life. He never even wanted to be a bloody lawyer. He'd simply been told, as far back as he could remember, that he would be one. "We need a lawyer in the family, Matthew. You're intelligent, a straight A student, so that's what you'll be."

With only one leg in his jeans, Matt had to sit down, overtaken by a sudden rush of nausea. Had he ever really worked out what he wanted for his life?

Tamsen found herself dithering in the kitchen, half out of her mind with worry. Whatever had possessed her to invite Matt over for dinner? For a start, the larder remained bare, no matter how many times she looked in it. It was official, there was next to nothing in the house to eat. Next she pulled the freezer door open, destroying her vain hope that the quarter loaf of multigrain bread and freezer-burned fish fingers, both of which had been a permanent fixture for as long as she could remember, had miraculously done a 21st century impression of the loaves and fishes and turned themselves into a gourmet meal.

"No such luck, eh, Azriel." Tamsen picked up the purring black ball of fluff, who affectionately nuzzled her under the chin. She adored the feeling of his purr, his vibration rattling through her throat.

Azriel's love was what Tamsen called "cupboard love" because he wanted feeding, but nevertheless she enjoyed the furry adoration. Cat food was one of the few things they did have a ready supply of - neither she nor Gina were prepared to risk the wrath of the affectionate stray who'd adopted them shortly after they moved in.

Tamsen pulled a packet out of the pantry and Azriel weaved precariously between her feet as she covered the small distance to his bowl.

"Well, at least you're not going to starve, are you, boy?" She tipped the revolting goop into his bowl. "If only Matt was this easy to feed." She gave him his ritual stroke as he settled to eat, his back arching to meet her hand.

Maybe Matt was this easy to feed - she could order something in. Besides, it wasn't her culinary talents that interested him.

Tamsen turned her attention to the bathroom, checking for at least the fifth time that it had been scrubbed clean. A suitable number of candles were in place to provoke the right mood, and the aromatherapy burner sat ready and armed with water and essential oils. Tamsen had settled on rose and patchoulli. She'd dripped a couple of drops of each into the water on top of the burner, and even without the flame the water was warm enough for the oils to begin their magical work of permeating the room.

Feeling like a temptress laying an elaborate trap, Tamsen stood at her wardrobe debating what to wear, a nasty sensation of déjà vu surrounding her.

"This is ridiculous," she said to Azriel who sat cleaning himself on the bed.

It was time to just be herself. If Matt didn't like the real Tamsen, best she find out early. Decision made, Tamsen wrestled her pale-green Indian silk dress from the wardrobe - the one her mother insisted made her look like some Taiwanese harlot - and slipped it on. To hell with the world, she thought as a sense of ease came over her. She dabbed musk oil on her pulse points and hung her favorite piece of jade at her throat, the smooth stone heavy, cool and comforting.

Azriel stopped washing himself, took one look at her and smiled the way cats do.

"Well, I'm glad you approve, Azriel."

He resumed washing himself, oblivious now to anything except taking care of his own needs. Tamsen studied him through the mirror on her dressing table; she could learn a lot from that cat. She turned her mind to applying a light dusting of makeup - just enough to not look pale, but not so much she ended up looking like the creature from the black lagoon when she got in warm water. Oh, the trials of being a woman.

"Be grateful you're a male, Azzie. I think I'll come back as a man-cat next time."

He settled down, cocooned in amongst crumpled, dirty clothing at the end of her bed, sleeping off dinner. What a life, she thought.

Matt knocked at the door of apartment 4C, a bottle of wine in his hand - his compromise, having resisted the urge to stop at the pub to medicate his emotions. He'd almost had to push Marguerite aside to get out the door. The gall of the woman. Thinking he'd cancel his plans just because she'd arrived unannounced.

He'd fumed most of the way over, a sense of injustice creating havoc in his guts. Anxiety and conflict had always cut a direct path to his digestive system. He was tormented by far too many unhappy memories of raging cases of diarrhea, or hours spent puking for no apparent reason. It had taken him years to work out the root cause of his illness was unresolved conflict - and now, he thought ruefully, it lay in wait for him at home. He shuddered.

Tamsen opened the door and his mother worries vanished. "You look stunning."

"You think so?" Her skin colored as a blush stole across her even features. "I was worried you might think I looked like a harlot."

"I don't have problems with harlots."

He couldn't help grinning. He'd made the right decision to leave Mother home alone. Tamsen was the most captivating creature. He'd never seen a dress like the one she wore; it gave her an exotic aura, appealing to him on levels he hadn't even known existed.

"Well, that's okay then. You'd better come in." She stepped aside, allowing him to enter her apartment.

"I thought you'd never ask." He could scarcely wait to see what other hidden treasures lay beyond the threshold.

"Wine, that's thoughtful of you."

He handed her the bottle and leaned forward, pressing a light kiss on her luscious lips. The touch was gentle and intimate, her lips soft and relaxed. He felt as if they'd known each other for years, not mere days.

"You'd better show me where the kitchen is so I can get the cork out of that bottle, get you drunk, then have my wicked way with you."

"Isn't it polite to eat first?"

"Maybe we could eat after, when we've worked up an appetite?"

Laughing, she took his hand. "I could go for that. We're going to have to order in 'cos I gave up on the cooking idea."

She led him into the kitchen. Sudden visions of her naked on his kitchen bench invaded his mind, a corresponding recollection and interest registering in his trousers. "Hmm, nice kitchen. Shall we christen this one too?"

"Can you talk about anything except sex?"

He needed to behave himself - he could be such a jerk. "Yes. If I want to."

"Why don't you try?" She rummaged in a drawer and found a bottle opener.

"Have I discussed with you the advantages of investing in unit trusts?"

"Forget it, talk more smut."

It was his turn to laugh. "I can't talk investment strategies then?"

"No, it's deathly dull and boring." She handed him the corkscrew and he made short work of the opening, the cork coming out with a resounding pop.

"Don't you love that sound?" He looked round for glasses. "Come on, out with the best crystal then."

"A nothing-but-the-best man? I have to wonder what you're doing with me then." She held his gaze, passing him a flute as unconventional as her. It was made of stained glass, with small green, yellow and red triangles made to look like tiny leadlight windows.

Disentangling himself from her gaze, Matt poured the wine. "You, beautiful lady, happen to be the best thing that's happened to me in a long time."

"Such a flatterer."

"Well, don't tell me you weren't hunting for compliments."

"I won't." She gestured toward the terrace. "You want to sit inside or outside?"

"You decide."

"You're the guest, so it's your decision."

"Outside." He threw her a devilish look. "So does that mean I get to decide where we do what all night?"

"You plan to go all night, do you?"

"Stop it." He was giddy at the thought of wallowing in her body all night. "You know what I mean."

"It depends." She sat herself down on the wicker two-seater facing the beach, patting the red-and-white-striped cushion next to her.

Being defiant, he leaned up against the glass panel that saved him from plummeting four floors to the ground. "On what?"

"On how well you behave yourself."

"Oh, I see." He took a slow sip of the wine, eyeing her over the rim of the glass. She reminded him of a porcelain doll, her legs tucked up under her, bare feet poking out from under the ornately embroidered material of her dress. "And what happens if I'm naughty?"

Mirroring his movements, she took a sip of her wine, eyeing him over the rim. It intrigued him, the way she played this version of Simon Says with him. "Maybe I'd have to spank you." She said.

His pulse raced. All manner of depraved thoughts played in his head. "I don't believe you'd do that."

"Well, behave - " she patted the seat next to her again " - and you won't have to worry about it, will you?"

He decided to park himself next to her. "Now I don't want you thinking I'm a pushover, all right?"

"I know you're a pushover. Her eyes never left his. "But don't worry about it."

They packed the last of the takeout curry boxes in the rubbish. Tamsen was stuffed and she hadn't laughed so much in a long time; Matt was funny, intelligent, articulate, caring and sensitive. How the man who'd carefully lectured her on the benefits of owning a worm farm could be the same man Gina swore and cursed about was hard to see.

She was giddy with wine, but her careful attempts at engineering a retreat to the oasis that was her bathroom were failing.

"Hey, you." Matt's hands were streaked in curry sauce. "Lead me to yonder bathroom - I recall that this morning you promised me a sensual soak."

"Girly manipulation's lost on you. I've been trying to get you there for the last twenty minutes, in case you hadn't noticed."

"All you had to do was ask."

"Where's the romance in that?"

"Ah." He smiled. "The lady wants romance. I can do romance. I can do anything you want me to do."

Her insides went to jelly. She took his hand and led him down the short hallway to the bathroom. The room was small, the sunken bath dominating, with a shower and vanity on the opposite wall.

"This is gorgeous."

She was pleased he appreciated the room - it was one of her favorites and she was happy to share it with him.

"Smells great too. Have you been burning oils?"

A man who enjoyed scent; she was in heaven. "No, but I will be soon. You deal to your vindaloo leftovers and I'll prepare myself and the candles."

He pulled her to him, being careful not to trail vindaloo over her dress. His presence was sure and demanding, it so turned her on. Looking up into his deep brown eyes, she realized the light made it difficult to see where his pupil and iris met – they were just pools of darkness. She was overwhelmed by his beauty and the thought that she would soon have the pleasure of exploring every little nook and cranny of him at her leisure.

"Might not be the only things burning by the end of the night if I have anything to do with it." He kissed her with a force and passion that left her breathless with desire.

A shiver ran down her spine as she lit the candles. He was glorious. She poured a dab of scented bubble bath into the rapidly filling tub, then positioned herself on the top of the toilet lid, intent on watching Matt. He was surveying the water, a distant look on his face. Maybe he was having some small out-of-body experience, scent could do that for you. She couldn't fail to remember her grandmother whenever she smelled mint; it brought back happy memories of preparing sauce for Sunday lamb lunches. A quiet moment of being somewhere else, with someone else, locked in an aroma.

When he at last snapped out of it she asked him, "Where were you?" She idly swung her legs backwards and forwards, her bare feet catching on the heated tiles underfoot.

"Right here."

"No, you weren't."

He looked puzzled, then cocked his head and looked up at her as if peering over a pair of imaginary glasses. "I was sitting in the bath as a child and my mother was banging on the door, trying to get me out, but she couldn't. Doesn't really make much sense."

He straightened up. "I don't particularly want to talk about my mother anyway. I've got better things to do."

"You have?"

He turned the taps off. "I have. I'm about to strip you naked and have my wicked way with you."

"Is that right?" She pulled her legs up under herself and sat perched atop the toilet like a pixie on a toadstool. "I'm afraid I've got news for you. You're going to stand over there and strip."

"I'm sorry?"

"You heard. Start ripping it off. I haven't got all night."

"I was good. This is a vile and evil punishment I don't deserve."

"True, but you'll do it anyway."

"I will, will I?"

"Oh yes."

"And why's that?" His voice was menacing, but she could tell by the look in his eyes that he was happy playing her game.

"Because of your reward."

"Reward?"

"I'll make it worth your while." She dropped her chin on her knees and hugged her legs, pressing her advantage home. "So get on with it."

He was a vision with his clothes on, but she looked forward to viewing him at leisure with them off.

"You're serious, aren't you?"

She nodded.

"I want you to know that I'm an amateur and I don't do this."

"There's a first time for everything. Now hurry up. Or do I have to go and get a whip?"

His features froze in shock for half a second; then he looked at her, took in her grin and relaxed. "You had me going there for a minute."

"I'll have you going for longer than a minute."

"I need you to come over here and help me. The hands-on approach."

"You're having those mummy fantasies again, aren't you?"

"Don't." He grimaced and she couldn't help giggling. "Get that tidy ass of yours over here and be my hands. I can undress myself any old time - I want you to do it."

"I suppose that could be fun, and since you asked so very, very nicely..."

Having uncurled herself from the toilet, she padded over to him. "You've got to take off your own shoes and socks. I don't do the shoe thing."

"I don't have to worry about finding you bonding with my boots, huh?"

"Gross. Hurry up and get them off - you've wasted enough time tonight."

He slipped his shoes and socks off, throwing them to one side. "So I could still be up for punishment then?"

"Very brave now that I'm off my pedestal and over here, aren't you?"

He reached out, pulling her to him by the shoulders, their faces millimeters from each other. "I am, so be very afraid."

With that he kissed her hard, his tongue snaking into her mouth, searching and demanding. She felt on fire; her entire body responded to him, her heart pounded. She wanted to slap him, run from him - his treatment cruel and savage - but she also wanted more.

She felt herself get wet and slick, just from a kiss. She craved him, desired him like she'd never desired before; it was overwhelming and frightening.

He pulled away from her abruptly. She was left stunned and gasping.

"Now undress me."

His eyes bore down into hers. He took her trembling hands and placed them by the top button of his shirt. Her knees were weak; the orange-and-blue pattern swam before her eyes. Her clammy hands seemed to stick to the silk. Half of her wanted to tell him to get lost, but the other half was giddy with delight.

Undoing his shirt, concentrating on the buttons, she attempted to let go of the conflicting thoughts and emotions raging within.

She slid the shirt off over his broad shoulders, allowing it to glide down his arms, then flicked it to the side of the room where his shoes and socks lay.

"Good." His voice was deep and creamy; she could tell he was equally turned on. "Suck here, I want to feel your mouth on me."

A small gasp escaped her lips as she latched onto his nipple. He allowed the finger he'd pointed with to trail slowly down her cheekbone, stopping to stroke her under the ear - the way she stroked Azriel. She rolled his nipple in her mouth, tasting, tormenting. She understood why cats purred, his touch was intoxicating.

She didn't need him to tell her to continue; she was wild with lust for him and wanted nothing more than to have him naked. She wanted to feast on his body. Explore every scented centimeter leisurely with her mouth and tongue and teeth.

She unbuckled his belt with hands trembling now with desire; he'd wound her up and there was no going back once she'd been wound. The black leather belt was new, the smell strong, and the leather caught in the buckle. She had to work hard to wriggle it free. He stood unmoving, watching her struggle, and she was furious he wouldn't help, yet it only inflamed her desire to disrobe him. The silver buttons on his fly were nearly as much trouble, compounded by the increasing pressure of his growing cock.

"I should make you undo those with your teeth," he growled.

"We'd still be here in a week." She looked up from her position on her knees. "You'd better hope like hell I don't break a fingernail, or you'll be in serious trouble."

He smiled. "Like I am at the moment, right?"

Bastard, she thought. She'd show him. By the time she'd finished he'd be pleading for mercy.

She dragged his jeans and boxers down and he stepped out of them. She sat back on her feet and surveyed the taut, tanned body in front of her. He was a fine looking man.

She leaned forward, placing a light kiss on his stomach, smelling and nuzzling that lovely part under his navel where the flesh was warm and soft, downy hair running in a dark line down to his pubic bone. He moaned a little and she felt his cock bobbing menacingly under her chin.

"That feels so good."

She kissed him again, just barely rubbing her lips over his hard stomach; the feeling was tingly and electric. "Hmm, it does, doesn't it?"

She moved away a touch and slapped him playfully on the rear.

"Oy, manhandling." The shock registered in his voice.

"Manhandling, my foot. Get thee in the bath, slave."

"Fighting talk."

"No." She spoke to him the way she'd address Azriel if he were misbehaving. "You're here for a soaking and I mean us to have a good one."

He lowered himself gingerly into the water. "And we might have a bath as well, right?"

"You just love twisting my words, don't you?" She started to peel her dress off provocatively; she was enjoying the ebb and flow of sexual tension.

"Hell, shoot me. I'm a lawyer - it's what we're trained to do."

Sliding her dress down to her waist, exposing her canary yellow bra, she noticed her nipples were standing proud under the material.

"Hey, Madam Spank."

She looked up, stopping what she was doing.

"You think you could get us both a jug of water before you do the lap-dance routine? Things could get a bit hot 'n' heavy once you get in here too."

Entirely lost for words, she found herself walking toward the kitchen. He was like no one she'd ever encountered before. One minute she was as horny as a rabbit on coke, the next she wanted to tear him limb from limb and store the pieces in her under-utilized freezer. What was going on?

Could be a long night; might as well take the fruit bowl too, she thought – we might need something to keep the blood sugar levels up.

"Yay, food too. You're an angel."

She couldn't even stay mad with him; he was quite a sight sitting there amongst the bubbles, soft light from the candles taking the edge off the stark room.

She quickly dropped the rest of her clothes to the floor and popped into the fragrant water opposite him.

"Hey, what happened to my private dancer?"

"You turned her into a waitress and she lost her nerve."

"Bugger." He reached for the fruit. "Can I make it up to you by peeling you a grape?"

"You may."

He set about peeling the skin off a grape with his teeth and she couldn't help laughing. He really was quite sweet.

She slid down into the warm, scented water, goose bumps prickling her skin. Loving the feel of the oily water and heat, she was also quite taken by the unsubtle leg rubbing up and down her calf. She headed off on an exploration of her own, wriggling her toes up the inside of what felt like a thigh, but it was hard to tell and the able grape peeler opposite wasn't about to give her any clues as to whether or not she was on target. He just kept working away at the grape.

"It doesn't have to be a perfect job, you know."

"Oh, but for you, my gorgeous creature, it does. Besides - " he grinned; she liked it when he grinned " - I'm a perfectionist. If a job's worth doing, it's worth doing well. That's the maxim I was brought up with."

He leaned forward, posting the juicy morsel in her mouth.

"So tell me..." She wriggled in the water again; it allowed her to surreptitiously reposition her foot - the one on the search-and-destroy mission. "How does a lawyer end up living in Titirangi?"

Matt looked puzzled. "I bought a house there."

"I figured that. I mean, like, I thought..." She wasn't sure what she was trying to ask.

"Why don't I live in the eastern suburbs? What's a well-bred man like myself doing out west?"

She flushed, realizing how ridiculous the question sounded. Stereotypical thinking annoyed her and here she was, indulging in it. "Sounds kind of lame, but I think that might be what I'm trying to say."

"To cut a reasonably long story short, I ran away."

"Ran away?"

"Yeah, the family are all resident in Sydney. I needed to escape the death-hold that my parents seem to think they should have over me, so I ran back here." He added as an afterthought, "And I hoped that going out west would keep them away. I didn't count on falling in love with the area."

"What do you mean, back here?"

"I was born here, educated in Sydney during my adolescent years, completed my degree between there and London, and once I'd graduated and done the big OE thing decided that settling here was the best of a bad bunch of options. London drove me nuts - too much concrete and damp. I quite like Sydney, but it was impossible being so close to my dysfunctional family after being away for a while. So here looked like a great compromise."

"But...Titirangi?"

"Don't knock it till you've tried it."

"I don't know if I'd be able to be so far away from the sea. That's the thing I love about the Shore - you don't have to go too far before you hit water."

"Bethels and Piha are just down the road. They're seriously wild and untamed too."

She smiled. "Wild and untamed - sounds nice."

He splashed her. "Wild and untamed - that's what I like about you."

"Me? I'm not wild and untamed."

"You seemed pretty wild and untamed to me last night." Matt's eyes narrowed. "I was hoping for a repeat performance."

"Were you now?" She hunted around with her foot and managed to find a sensitive spot; he winced when she wiggled her toes.

"Keep doing that - you're on the right track."

A sudden movement disturbed the water and she felt his foot plant itself firmly against her pubic bone. "You're pretty on track yourself."

"So what about you?" Pulling grapes from the bunch, he then devoured a couple. "Now you know I'm on the run from an over-controlling family, I want to know how you ended up installing fish in workplaces."

"It's a long story."

"Try me with the condensed version."

She thought about it for a while. "Really, our stories aren't that dissimilar, except that I haven't been gallivanting all over the world and my parents are still living just up the road, which makes for interesting dynamics." She pulled a face. "Especially when I'm not performing like the trained seal my mother expects."

"Ah. So you're the poor little rich girl who's tried to rebel but just doesn't seem to be able to divorce herself from the gravy train."

"That's a bit harsh." She was torn. If anyone else had summarized her life in those terms she'd have been appalled and angry. But Matt didn't seem to be judging her, or being malicious. He was just stating the facts.

Maybe it was her truth, and maybe the truth did hurt.

Tamsen countered. "Well, console yourself with the fact that at least you managed to get yourself some sort of higher education and your parents don't expect you to just fill in time with some sort of job to keep you out of trouble until you manage to catch yourself a decent man. And after that you're supposed to spend your time doing whatever it is that young ladies are supposed to do."

"Which is?"

She sighed heavily. "Give them grandchildren, preferably boys."

"Of course."

"Who can be sent to the right schools - "

"And become doctors and lawyers."

The conversation was absurd. Looking at each other, they burst into laughter.

When he'd calmed down Matt watched her trying to stifle her giggles. "So they've set you up in a business where you can meet the right sort of people."

She nodded.

"And instead you're sitting naked in a bath - "

"In their apartment."

"Nice touch. Their apartment with a lawyer - "

"A rebellious westie lawyer." She could see where the conversation was going.

"It's too bizarre."

She laughed again. "But it's great. Don't you see? Somehow, no matter how they try and control and manipulate, it keeps coming back to bite them." She slid forward between his open legs so she could trace her finger down the middle of his chest. "It's as if the universe conspires against them."

He pulled her closer to him, up onto his lap, her legs wrapping around his back. "Well, I just think it's wonderful. The universe can do as much conspiring as it likes as far as I'm concerned, especially if it means I get to sit here, hot and horny and naked with you."

With that he kissed her and she swore she saw stars.

Matthew was feeling prune-like. "That was nice, but why don't we adjourn somewhere a little drier and see where this is going."

"I thought you knew exactly where this was going." Tamsen kissed him on the tip of his nose. "In fact, I thought you were in the driving seat."

"Baby, I'll give you driving."

"I bet you will." She stood up and bent over in front of him, fumbling for the plug.

"Jayses, woman, a man could get arrested for what I'm thinking at the moment." His cock was at instant attention; the provocative view of her rear - coupled with bubbles snaking their way down her upper thighs - being more than he could stand. "Lead the way to the bedroom, babe, and I'll lick you dry."

Pleased to see her actions were having the desired result, she shivered involuntarily, and his cock bobbed in response.

He loved the chase, especially with Tamsen. She was so very erotic, yet seemingly oblivious to the fact she was doing incredible things to him. A heady mix that had his senses on high alert. He'd made love to her so many times in his head since their encounters last night, but the thrill of actually being with her - her scent, her warmth, her taste... Heaven.

She padded across the floor, leaving little watery footprints on the tiles. "I hate this floor - it's the only part of the room that puts my teeth on edge."

"What are you going on about?" He was thinking seduction and she was talking décor; there was something wrong.

"The tiles - feel them." She pulled a face and threw him a warm fluffy towel from the heated towel rail. "They've got grit embedded in the glaze so you don't slip over with wet feet. Gives me that awful feeling - you know, like when someone rubs their fingernail over a blackboard."

He felt the hairs over his shoulders and up the back of his neck come up on end. "I do." He shuddered. "Don't take me there, you'll kill the mood. Talk dirty to me."

She threw him an evil grin. "The toilet could do with a clean."

"Bitch."

Blowing him kisses, she began extinguishing the candles in the room, one by one. It wasn't the sort of blowing he had on his mind.

"Come on," she said as the last one died. "Follow me."

"Hell, it's a cave in here. Where's the light?" He was amazed at how black it had suddenly gone. "I'm in danger of breaking my neck."

She giggled and he saw a small shadow cross in front of the muted light coming from under where he assumed the doorway was. He'd been in such a hurry to get her naked he hadn't taken too much notice of their surroundings. Cursing his one-track mind, he told her, "The occupational, safety and health people would shut you down for this sort of inappropriate behavior, you know that don't you?"

"Give me a break - this is a private home, not a brothel."

"I'm glad you cleared that up for me." He made a tentative movement to get out of the bath, but decided against it. "Come on, get moving so I can see where I'm going."

"I thought you worked on feel."

"Listen, woman, I'll give you feel when I get my bloody hands on you. Now open that door so I don't break my neck trying to get out of this godforsaken tub."

She opened the door and in the light he saw her sashay out. "Tetchy, tetchy. Don't be long now." Her voice floated down the hallway, "I'll leave the boudoir door open so you can find your way. Wouldn't want you getting lost now, would I?"

After climbing out of the tub he vigorously toweled himself dry. He was tempted to dress, pop in the bedroom and peck her on the cheek just to show her she couldn't push him around. But on reflection he decided that would be idiotic, especially with the case of lover's balls he was developing. Jesus, she could be utterly infuriating.

He had no idea whatsoever how to handle her. All his usual tricks were just that -, tricks. Idiot, schoolboy, macho crap. He was seriously winging it with this woman and that was unsettling.

Right, he thought, time to take some positive action and get this little dance with yonder devil-woman underway. Pulling himself up to his full five foot ten and one-quarter inch, he set out for the bedroom. She was right about the tiles, he thought - a serious case of burn would be the result if you shagged on this floor and it wouldn't be due to the under-floor heating.

Her trail was easy enough to follow: a towel lay half out of the second doorway on his left. It amused him, reminded him of Hansel and Gretel. What did that make him - Hansel or the male version of a wicked witch? He chortled at his own insane thoughts. He certainly felt wicked anyway.

She lay on her bed, a vision in a ginger silk negligee, shoestring straps draped in an alluring manner off her shoulders. The room made him think of a gypsy caravan - beautiful and colorful textured fabrics adorned the walls, gathering in a rainbow of color on a circle of silver above the central ceiling light. He felt as if he'd been transported to another time and place. It was surreal, but so totally Tamsen it took his breath away.

"This is gorgeous. I've never seen anything like it." He threw himself on the bed next to her.

The room even smelt exotic - or was that her? He wasn't sure anymore. He felt as if he'd just walked into the set of some Arabian Nights movie, only this was real - she was real. "You are truly amazing. You know that?"

"So you keep telling me." She smiled; it was dazzling. The light from the candles she'd placed around the room danced in her eyes.

He was in serious trouble, he could feel it. A connection was being forged between the two of them he didn't understand. He kept trying to remind himself he was just here for a good time, but it felt as if more was happening. He couldn't describe how he was feeling.

Confused. Yes.

Attracted. Absolutely.

Connected. A definite possibility.

Horny. An absolute certainty.

The combination had him feeling all the more like a fumbling teenager.

He licked her on the shoulder, nibbling at the shoestring strap of her negligee. "Sexy lady," he growled. She was lightly oiled and smelled musky. "When did you put that oil on? You smell gorgeous."

"In the dark in the bathroom."

"Aha, so that's what you were doing. Prepping."

She giggled. "If that's what you want to call it."

"I do." He was touched she'd gone to so much trouble for him.

"So -" he ran a finger lazily up and down her front, stopping to circle her rapidly hardening nipple " - do you go to this much trouble for all the boys?" He flicked his fingernail over the nub and she shuddered in response. "Or am I getting special treatment?"

"You're getting special treatment. There's not many who make it into my sacred space."

"Sacred space, hmm?" He was rolling the nipple between his thumb and forefinger now, watching her breathing quicken and enjoying the power he was exerting over her stunning body. "Not many get to worship at the temple of Tamsen?"

"No." Her voice quivered. "Count yourself very lucky."

"Oh, babe, I do. You have no idea how much."

With that he released her nipple, slid his hand down to the dip in her belly and found her mouth with his.

CHAPTER EIGHT

Tamsen lay snuggled against Matt's chest. His breathing was regular and she was comforted by the scent of a man between her sheets. It had been a terribly long time since anyone had stayed with her. She lifted her head, looked at the clock and realized the birds had woken her.

"Matt, it's ten past five. You'd better wake up."

"Hmm?" He wriggled, drew her closer to him and attempted to haul the sheets up over them again.

She pulled away, shaking his arm gently. "Matt, you need to wake up - it's morning."

He opened one sleep-laden eye and looked at her. "What you saying, gorgeous?"

"We fell asleep. It's ten past five. You should probably shower - you'll need to get home and head for work."

"What?" He looked at the clock, comprehension registering on his features. "Aw, shit." He sat bolt upright. "I knew you'd be trouble. What did you do, put a spell on me or something?"

Oh, how she wished. "No. You slept like a baby – well, we both did." She pushed him playfully down on the bed, "No damage done, though. You've still got time to get home and ready for work and no one will ever be the wiser."

He flipped her back up on top of him; his hard cock pressing against her stomach. "We could always have a quick refresher course before I go."

She couldn't believe how much he turned her on; she could feel herself getting wet again. "Hm, sounds like a great idea."

He grabbed her hair, pulling her down to him so he could plant a kiss on her willing lips. God, she liked it rough - it was such a turn on. Then he hesitated.

"What's the matter?" Tamsen asked. He seemed to be losing interest and she hadn't a clue why.

"My bloody mother's in town."

"So?" She was confused.

"She arrived last night with some idiotic notion of getting me back with my ex-fiancée."

"Well, she hasn't got a hope, has she?" Tamsen kissed him passionately and he responded, fully aroused again.

"No - " he tried to talk around her insistent kisses " - you don't understand."

"I do." She continued the kissing barrage. "You can't come and fuck me tonight, you're seeing your mother, so you'd better give me a good one now before you go."

He struggled vainly under her. "Tamsen." His tone was stern and he sounded troubled.

She stopped being obstructive, a pending sense of doom filling her heart.

"It's not that, babe."

He really was disturbed. She felt sorry for him.

"What is it? You can tell me."

"Mother's parked in my spare room at the moment. She'll know I haven't been home."

"You're a big boy - you can stay out all night if you want too." She kissed him playfully on the nose. "And besides, wasn't I worth getting into trouble for?"

He smiled. "Oh, hell, yes."

"Well, then, stop your whining, give me the shagging I deserve for keeping you out all night, rush back home and tell Mother a huge pack of lies and all will be well."

"You're evil."

"I know. Now shut up and get to work."

He grinned. "But what'll I tell Mother?"

She gave him a wicked grin. "You'll think of something. You're a lawyer."

Tamsen sprawled across her bed, wrapped in a sheet, feeling deliciously used and abused. She'd just seen Matt out the front door; he'd refused all offers of a shower, citing in his defense that her bathroom was too much of a risk. The chances of him spending any more time around her naked and ever getting home for a change of clothes were apparently two inconsistent concepts.

She'd pouted, but he was probably right. If he'd showered she'd have joined him and they'd have had another marathon session. So he'd left - probably smelling like he'd spent the night shagging.

Tamsen wondered how the scene would play out when he got home. By all accounts his mother was a battle-ax. Poor Matt, he was in for a hell of a time. Part of her felt guilty, the other part was too busy drifting off into post-coital bliss. She didn't have to be up for at least another hour.

Life, she decided, was definitely looking up.

Matt couldn't believe he was sneaking into his own home. With any luck his mother would be asleep and he'd be able to fudge the time he got in. Why he thought there might be a chance he could manage that now when he'd failed miserably as a sixteen-year-old he couldn't fathom.

So far, so good. If he could make it to the bedroom, without bumping into her he was sweet.

Safe inside his bedroom, he could feel his heart beating rapidly. He leaned up against his closed door and stifled the overwhelming desire to giggle hysterically. He'd pulled it off. All he had to do was make the bed look slept in and get himself in the shower and then even he would almost believe he'd been here all night.

He threw the pillows around on his bed, feeling ridiculous. How the hell had he managed to get to this stage in his life and still be trying to pull the wool over his mother's eyes? Maybe because it was easier than fronting with the truth.

The evening he'd just had with Tamsen was one of the best he'd had in a very long time. She was great. They'd laughed, enjoyed each other's company, had plenty to talk about - and then there was the sex. Lord, the sex.

Showered, he climbed back into corporate battledress, checking his watch and debating whether or not he had time for breakfast. A quick coffee would have to suffice.

Matt realized he was happy and content - he'd forgotten what that felt like. It was amazing what good company, good food and great sex could do for a man's outlook on life. He really was a simple man with simple needs.

He cast a backward glance at his "slept in" bed. Best leave it as it was, as much as that grated; he might as well make the charade convincing.

He'd half drunk his coffee and was just looking for a pad and pen to leave a note for his mother when she walked into the kitchen.

"And what time did you get in?"

"Good morning to you too, Mother. Lemon looks really great on you. Is the robe new?" He leaned forward and planted a kiss on her forehead.

Marguerite's petite, delicate frame sheathed an iron will. Many were fooled by her fragility; Matt was not. He knew the warrior woman within.

He asked, "Would you like a cup of coffee? The jug's just boiled."

"You know I don't drink that instant muck, Matthew."

"Well, there're beans or grounds in the pantry, and you shouldn't have any trouble with the machine - you did buy it."

She looked hurt. He still hated it when she played the I'm-a-victim card with him; she was not and had clearly never been a victim in her life. "Aren't you going to have breakfast with me? I travel all the way from Sydney and my only child can't even find the time to sit down and have a decent discussion with me."

He sighed, looking at his watch. If he didn't get away soon he was going to get stuck in rush-hour traffic and he detested that. "Mother, I've got to get to work. I promise, I'll be home about six tonight and I'll take you out for dinner. We'll catch up then. How does that sound?"

She brightened. "That sounds fine, Matthew. I'll keep myself busy until you get home. It's pretty clear I haven't been uppermost in your mind since I arrived."

"I've got to go." He hugged her awkwardly. "I'll see you at six."

She called after him. "What shall I wear, Matthew?"

"Whatever you're comfortable with, Mother." He'd work out where to go for dinner based on what she chose; it was easier that way. "Casual" was a concept his mother neither acknowledged nor chose to understand.

Tamsen's foot tickled. She was vaguely aware of a raspy feeling, followed by sudden and intense pain.

"Ow, Azriel. Stop it, you beast." The cat was licking and chewing her foot, a sure sign she'd slept in past the little horror's breakfast time. "No need to worry about an alarm clock when you're around, is there, boy?"

He padded up the bed and started rubbing himself insistently against her hand. If she didn't get up he'd move to her face and start chewing her chin. It was an amusing ritual she'd grown used to, but she didn't particularly want to get out of bed this morning. Far too many shenanigans during the night, she suspected.

Locating her negligee on the floor, she smiled at the memory of how it got there, popped it on and headed to the bathroom, Azriel darting between her legs and in danger of tripping her up. He was an affectionate little man and she was grateful for his company.

I'm late starting the day today. Her friend, the blank page, waited patiently for an explanation while she collected her thoughts. Only Azzie and I at home. Gina's God knows where, and for the second morning in a row I can hardly close my legs due to the amount of time they spent with gorgeous Matt between them. I feel like such a decadent creature but he's wonderful. I've never met anyone like him. I can't wipe the smile off my face. He just has to be the most amazing person. We've got so much in common it's scary. Horror of horrors, I'm not going to be able to see him tonight. His mother's in town. Some desperate attempt to get him and his ex back together. Over my deceased body! This one's worth fighting for. I hope she's up for it. Sounds like it could be Prada handbags at fifty paces.

Tamsen set about locating something that resembled food for breakfast. The food fairies hadn't been in during the night and restocked the cupboards. A lone and battle-weary banana was all that was left of the fruit bowl after Matt's grape assault. It would have to do. At least there was still some dandelion tea on hand. She poured boiling water over the leaves and made short work of the banana.

Azriel mooched back to his bowl, giving her another one of those is-this-all-there-is looks that cats perfect in order to keep cat-food companies earning billions of dollars per year.

She giggled at him. "'Fraid so, pal. I'll do the shopping on the way home. What would you like this week - salmon or chicken?"

He looked at her as if she'd lost the plot. Today, she decided, he could be right.

Life was good. There was an industry gathering coming up in Wellington this weekend and Gina was heading down with her on the train. They had both decided a side of shopping and girly fun should be thrown in for good measure.

Matt pulled as far down the driveway as he was able. He really must get onto the workmen again - the landscaping was taking forever. How tough could it be, building a couple of retaining walls and planting a few more trees? Admittedly the site was steep, but these guys were supposed to be the best.

His tolerance levels were shot. The day had been crap and the prospect of fending off his mother's concerted attacks didn't appeal. He'd resigned himself to a fight. Best see what she was wearing and work out where to for dinner.

He had in his mind a little intimate upmarket restaurant in Parnell a client had recommended. Reservations were pretty tight, but his man had called and put in a good word. If they could be there within the next two hours a table was theirs.

Dropping his briefcase in the foyer, he heard voices coming from the kitchen. Strange.

"Ah, darling Matthew, I thought I heard your car." Marguerite met him in the lounge, a glass of champagne in her hand. She never drank alone.

He looked around but couldn't see anyone. "Is there someone here? I thought I could hear voices."

"Hello, Matt."

Every hair on the back of his neck came to attention. His palms broke out in a sweat and he had the urge to run out of the house. He had to check himself; it was his house.

"Angie." Her name stuck in his throat. "Fuck!"

"Matthew. Language, please." Marguerite had a pained expression.

He'd give her pain, he thought. "What the hell are you doing here?"

"I invited her, Matthew. She's graciously consented to come out to dinner with us so we can tidy up this whole misunderstanding."

"Over my dead fucking body." Matt felt a flush of rage rising in a torrent from his aching gut. All the frustrations of the day had been looking for an opportune moment to unburden themselves, and this was it. "You can get the hell out of here." Matt directed the stinging missiles of his words at Angie.

Angie just stood there, an infuriating, superior look on her face. Matt had resigned himself a long time ago to the fact she and his mother worked hand in hand. But the audacity of her, to arrive here now and expect...it was too much.

"Now, Matt, don't be like that, darling." She even sounded smug.

"Don't fucking darling me." He shot her a look he hoped could kill but she didn't even flinch. He was swimming in shit, no match for their combined talents.

"If you're not going to leave, you two can do what you like. I'm gone." No way was he spending an evening with arsenic Angie. "And you - " he jabbed a finger in Angie's direction " - had better be off the property when I get back or I'll call the police and have you physically removed."

"Matthew!" His mother looked mortified.

"I'd advise you to stay well out of this, Mother. The Angel Gabriel will be welcoming Lucifer at the pearly gates before I get back with this bitch."

Blinding, white-hot anger fueled his return to the car. Only as he backed out the driveway did he realize he had absolutely no idea where he was going.

Tamsen busily unpacked the groceries, a chore she hated. It was bad enough she'd had to spend all that time dragging herself around the supermarket aisles, dodging pensioners and children. And the men! Those same men who were able to park cars on ten-cent pieces, but didn't seem to be able to apply the keep-right rule in a simple supermarket aisle. Now she had to haul the darned stuff into the kitchen and unpack it. Where was the justice?

The intercom buzzed. She wasn't expecting anyone. Surely it wasn't Gina being delivered home drunk again?

"Hello?"

"Tamsen, it's Matt. Sorry to arrive unannounced."

"Not a problem." She punched the security gate lock to let him in the building. "Come on up."

Oh, joy. She felt like jumping up and down on the spot. He was supposed to be going out for dinner with his mother. What could have happened? Did she really care? The point was he was here. Her mind ran off in all sorts of dirty directions. What a bonus.

She cast a glance over the kitchen - the mass of displaced food items plus plenty more still waiting to be discovered hidden inside opaque plastic. What the hell, the mess wasn't too bad.

At the knock on the door she almost sprinted to greet him.

"Azzie, get out the way." The black ball of fluff was sitting patiently at the door so she picked him up. "You know it's not time to go out yet."

"Hey." Matt looked strung out. His tone was jovial but it didn't match the sadness that Tamsen saw in his beautiful brown eyes. "Didn't know you had a cat."

She was touched to see Matt tickle Azriel under the chin. Azzie purred in appreciation, a good sign. The little man had always been quite the judge of character.

"Yeah, he loves it up here on the fourth floor. He'd like to get out at this time of night though. I take him down with me in the morning. He gets to gallivant around all day and then he spends the night up here with us. He's rather cool, don't you think?"

"I do."

Tamsen shut the door and put the cat down. Azriel had got no more than a couple of feet from them before Matt collected her in a huge bear hug, his whiskers scratching the side of her neck as he nuzzled her. He felt good, even if his scent was strong and acrid; he still wore the stress of the day.

It made no matter. She longed to crawl inside him, be devoured and consumed by him. He made her crazy with lust. His mouth found hers. His kisses were urgent, angry even. She didn't care. Her body reacted instantly to his frenzy, her core temperature rising with the flush of desire. As he pressed her against the wall of the hallway she felt alive, vital, lost in the moment.

"God, I need you," he gasped. "It feels like I need to kill someone, or fuck."

"Fuck away."

CHAPTER NINE

Afterward they both slid down the wall until they were sitting on the cool floor, having taken care to untangle a mass of sweaty limbs and twisted clothing. Tamsen noticed beads of sweat running in small rivulets in front of Matt's ears. His chest heaved as his breathing slowed.

Tamsen laid her head against his damp upper arm and asked, "What that was all about?"

He looked across at her, a sheepish grin taking shape. "Er, I'm not actually quite sure." He kissed her on the crown of her head.

"Maybe we should get cleaned up and you can tell me why you're here and not having dinner with your mother, hmm?"

"A very good idea." He grinned wickedly. "You just want to get me in that bathroom of yours again - I know your game."

She laughed out loud. "You don't think there's much chance of seduction after that little performance, do you?"

"I have to admit, you might have a point there."

He looked around, searching for the remains of his clothing. "What is it about you? I seem to be developing this habit of tearing my clothes off in the most inappropriate places." Matt's shirt buttons lay scattered across the room - he'd been in such a hurry to get his clothes off he'd almost shredded them.

She stood up, searching for her missing panties, which seemed to have vacated her jeans in the rush. "I'm just a devil woman is all."

"You're not wrong there." He was collecting buttons off the floor. "Don't suppose you're much of a seamstress, are you?"

"I'm sure I've got a sewing kit stashed somewhere."

"Stolen from some unsuspecting hotel, no doubt."

"How did you know?" She laughed.

"Just a wild guess."

"Come on, you." She smacked him playfully on the bottom. "Bathroom."

Matt sat shirtless on the leather sofa watching Tamsen sew the few buttons he could find back on his shirt.

"My, you're a woman of many talents."

She stopped work and smiled. "I am and you haven't even seen the start of them yet."

"Is that right? Keep up with that sort of dirty talk and you might have another bout of raping and pillaging on your hands."

She laughed. "I thought it was the victim, not the perpetrator, whose clothes got shredded."

"Ah, so I'm lousy at role play." He shrugged. "Maybe you can teach me a few tricks."

"I'm sure I can."

He knew she could. He'd had no intention whatsoever of having sex with her when he walked in the door. He hadn't even realized quite how uptight and angry he was with his mother until he got here. In fact, he'd been surprised to find himself on the motorway coming in this direction. His anger and humiliation at the scene he'd come home to still burned deep. His mother had gone way too far this time.

Tamsen cut into his thoughts. "So, are you going to tell me what happened?"

"We just had the best sex."

She threw the pincushion at him.

"Hey, watch it. Lethal weapon. That could take somebody's eye out."

"You were supposed to be having dinner with your mother, remember?"

"Oh, right, that's what happened." He rubbed his chin thoughtfully, certain it would push some more of her buttons. He liked it when he got a reaction from her - not just a sexual response but any kind of retort. He could almost refuel from her vital life force.

"Oh, right, that's what happened," she mimicked him, even down to the rubbing of the chin.

He couldn't help but laugh. "Woman, you are glorious."

"Stop trying to change the subject and tell me what happened tonight. You arrived like a bull at a gate." She threw him a sly smile. "Not that I'm complaining, of course."

"Me being hung like a bull and all."

"Absolutely." She nodded her head vigorously.

"You're mocking me, aren't you?"

"Would I?"

She was a goddess. He'd never felt so at ease with a woman - she drained all the tension from any situation. Yet he also liked the way she stood up to him, challenging him at every turn.

"You should be a therapist, you know that?"

"Nah, couldn't do it." Tamsen bit through the last of the thread, all the buttons they could find now firmly sewn back on his shirt.

"Why not? You'd be good at it. Look how much more relaxed I am now - you just have that effect on me."

"That's not me, it's the sex." She threw him another provocative grin. "And therapists aren't allowed to fuck the patients, so it'd never work."

She really was a gem. "Most women would be incensed if anyone suggested it was just a shag that had changed the mood."

"I'm not most women."

"Ain't that the truth." And wasn't he grateful.

She threw the shirt back at him. "You're still missing a couple. Be more careful next time you undress."

"I'm not worried - I've another fifteen in the wardrobe exactly the same."

"Well, you don't have to wear them." She had that wicked look in her eye again; he had a vision of the entire office naked.

"I'm afraid casual Friday's not ever going to be part of the doctrine where I work."

"Maybe you need to change where you work."

"What makes you say that?" He was puzzled - not at the question, but at his own reaction to it.

"I don't know. You strike me as someone who's searching for something but you're not quite sure what."

He stood up, a gamut of conflicting thoughts running through his head.

Tamsen crossed the room and was in front of him in an instant, helping him do up what was left of the buttons on his shirt.

Aware of her scent, the clean smell from their showering, he stopped what he was doing. "Is it me, or does this shirt stink?" He lifted up his arm and sniffed.

"It stinks. Why don't you let me wash it?"

"But that means I'd have to stand around here half naked for the duration." Raising her arms, he checked out her petite frame. "I don't think you'd have any shirts in my size."

She grinned. "I think I could stand having a half-naked gorgeous man lying around my apartment for a few hours. I'm prepared to make a sacrifice for the good of the cause."

"You think you'll be able to keep those lust-crazed hands off me?"

"I think I'll manage." The sarcasm in her voice made him want to laugh.

Smelly shirt in hand, Tamsen left the room. Matt ferreted in his pants pocket for his cellphone. Best cancel the reservation for dinner. It would have been nice to take Tamsen out, but smelly, disheveled shirt aside, he wasn't dressed for the occasion and he had no intention of going home to his mother's carefully set trap. As much as the option appealed, taking Tamsen back there and wiping the smug looks off Marguerite and Angie's faces was out of the question. He wouldn't put her through that.

She'd disturbed him, though. Suggesting he was looking for something different. Perhaps his disenchantment with the job was more than general malaise.

"All done." Tamsen arrived back in the lounge, Azriel trotting behind. The cat behaved more like a dog, he thought.

She added, "It's washed and in the dryer, so I'm only going to have the pleasure of your nakedness to feast on for half an hour or so."

"Damn, is that all? And here I was thinking I should break out the baby oil and we'd be able to have hours of fun playing naked Twister."

"Don't know about naked Twister, but you've had such a lousy day why don't you let me give you a back rub?"

He cocked his head. "Does that involve baby oil?"

"Better." She ran a fingernail across his chest and he shivered in response. "Go settle yourself on my bed and I'll be right with you."

"I don't need asking twice."

Towels in hand, Tamsen turned her mind to oil combinations. Let him think this was a nice "touchy feely" session – she was in the mood for more sexual gratification and bodice ripping. On her terms. So what if the price to pay was being seamstress again? Slow and sensual was off the menu, hot and heavy was on. Lavender oil for stress and tension, ylang-ylang for heat and passion.

Armed with supplies, she discovered the only thing missing from the bedroom was Matt. Where the hell could he have got to, she wondered. He couldn't have got lost, could he? She heard voices from the kitchen and went to investigate.

"Bleedin' hell, a woman gets home and finds a half-naked boss lounging in her kitchen."

A very drunken Gina was holding herself up on the kitchen bench and leering at Matt. A certain practiced huntress stare Tamsen knew well and disliked and one Gina normally reserved for the female of the species.

Matt was clutching a glass of water and inching backwards, the look of a trapped animal in his eyes.

"Gina, I wasn't expecting you." Tamsen wasn't sure whether to try and distract her or belt her.

"I can see that." Gina's voice took on a predatory tone. "He's rather tidy with his clothes off, isn't he, Tams?"

Matt looked across at Tamsen, a flash of fear crossing his features. "I was just getting a glass of water before we..."

"Before you what, gorgeous?" Gina had him cornered, the microwave at his back. She reached out and ran one finger down the middle of his chest, the gesture lewd and suggestive.

Matt went pale. Tamsen's stomach clenched. "Gina!" she snapped.

Matt jumped but her drunken friend didn't seem to register her own name. Tamsen stifled the urge to cover the space between them and pull Gina away by the hair.

"What?" Unsteady on her feet, Gina turned to face her friend. Matt took the opportunity to slip quickly out of the tight spot by the microwave and was at Tamsen's side in an instant.

"Just wait for me in my room, Matt." Tamsen touched him reassuringly on the arm. "I'll deal with her, she's just drunk and out of control - " she threw Gina a steely look " - as usual."

Gina stumbled backwards, just managing to catch herself on the bench top, and slouched against the microwave, filling the space Matt had vacated. "Not as usual. Don't believe a word of it, boss man. Come on, Tams, share. Since he's here he could fuck us both. You'd like that, wouldn't you, boss?"

Matt looked at Tamsen, fear replaced by horror. "I think you're right. I'll just wait for you." He cast a despairing glance at Gina, shook his head, and escaped down the hallway.

Tamsen called after him, "Don't worry, I won't be long."

"Don't worry, I won't be long." Gina's mocking singsong tone only fueled Tamsen's fury.

She turned on her friend. "What the fuck do you think you're up to?"

"Why do you want him, when you can have me?"

Tamsen fought another urge to slap her. Gina was always like this when she got drunk - over the top and amorous, especially whenever Tamsen had a man around. "You can't even stand the man. Why'd you have to do that?"

"Do *what*?" Gina seemed genuinely perplexed by the question.

"Treat him like a piece of meat."

Gina's bottom lip started to tremble. "That's what he is, isn't he? That's what they all are. It's me you love, isn't it?"

Tamsen felt some compassion for her friend. It wasn't her fault she kept on screwing the wrong women. Take her latest - she was a complete and utter piece of work.

"Oh, God, Gina. We've been through this. Why do you keep doing it?" But it was useless talking to her when she was drunk. And in the morning she'd either deny this had ever happened or wouldn't remember anyway. "Come on, why don't we get you into bed."

Gina looked at her, makeup smudged across her cheek, hair tousled; she looked as if she'd been ravaged tonight anyway. Why she thought she needed her and Matthew, Tamsen had no idea.

"I suppose, if you're sure you don't want him to share." All the fight had gone out of her.

"Quite sure."

Gina laughed, high-pitched, one of those laughs only drunks seem to be able to find inside themselves. "Well, he seems to have put a smile on your face. He must be bloody good."

The tightness in Tamsen's stomach returned. "I'm not going there with you, Gina. Just shut up about it."

She laughed again. "Ooh, that good, huh? Wait till the girls in the office hear about this."

Tamsen half dragged, half carried Gina down the hall and dumped her unceremoniously on her bed. Her friend's eyes closed almost on impact. At least Tamsen and Matt wouldn't have to worry about being disturbed.

It was an impossible time of the evening for her to be coming home drunk. 7.30? She hadn't exactly been out on the town all night.

Tamsen entered her own room and closed the door. Matt sat unmoving on the bed, a look of thunder etched on his even features.

"So, that'd explain why she wasn't at work today. Out somewhere getting pissed."

Tamsen's stomach fell. "She wasn't at work?"

"Nup." His expression hadn't changed.

Tamsen sat gingerly on the bed beside him. Why she felt responsible for the idiot choices Gina was making she didn't know, but for some strange reason she did.

"No doubt there's a good explanation for it."

Matt shot her a disparaging look. "Tamsen, don't."

"Don't what?"

"Try to defend her. You could see how drunk she was. And from the way you dealt with her, it's not the first time she's behaved like that."

Tamsen shrugged.

"It's certainly not the first time she's been absent from work without any kind of explanation."

Tamsen decided she'd heard enough. "You want that massage, or do you want to talk about my reprobate house mate?"

He nearly smiled and she thought she saw some of the anger drain away.

"I'd never turn down the offer of a sexy woman's hands on my body."

Matt tried to keep his mind off the troubles of the day, which seemed to be increasing at a rapid rate. The brief sexual interlude with Tamsen had lowered his tension levels and the massage further eased his strained nerves, but the thought of his mother brought it all rushing back at a rapid rate of knots. He wished Tamsen hadn't brought it up.

Neither did he wish to turn his mind to the comatose drunk passed out down the hall. No wonder Gina hadn't turned up at work this morning. It started to make sense too - the number of sick days, her inability to take instruction, her "not being with it" when she was on the job. The thought of having to deal with her in the morning, armed with the knowledge gleaned here tonight, made him feel physically sick. Never mind the potential damaging fallout with Tamsen.

As for Gina's exhibition in the kitchen, he almost shuddered. He'd never felt so trapped in his life. Well, except around his mother. Which brought him neatly back to the reason he was lying here in the first place.

"You haven't answered me. So what happened with your mom?" Tamsen clearly wasn't going to give up on the discussion.

He sighed heavily. "I think I mentioned to you she was the control freak from hell."

"Something like that." She continued to massage his belly.

Even thoughts of how hellish the day had been weren't cooling his ardor. Tamsen had the most magnificent hands; it was as if a soothing, healing current ran directly from them. Just a touch and he was putty in her hands.

"When I arrived home from work today..." He lifted his head up so he could look her in the eye. "Some of us do work, unlike your drunken friend out there."

"We can talk about Gina later. It's you and your mother I'm interested in at the moment. Why don't you stick to that?"

"Ever considered being a barrister? Your approach to a direct line of questioning's right on the mark."

She laughed. "Stop trying to change the subject."

He dropped his head back on the pillow. "Right. Mother." He took a deep breath and closed his eyes, focusing on the pleasurable sensations coursing through his body. Maybe it wouldn't be too bad sharing with Tamsen, he thought. She seemed to have this knack of making him feel like everything would be okay.

"So you got home from work," she prodded.

"I'd arranged dinner for the two of us at the most expensive restaurant I could find - had to call in a couple of favors for the bookings, but that's beside the point. But then I arrived home and my bloody mother was entertaining my ex-fiancé."

"Ooh. Nice!"

He loved the way she had of making the right comment, in the right tone, at precisely the right moment. "Exactly. To say I was thrilled would be an understatement."

Another tingle of pleasure ran through his body. She was massaging his pectoral muscles. He'd have happily shut up and shagged her again but there was little chance of getting away with that. Not yet, anyway.

"So the two of you had a little show-down and you left in a white-hot rage."

"How did you know that? Have you been stalking me?"

"Elementary, my dear Watson." She giggled. "You were pretty angry when you got here."

He wiggled his aching cock against her. "Parts of me were."

She wiggled back. "No more than a natural reaction to the frustration and anger you felt at your mother. You're just lucky I'm understanding."

"And a bit of a whore."

She slapped him on the thigh. Hard.

"Sorry. I deserved that. Though I meant it in the most flattering way."

She smiled seductively. "I know. It pays to keep you on a short leash until I have you trained right."

Another bolt of desire shot to his nether regions. "Stop talking dirty to me. I'm having a hard enough job as it is trying to relax."

"Would you like me to stop?"

"No."

"So, your mother. I take it she doesn't approve of the cancellation of the wedding she had planned?"

"We didn't ever get as far as the planning stage. Some of the ideas Angie had about marriage woke me up to the fact I was looking at a lifetime union that would be a living hell."

"You weren't compatible?"

"On paper we looked perfect. It was only when I started imagining waking up with her every morning, the same old daily grind..." He was having trouble finding the words to describe the discontent he'd felt every time he turned his mind to being with her for the rest of his life.

An anxious feeling began to stir in his stomach. He realized it was the same one he had when his mother was around. Why had he never put the two together before now?

"It couldn't just be called pre-wedding jitters then?

"No. I could tell it was all wrong. The day I found myself down on the waterfront looking at apartments I knew it was all over."

"Looking at apartments?" She sounded puzzled. "But you love gardens – you can't have a garden in an apartment."

"Exactly. That's how it was."

She giggled. "I see now."

"So you can imagine how pissed off I am that Mother's decided to put her paddle in and try to resolve the 'little misunderstanding'." His tone of voice went up a couple of octaves in imitation of his mother.

Tamsen couldn't help laughing. "And I'm sure she'd beat you if she could hear you taking the mickey out of her."

"I'd rather you did." He drew her to him, his lips finding hers in an instant. His tongue probing the warm recess of her mouth.

She met his passion, rubbing her body against his with reckless abandon. He couldn't stand not to be inside her. The power she had to make him want her was terrifying. His desire churned inside, insatiable, like a terrible addiction - the more he fed on her, the more he wanted her.

She pulled away from his mouth, gasping. "You'll devour me."

"That's the idea."

He enjoyed watching her struggle with herself. She'd been driving him wild long enough. It was satisfying watching her self-control crumble.

"Come on." Her words conveyed a sense of order her body did not; he could still feel her trembling. "That shirt of yours must be dry by now - why don't we head out for something to eat?"

"I thought you were hungry for me."

"Oh, sir, but I am."

"We could eat in."

"Except we wouldn't eat anything."

"Except each other." He couldn't resist.

"Stop right now." She looked flustered. Her tangled hair hung seductively over her bare shoulders, the thin cheesecloth top scarcely covering her erect nipples. "You can do what you like, sunshine, but I'm going out for dinner."

CHAPTER TEN

He was a horror, Tamsen thought. At this rate she'd lose pounds. So much sex and hardly any food. Though it was the nicest possible way to slim down – beat starving herself into osteoporosis any day.

One look in the bathroom mirror confirmed her suspicions: yep, no doubt about it, he made her hot. Her cheeks were flushed and she looked like she'd just run a marathon, not given someone a relaxing massage. She beamed at herself. Like there was any chance anyone could relax with that half-naked god underneath them. An involuntary shudder ran up her spine.

"Someone walk over your grave?"

She spun around and he was in the doorway, buttoning up his clean shirt. "Out you." She wagged a pointed finger at him. "You and me and bathrooms are a bad combination. You'll have your clothes off again in no time and I'll never get fed."

"You and me and anywhere's a bad combination. Maybe we should stay in - then it wouldn't matter if our clothes came off." He grinned wickedly. "Unless, of course, you're an exhibitionist."

"Be off with you." She slipped past him in the doorway, not daring to let any part of their bodies touch lest she end up naked and starving.

He followed her back into the bedroom. She quickly changed her top - she was going to have a devil of a job getting the oil out of it. The muslin blouse was one of her favorites too; the material caressed her skin like the wings of a thousand angels. She made a mental note not to offer a massage to him again unless she was naked too. Another involuntary shudder.

Quelling that thought, she turned to him. "So. Where we eating?"

He held his hands up in mock surrender. "I'm not even going to answer that question on the grounds that whatever I say will get me into trouble. You decide."

"There's a café just down the road, nearly on the beachfront. You want to try there?"

"Sounds fine to me. I figure the sooner I get you fed, the sooner I can get you back here and we can start again where we left off."

Matt tried to sneak into his own home for the second night running. This time he couldn't escape his mother. She sat waiting for him, as she'd done so many times in his youth.

"Mother." He knew better than to simply walk past without acknowledging her presence.

"Matty. I'll never understand you." Marguerite wrung her hands. He hadn't seen her do that since his father died and an unexpected pang of guilt stopped him in his tracks. Sometimes he hated being her only offspring.

Matt sighed, all the fight knocked out of him - or maybe he'd fucked it out. "There's not a lot to understand, you need to accept that Angie's not going to be a part of my life and we'll be fine."

"But, Matty -"

Matt held up his hands. "I won't argue with you on this, Mother. I'm not backing down and that's the end of the matter."

Marguerite, sensing the undermining of her position, crossed the room and laid a cool hand on his cheek. "You so remind me of your father when you talk like that." The woman was a masterful manipulator, but something about her seemed to have softened, or maybe he was looking at her through new eyes.

"I miss him too, Mom."

"Yes, well - " Marguerite turned her back on him, " - let's not go there, emotions have run high enough around here today."

After years of watching his parents, Matt knew that signaled the end of their conversation. He could only hope that this time she would listen to him.

Why should this time be any different, he wondered?

Matt was having increasing difficulty concentrating on the file open in front of him. It was happening more often. The Tamsen factor. She'd destroyed his work ethic and really gotten under his skin.

Gazing out his 14th floor window over the glass-like harbor, he watched yachts and pleasure boats jockeying for position with ferries and naval frigates. He usually found the vista calming; today it only highlighted the intense confusion milling within him.

"Don't tell me she's dumped you already?" Danni's enquiry as she unceremoniously placed a flat white on the only vacant space on his desk brought him back to the present moment.

"No." He couldn't help sounding indignant. It wasn't even Tamsen who concerned him. It was the scene in her kitchen that was really getting to him. How the hell was he to deal with Gina's absences now?

"Danni?"

"Yes, Matt?" She was busying herself filing again. He found himself uncharacteristically avoiding following the slim line of her legs up to the hem of her skirt. He obviously had Tamsen fever bad.

"What's your opinion of Gina?" He decided to close his office door; there was no reason anyone else should hear them discussing another staff member.

She looked concerned. "Is there a problem? It's not like you to shut your door."

He shrugged. "Just wouldn't like it to get back to her that we were having this discussion."

"Not much chance of that - she's not turned up yet and she's nearly an hour late most mornings."

"Have you had anything to do with her socially?" He felt lousy digging for information, but he needed to confirm his suspicions.

"She's been out with us girls a couple of times. Gets blind drunk and usually ends up having a fight with one of us."

"What, physically?"

"No, verbally. She's only a little thing, but she's got a mouth on her. Some of the things that have come out of it - man, what an education."

"So what are the fights over?" Matt couldn't imagine his staff brawling, or yelling at each other; most of the girls were really friendly and conservative.

"She usually comes onto one of the girls or their boyfriends and it doesn't take long to get ugly. She doesn't like anyone saying no to her, that's for sure."

Flashes of his own brush with her in Tamsen's kitchen came rushing back. Matt shuddered.

"Don't know how that lovely girlfriend of yours puts up with her. Though I have to say, she's been her saving grace a couple of times."

Matt paid more attention. "What do you mean?"

"When things have gotten really ugly, it's usually Tamsen who calms her down and manages to smooth things over with the other girls." Danni looked thoughtful. "She has this way of managing to disperse bad feeling. It's almost as if she casts a spell over everyone. Hard to describe unless you've seen her do it."

He was interested. "She's done this a few times, smoothed things over?"

"Absolutely. Everyone thinks Tamsen's great. I'm surprised it took you so long to notice her."

He felt himself flush. She was right. He wasn't usually backward at coming forward as far as women were concerned.

"But then, as I've said before and I'll say it again - " she winked at him " - she's not your type, is she, boss?"

Matt's tone was teasing. "Thanks, Dan. I think that's about as much as I need to know." He knew Danni enjoyed the banter.

"Watch yourself, Matt. That Gina - she can be an evil piece of work when she wants to be."

She went back to her filing and he continued on staring blankly at the pages in front of him. What the hell should he do now?

Tamsen had finished her morning rituals and changed the sheets on her bed. They could damn near walk themselves to the laundry room, she thought as she loaded them into the washing machine.

She couldn't help sniffing the pillowslip before she popped it in. It still smelt of Matt. Breathing in his pungent scent filled her with joy. It was almost a shame to wash him away, but there was nothing like freshly laundered sheets either. If she had the time she'd change her sheets every day.

Skipping down the hallway, thoughts of the blissful night she'd had with Matt coursing through her head, Tamsen almost collided with the walking train wreck that was Gina stumbling toward the kitchen.

"God, do you have to be so happy in the mornings?" Gina sounded as derelict as she looked.

"You could be too if you'd stop abusing your body the way you do."

"What, and risk living the dull and boring life you do? Never."

Gina's comment stung. Tamsen didn't think her life was dull and boring. In fact, it was anything but. How getting trashed night after night to the point of not being able to turn up for work, being carried out of parties and – Tamsen's stomach turned at the thought - stealing other people's partners could be considered a better way of living was beyond her.

"Really, Gina. I think after last night's little performance you should be taking a good look at yourself."

Gina was rummaging around in the pantry. "Fuck, where's the coffee? All I can find is that dandelion crap you drink. I need caffeine."

"We must have run out."

"Why the hell didn't you buy any?" Gina's tone was derogatory and offensive.

"Because it wasn't on the list."

"Jesus. You'd be fucking useless, wouldn't you?"

Tamsen's blood pressure rose. "It wasn't even my turn to do the shopping. You haven't done it for months. So don't complain about things not being in the cupboard if you didn't even bother to put them on the list."

"If you drank coffee like a normal person you'd notice that we'd run out."

"And if you shopped like a normal person you might buy your own." Tamsen was over the abuse Gina threw around when she woke up with one of her stinking hangovers. Though now she stopped to think about it, the hangovers were becoming a daily occurrence. There was only so many times you could blame getting stinking drunk on having a dysfunctional childhood.

"Shit, look at the time. I'm late for work again."

"Wonder how that could have happened?" Tamsen couldn't help sounding snide; she was way past being the dog that Gina kicked.

"Don't be like that, Tams, your precious boyfriend's going to have it in for me."

"And you deserve it, especially after the way you behaved last night."

Gina went pale. "What are you talking about?"

"Don't give me the 'I don't remember routine'. You know exactly what you did – it's what you always do."

"Fuck." Gina swore under her breath. "I didn't try and shag the boss, did I?" Her pallor took on an almost green shade. Puking in the kitchen sink was a very real possibility.

Tamsen felt almost sorry for her. "One of these days you're going to get yourself smacked over. For a moment last night I even thought Matt might punch you."

"Oh, God. How...well, you know... How was he about it?"

"Livid."

"Fuck."

"I'd say you're not his favorite person right now. In fact, Gina..." Tamsen sighed. It really had to be said. "You're not my favorite person at the moment either. You need to look at yourself. You crossed the line last night. I'm tempted to wash my hands of you."

"Just like my family did." Gina spat the words at her. "I don't need them and I don't need you either."

Punishing blow leveled and one received in return, Tamsen headed for the door thinking it would be wise to get herself out of the flat. She didn't need the crap Gina was bringing into her life anymore.

"Don't you fucking walk away from me after a sanctimonious speech like that, little Miss Perfect."

"I'm not going to argue with you, Gina. I won't argue with you when you're drunk and I'm not arguing with you when you look like death warmed up either. Get yourself some breakfast and go to work and maybe we'll talk about it later. I've got a business to run."

Grabbing her bag and keys off her unmade bed, Tamsen legged it for the front door, Gina's ranting following her thick and strong from the kitchen. Tamsen usually spent hours trying to calm Gina down after spells like this. Today she just wanted to run – though going back into the kitchen and slapping her also appealed. What had changed?

She was confused and nearly in tears by the time she reached her van.

"Danni!" Matt's bellow brought his assistant bounding into his office.

"Yes, Matt?"

"Has Gina arrived?" The sooner he got this out of the way the better.

"She staggered in about ten minutes ago."

Staggered, no doubt, being the appropriate term, he thought. "Would you send her in, please, and cover for her on reception until I'm done."

"Aw, but..."

"Don't pull that face. I'll take you out for a sticky bun for afternoon tea to make it up to you - how does that sound?"

"You know I'm a pushover for sticky date buns." Danni left him alone with his anxiety.

Matt waited for Gina, feeling sick to the stomach. He hadn't wanted to be lumped with the role of partner overseeing clerical staff in the first place and he hated dealing with difficult staff.

His thoughts were interrupted by a tentative knock on his door.

"Come in, Gina, and close the door please."

She looked like death, pale and drawn. If he didn't know any better, he'd have sworn she hadn't had a single minute's sleep. She wasn't front desk material, not in this state.

"Take a seat, please." He gestured to the chair in front of his desk.

She sat down gingerly. Her eyes hadn't met his since she'd walked into the room and she didn't say a word. A far cry from the aggressive huntress who'd had him holed in up in the kitchen last night. He had a stab of sympathy for her; she was a completely different person when she was drinking.

"Now, Gina-"

"If it's about last night, I'm sorry. So very, very sorry." She looked at him pleadingly and his sympathy ratcheted up a notch. "It won't happen again."

Too right it wouldn't happen again - he was planning never to be anywhere near her if she was drinking. "It's not about last night, Gina. Well, not directly anyway."

"I was hoping we could keep our personal lives out of the office." She looked more uncomfortable than he felt. "I know that's difficult with you and Tamsen being..."

A knock on the door broke the uneasy silence hanging between them.

"Come in, Catherine." Matt was relieved to see his efficient office manager. The less time he had to spend alone with Gina the better.

All beige business suit, the towering form of Catherine Brooks dominated the room. Her no-nonsense approach was one of her most endearing qualities though even Matt often found himself squirming under her steely gaze. He couldn't begin to imagine how Gina must be feeling.

It had been tough approaching Catherine to discuss the glaring anomalies in Gina's behavior. Which, upon inspection seemed to have become almost predictable. Four days on work with one day off sick – but never the same day off, which Catherine had suggested was the main reason she'd not noticed the pattern. She was distressed to hear Matt's rather toned down version of events at Tamsen's last night, but wasn't surprised given that a couple of calls to prior employers confirmed the same pattern.

"Take a seat, Catherine." Matt cleared his throat and looked directly at Gina. "Now, Gina. Catherine and I have been going over your absences since you joined the firm six months ago and we've found a disturbing trend. You seem only to be able to work a four-day week, or even three in some cases."

Wanting to avoid her ravaged face, he leafed through a couple of pages from her personnel file. How was it going to impact on Tamsen? None of his business, of course. The potential for conflict with her over the pathetic image of the woman sitting in front of him sparked a surge of anger and resentment. Though how Gina could possibly be such a threat to a barely-off-the-ground relationship, he didn't understand. Even more terrifying was the intensity of his evolving feelings for Tamsen. The inner turmoil made his head spin.

"What, if anything, do you have to say for yourself?" His question sounded pompous and conciliatory and he could have kicked himself. Nervousness doing nothing more than making an unbearable situation more hideous.

"There's nothing much to say really, is there? By the sounds of things - " she threw a look of contempt at Catherine " - you've both made up your minds already and nothing I can say is going to change that." She shrugged. "Happens to me all the time - convicted without trial."

Matt shifted uncomfortably in his chair; the sooner he got this over with the better. He handed Gina the written warning he'd prepared earlier and waited.

"What's this?"

"I suggest you read it, Gina." And quickly, he hoped.

She read the letter, put the paper down and looked at him with such despair Matt's insides seemed to shrivel in response. He hadn't seen so much pain emanating from a person since he'd thrown his kid sister's Barbie doll on the open fire and laughed as it melted in front of her mortified eyes.

"You bastard." The despair was quickly replaced by anger. "A written warning. This is not about work - this is about last night."

"It's not about last night, Gina. I told you that and I'm a man of my word." He was having a hard time keeping his voice composed.

"This is not about work. This is about you shagging my Tamsen and wanting to get me out of the way."

Matt glanced at Catherine, whose face held its mask of composure. He was grateful he'd come clean with her about Gina's atrocious behavior, albeit leaving out a few of the gaudy details.

Catherine cut in, completely unruffled by Gina's outburst. "Gina, Mr Solomon came to me and discussed his relationship with your room mate. I don't believe that has anything at all to do with the situation we find ourselves in this morning."

She adjusted her horn-rimmed spectacles; Matt realized in that split second the woman was beautiful. "You will be well aware of the number of occasions I have had to check your behavior and the number of times I have warned you about your tardiness in getting to work. Mr Solomon's explanation as to the delicate situation he found himself in yesterday really just completes the picture."

Gina shuffled in her seat. Matt felt a similar urge and he wasn't on the receiving end.

Catherine continued. "I spoke to a number of your former employers this morning, and they all confirm that you were dismissed from their employ for exactly the same reasons."

Gina shot another look at Matt but Catherine intercepted it. "You should be grateful to Mr Solomon. If it been left to me, in view of your lateness and the states you have arrived at work in recently I would have dismissed you on the spot." She held up a hand as Gina opened her mouth. "And don't even try to protest - it's clear you're drunk on the job now. Sleep does not a sober person make. However, Mr Solomon has insisted we give you another chance - against my advice, I might add."

"Well, he doesn't need to bother." With contempt pasted on her face, Gina stood up. "I quit."

She headed for the door, nearly ripping it off its hinges as she tore it open. "I wouldn't waste my time working for you, you manipulative bastard. I don't need your sympathy, or your condescending attitude, so you can just go to hell. Find yourself some other unlucky bitch to feel all magnanimous over." With that, she stormed out of his office.

Matt's stomach tied itself in an even tighter knot and he suppressed the urge to vomit.

He tried hard to compose himself. "Well, that went swimmingly, don't you think?"

Catherine gave him a wry smile. "Don't beat yourself up Matt. I was expecting it. Everyone I spoke to this morning said she'd react like that. If she's got a drinking problem, as you suspect, it's textbook really. She's just looking for someone to blame. Unfortunately, for you, you're it."

She stood up and collected the personnel file off his desk. "We're better off without her. For every bad receptionist out there, there are hundreds of good ones to take her place. I'll have the spot filled in a jiffy, don't you worry."

"Thank you, Catherine. Now I know why we hired you."

"Yes, well, I don't know how she slipped through my net. I must have been having a bad day." She shrugged. "Never mind, onward and upward and all that. Oh, and Matt..."

When he looked up Catherine had a strange, knowing look on her face. She said, "I don't usually comment on personal matters..."

"But - " he smiled " - in my case you'll make an exception." He thought he saw a slight chink in her office armor.

"Yes, in this case I'll make an exception. I suspect your lady knows exactly the beast she's living with and you won't have to worry about any poisonous remarks coming out of young Gina's mouth."

He laughed. "It's unlikely she'll be my number one fan now, is it?"

"Precisely."

When Catherine left his office Matt felt suddenly drained and very alone. He peered out the window, the view of the ocean calming his jangled nerves. Gina was probably heading home, boiling with rage, to tell Tamsen what had happened.

The dilemma. Should he call her first and warn her? She was involved. Well, sort of. Wasn't she? Why was he never able to have anything that resembled an uncomplicated relationship? Was he some sort of freak who attracted drama?

His gut ached. It was always the way. Where the hell was that antacid? He rummaged around in his drawer, certain there was a half-open packet lying around. Nothing like tension to bring on another atrocious acid attack.

Locating the desired tablets, he popped a couple and tried hard to think about what he should do next. Gina was a loose cannon and he'd just given her a hundred and one reasons to explode shit all over him. No matter which way he looked at the situation, anything he did could be construed as wrong. He was fucked.

His door burst open and Danni shattered his thoughts. "Whoa, she took that well. *Not.*"

Matt sighed. "I thought I asked you to stay on reception."

"Catherine sent me on my way, so I thought you could take me out for the sticky bun you owe me - you know, for covering for the wicked witch from the west."

"Danni, don't be so frivolous." He was feeling lousy and the post-execution reports weren't helping.

"What did you do to her? She left with a hiss and a roar - positively toxic."

"*Danni.*"

"Come on. You can debrief me down the road. We're better off without her, you know that."

He did know that. He was just worried about Tamsen.

CHAPTER ELEVEN

"He's a fucking creep. You should be ditching him."

Gina's bellowing was so out of order. Tamsen had been late for an installation and knew her customer wouldn't be happy.

"He's nothing of the sort and I won't be ditching him."

"But you don't understand. He sacked me."

"You quit."

"Only before he had the chance to sack me."

"Gina, hasn't it ever occurred to you this is what happens with every job you ever get? Matt and I have nothing to do with it."

"If you weren't shagging my boss this wouldn't have eventuated." Gina guzzled a glass of wine, then hastily refilled her glass from the cardboard cask on the kitchen bench. The ruby liquid formed a tiny whirlpool in her goblet.

Tamsen watched her with a mounting feeling of dread. Why didn't Gina simply stick her mouth under the cask tap and save on the washing up? The amount she drank was phenomenal and must be adding to the chaos in her life.

She told Gina, "Your problem is not the job, nor my boyfriend."

"Boyfriend, now. We're past the casual fucking stage already, are we?"

"I'll treat that with the contempt it deserves." Tamsen could have quite happily clobbered her, but pressed on. "Your mother's right, your problems come out of that cask and from those druggie girlfriends you spend all your time with."

"Great. So now you're going out with a fucking lawyer you think you're a cut above me, do you?" She added as an afterthought, "And you can leave my slag of a mother out of this as well.

Tamsen sighed. "Gina, you must be able to see how out of control your life's getting. If you're not drunk you're hung over, or out looking for something to take the edge off. It's not surprising Matt put two and two together. How many days have you had off sick in the last six months?"

"You would spring to his defense, and after all the years we've been friends. If you were any sort of a friend you'd get rid of him. He's a bastard."

"Gina, he's not a bastard." Tamsen was getting tired of the argument and began to think Gina would never see sense.

"Well, if you're not going to dump him you can forget all about our trip to Wellington."

"What!"

"You heard me. It's him or me."

"Gina, don't be ridiculous."

"I'm not being ridiculous. If you want me to come away with you, you'd better kick him into touch."

"I won't be blackmailed."

"Fine, then." She had a look of utter disgust on her face, one Tamsen hadn't seen in a very long time. "You've made your choice. You'd better see if Mr Wonderful will accompany you, 'cos I certainly won't be." Gina stormed out of the kitchen, but not before snatching up the cask of wine Tamsen noted with dismay.

The kitchen looked like a bomb-site with half-eaten scraps thrown over the bench and red wine dribbled down the cupboard doors and over the floor. No shock there, Gina got nearly as much over the floor and herself as she got down her throat these days. When had it all started going so horribly wrong? They'd been friends for years. Was it something that she'd done, Tamsen wondered. Did it really matter?

Anger burning in her gut, she set to work cleaning up the mess Gina had left.

How many of these messes - actual and metaphorical - had she cleaned up? Her own life was beginning to look up, yet here was the same pattern kicking in again - Gina having a crisis, and Tamsen putting her own life on hold to bail her out. Maybe it was time to take a stand.

"Stuff it." Tamsen addressed the black ball of fluff who was busy licking a hardening blob of peanut butter off the tiled floor. "It's time to look after me."

The cat looked at her with his huge yellow eyes. "And you, of course."

Azzie twined himself around her legs, making her think of a quote she'd heard somewhere, something about carrying a cat by the tail and the lesson learned. It all became clear: she would do nothing about Gina. Gina would have to sort out her own problems.

She took another look at the shambles that was their shared kitchen and decided she hadn't made this mess either and set out for her room with a new lightness of spirit.

"Come on, Azzie. You and I have got plans to make for the rest of our lives."

The drive home hadn't eased Matt's guilt. All reason and logic assured him he'd done the right thing but his insides still howled at him. The afternoon had dragged. Part of him wanted to the day to end so he could see Tamsen and explain; the other part never wanted it to end so he wouldn't have to.

"Matt, is that you, darling?"

Shit, Mother. He'd almost forgotten she was still here. If she'd dared to have Angie here again he really would just throw himself off the nearest retaining wall – if he could find one. Why were the gardeners taking so long to finish the job? He made another mental note to get on their case tomorrow. Tamsen had walked into his well-ordered life and everything seemed to be falling apart.

"Yes, Mother, it's me."

He walked through the open door to be assaulted by the tantalizing scent of cooking bacon. His mother appeared in full kitchen regalia, complete with his barbecue apron.

He couldn't help laughing. "Smells as if you're cooking my favorite."

"Well, darling, that is if Beef Wellington is still it." She smoothed her hands over the rough surface of the apron. "Things seem to have changed so much it appears I hardly know my son anymore, and he's not willing to share with me what's going on in his life."

Matt set his features, resolving not to react to anything she had to say. He'd learned the best way to keep her out was to never allow her to see what had got through his defenses.

Thwarted by his silence, Marguerite said, "So can I assume that you'll be staying home tonight and your dear old mother can have the pleasure of your company? Or are you likely to run off again?"

Matt could almost taste the blood in the back of his mouth from biting his tongue. "That's fine as long as it's only us, Mother."

"There's no need to use that tone, Matty. Angie's a lovely woman and I still can't see why you've decided that you'd rather spend time with a fish breeder than with her."

"Who told you about Tamsen?"

"It doesn't matter who told me. The point is I'm just trying to prevent you from running your life."

"More like stop me bringing the family name into disrepute."

"Well, I'd be lying if that wasn't a factor."

"Mother, do you realize how shallow you sound?"

"Quite frankly, Matthew, somebody's got to keep an eye out. You seem hell bent on destroying yourself and everything that this family's worked for all these years."

He could have kicked himself; he'd been sucked in again and now he wasn't able to let it go. "I. Am. Not. Destroying. Myself."

The knot of tension in his stomach was crippling and the gorgeous cooking smells coming from the kitchen weren't helping. He had a ludicrous desire to laugh. His mother was accusing him of destroying his life and all he could think about was that he hadn't had lunch.

"I'm not discussing this with you any more, Matty. I don't intend tarnishing our evening. And I'll certainly not be responsible for driving you back into that unsuitable woman's arms two nights in a row."

Despite the goading he held his tongue, and secretly had some pride in himself for doing so. "I'm assuming we've got at least an hour before dinner so I'll be going downstairs for a quick workout."

He pecked her unceremoniously on the cheek and shot through to change.

Matt lay in bed, aware he was grinding another layer of enamel from his molars. His stomach was full, but so was his head and the dual combination was giving him trouble. Tamsen hadn't called all night and he was paralyzed with fear, torn between an urge to ring her and fear of making their situation worse. Though how much worse could it be?

He had no idea what Gina might have said. He was a lawyer who supposedly dealt with facts, concisely thought things through, and here he was behaving like a lovesick schoolboy. Unable to work out where the land lay with Tamsen because he was too scared to gather the simple facts.

It was far too late to phone now anyway. He'd just have to continue to stew about it. His specialty. Years of practice.

He sighed, rolled over onto his stomach and vowed to call her first thing in the morning. Now, if only his head would just shut up and his stomach would settle down he might have a chance of a semi-decent night's sleep.

Goddess, I'm lost.

Tamsen closed her journal, sighing heavily. She had a feeling of grief about her today, no doubt aggravated by Gina's noisy all-night drinking binge. The kitchen still looked like a bomb had hit it – well, it had, in the form of Gina. Tamsen had held firm on her decision not to enable Gina by picking up after her.

But it truly was a difficult thing, only looking after yourself when you were used to mothering another human being.

Two sharp beeps from his cellphone alerted Matt to the incoming text message. Please let it be Tamsen, he thought. He'd been pretending he was coping with her not returning his call but he wasn't fooling anyone, especially himself. He'd learned recently that if he couldn't be honest with himself then he really didn't have a chance.

He could have kissed his phone, - she'd agreed to meet him for coffee in just under an hour.

Thank God he didn't have to wait any longer; his stomach wouldn't hold out. He'd been through half a packet of antacids already this morning.

Tamsen sat waiting for Matt in the courtyard garden - early as usual, wanting to soak up its energy. It intrigued her the feeling of tranquility and positive energy this little space had. She was touched and reassured that Matt enjoyed being here too. His home exuded the same harmony, which she found interesting. How could someone who liked being here and had a home that oozed this kind of balanced energy work where he did?

She sniffed a piece of apple mint from the small herb garden, the fuzzy leaves tickling her nose. The scent of fresh, pungent citrus and mint was overwhelming. It amused her that it was called apple mint when it so reminded her of oranges.

"Hey. It's nice to find you admiring the fish and enjoying the garden."

His voice flowed through her, cool and soothing, running down her spine like the water down the small waterfall she'd been watching. She could listen to him all day.

"Hi." She looked up. The light - was it playing tricks, or was it his aura she'd glanced upon? She looked into the black wells of his eyes and felt a connection, a sensation so severe and sudden it took her breath away. He was in pain and unsure of himself - she could feel it.

"I'm not mad at you." She held out her hand, coaxing him closer. She wanted to touch him, to feel the physical manifestation of the dance their emotional bodies had been doing. He took her hand and she sensed him relax.

"Why is it that when I'm with you everything feels right in the world?" He had a puzzled look on his face.

Her heart soared just hearing the words. "Probably because it is."

She realized she'd been waiting for this man for a long time and she'd be damned if she'd let a minx like Gina stuff it up for her. "I've ordered coffee for you," she told him.

"And some sort of herbal crap for you, I suppose."

She knew his gentle dig came from a loving place. "You know me, I get a big enough kick out of life without having to resort to chemical enhancement."

He bent and kissed her. She loved the feel of his lips on hers. She had an instant desire to tear his clothes from him and make love to him, right there in the courtyard. His ability to arouse her at a moment's notice bordered on terrifying.

"Stop it, you horror." Her words came out in ragged gasps. "I hate the way my body reacts to you sometimes. I feel like a slut."

He grinned. "I feel like a bit of slut. Want to head home?"

She felt her temperature rise. All decorum flying out the window, she had a sudden vision of him naked and wanting. What the heck, she was sick of being a good little girl.

"Hell, yes!"

The drive back to his home was hideous. He wanted to touch her, rip her clothes off her, take her in every way possible and then some more. He was grateful traffic was light and the journey took no more than twenty minutes. Twenty minutes that could have been a lifetime as far as his dick was concerned.

They hadn't talked much. He'd expected things to be difficult over Gina - but Tamsen, he discovered, much to his surprise, didn't seem to think he was the problem.

"Matt, when are these people going to be finished with your driveway?" Tamsen picked her way around a large mound of scoria that had appeared since he left for work that morning.

"Who knows?" He scratched his head. "Hard to believe that God could've created the world in six days. Good job these guys weren't contracted to Him - " he threw his arms out " – or we'd still all be floating round in space waiting for it to happen."

She laughed. He loved the sound of her musical laugh. He noticed he seemed less nervy around Tamsen, and he liked that too. She had an almost unflappable quality he envied.

"So is your mother likely to be around?"

Hell. In his haste to get Tamsen home he'd completely forgotten about his mother. What to do? Ah, stuff it. He'd just brazen it. He could bring home whomever he liked.

"I've no idea." He grinned an evil grin. "We'll just have to front up and see if she's home."

He pulled her to him; she was soft and compliant in his arms, and wore a fragrance that reminded him of the sea. "Hmm - " he nuzzled into the warm spot behind her ear " - you smell almost nice enough to eat." He tickled her neck with the tip of his tongue and felt an immediate surge of lust when she shivered in response.

"I love it when you do that."

"What, this?" He couldn't help doing it again.

"Yes. That." She rubbed herself up against his rapidly hardening cock, the movement cat-like, her entire body almost wrapping itself around him.

"Mother'd better be out or we're in serious trouble."

"Well, we'd best be on our way then." She untangled herself from him and made for the front door. "Unless, of course, you'd rather take me out here?"

"I'm tempted." The wrap-around skirt she wore exposed a tantalizing glimpse of her milky-white upper thigh every time she walked. She was the most sensual creature. Even her gait was unhurried. Matt had never met anyone who appeared not to be in a hurry to get anywhere, yet was always on time. An intoxicating mixture of paradoxes.

He found himself fantasizing about tearing her skirt away from that taunting thigh, rolling her in a pile of dirt and fucking her until their combined sweat created a sweet mud bath.

"Come on, slowcoach." She looked across at him, an evil glint in her eyes. "Stop dreaming about having me outside and let's get in before I'm tempted to tie you naked to the nearest tree."

He felt himself blush; how the heck had she known what he was thinking? And what's more, why was he blushing?

"The front door's locked. That's always a good sign." He fumbled through his keys, visions of her tying him to a tree flitting through his mind.

"I'm pleased to her that news." Her voice sounded low and soft. He could feel her breath on the back of his neck, never mind what she was doing with her hands around his backside. Her touch was electric, the energy around her intoxicating.

"Stop that, you tart." He could feel beads of sweat starting to form on his body and he knew it had nothing to do with the air temperature.

"You going to open that door so I can get inside and ravage you or am I just going to have to take you on the doorstep?"

"If you'd get your hands off me I might have a chance of finding the right frigging key." She turned his brain into mush.

"My, my. Typical man. Can't do more than one thing at a time, huh?" Her tone was teasing.

He practically fell through the door, pulling her in after him, their combined force slamming it shut. Sandwiching her against the rimu panel, he savaged her mouth with his, sorely tempted to strip her naked and have her on the spot.

She came up for air, gasping, "Oh, God, you turn me on."

"Babe, you have no idea how mutual it is."

"I think I might." She was stroking him through his suit pants, and all he could do was lean his head on the door over her shoulder and moan.

She giggled. "I presume Mommy's not here then?"

"Stop it, you wicked woman." He'd forgotten about his dreaded mother again. Where the hell could they go where he'd be sure to hear her if she came back and it wouldn't look too obvious what they'd been up to? Though the way he was feeling at the moment he was sure he'd end up with "just been shagged" running across his forehead in bold neon letters.

"Come with me." He took her hand and led her downstairs.

"Ooh, down to the dungeon."

"I'll really give you dungeon if you're not careful."

She lifted his hand to her lips, the touch sending shivers up his arm. "I can hardly wait. Lead on."

After unbolting the slide lock, he threw open the door at the bottom of the stairs to reveal a fully equipped workout room.

"My, no wonder your body's in such a delectable shape." Tamsen grinned. "How many hours a day do you spend down here getting sweaty?"

"Not too many." He pulled her toward him again and closed the door behind them. "Now, you over here so I can get hot and sweaty with you."

"Can't say I need asking twice." She pressed herself to him with an intensity and passion that surprised and excited him. He felt himself growing hard against her.

"Bet this doesn't usually get much exercise down here, does it?" She rubbed her hip backwards and forwards over his cock.

"Not usually. But for you, pretty lady, I'm even prepared to make an exception to my no-women-in-the-workout-room rule."

"Ooh. I am honored, aren't I?"

"You are." He pushed her toward the bench press and obediently she dropped herself across the bench, the inviting full view of her inner thighs making his head spin.

"You're an enticing creature," he almost moaned.

She smiled and the innocence of the smile touched him. There were no pretensions about her – and that was what he found so alluring.

He joined her, astride the bench, facing her. Taking her face in his hands, he leaned forward and touched his lips to hers. Another surge of something – though what, he wasn't quite sure - rushed to his head. She was like a drug and he couldn't get enough of her.

"Hmm..." she moaned softly, then opened her eyes and looked straight into his.

He felt as if he were naked under her stare. She reached forward, running a long fingernail down from his hairline, in front of his ear, and stopping to circle the sharp point of his jaw just below his earlobe. The sensation was a cross between arousing and annoying; if anyone else had touched him in this way he'd have been infuriated, but with her it ratcheted up the tension.

"You know, I've never been had on exercise equipment before. You're just full of surprises."

"Oh, you have no idea." The fire in his belly warmed to her words and he pulled her toward him, her skirt falling further away from her thighs, exposing the small pair of apricot satin panties she wore. He traced his finger down the silky material. Her responsive moan told him all he needed to know.

"You like that, don't you?"

"I like it very much." She mirrored his action, drawing her finger across the bulge in his trousers. "See, you like it too."

CHAPTER TWELVE

Tamsen was desperate for him to touch her again.

He had this way about him. Intense patches of activity, and then he'd slow down. He was driving her nuts, but whether intentionally or not she couldn't be sure. The mere thought of being taken by him in here, the place he spent hours sweating over himself, made her almost orgasm on the spot. Yet he'd scarcely touched her, just kept making promises with his eyes and his body.

His body.

Now she knew why he was in such great shape. All she wanted to do was rip his clothes off his back and here he was, vacillating between animal and chaste. Frustration fueled her lust.

"Come here, you heavenly creature, you." She clasped her hands around the back of his neck and shimmied herself up onto his lap.

Tamsen sought out his mouth and plundered it with hers. He had a wicked way of nipping her bottom lip between his teeth; it turned her on no end and she felt the beginning of her wetness. Grinding herself into the hardness beneath her, she felt his hands find her hips and assist with the rhythm.

"Hmm, that's so nice." She whispered the words beside his neck. She loved his neck, especially that little patch just behind his earlobe. She drank in the scent of his skin, his essence and energy rising to meet hers.

"I want you, Tams." Roughly he pushed her hair aside, the declaration aimed at the cleft between her shoulder and collarbone. He traced the dip with his tongue, then blew his way back to her throat.

"I want you too. Take me. Please. I don't want to wait anymore, just take me."

Matt didn't need asking again, but she would have begged if necessary. He struggled with the tie on her skirt, and - way past pretending she needed to be seduced - she pushed his hands away. This was about getting them naked in the fastest possible time.

"I love it when you tell me what you want." He was dealing to the large sliver buckle on his belt. She could barely contain her need to stop undressing herself and attend to him.

"I love it when you tell me what to do."

She slipped the thin lace top she wore off her shoulders and stared deep into his eyes. Releasing the clasp in front of her bra, she brazenly allowed the garment to slide down her back and off her buttocks. She felt powerful and alive while his eyes feasted on her, her nipples hardening in response to his intense observation.

She was completely naked and he hadn't yet touched her, but she was alive with longing. Every molecule in her being danced under his careful examination.

"I want you to lie down on the bench." His voice sounded deep and husky with desire.

Breaking out in goose bumps, she could barely wait to feel his skin against hers.

She lay back on the bench, the vinyl cool against her flesh. Steadying herself, legs on the ground either side, she felt wickedly exposed and vulnerable. He stood over her chest, his cock just inches away from her rock-hard nipples.

She reached up, hands caressing him, worshipping him. He sucked in a breath at her touch and she realized she'd stopped breathing too.

"Let me suck you."

Her words had an immediate effect; his pupils widened and an involuntary moan escaped his luscious lips. A small pearl of pre-come formed on his glans. She lapped at it with the tip of her tongue, teasing more from him with the promise of the warmth of her mouth.

He shuffled forward, resting his bulk on the weights above her head, allowing her to suckle him. She adored giving oral sex; the feeling of power was incredible, a real turn-on.

"You like that?" She expertly ran the head of his cock through her hand.

He nodded.

"You want to come in my mouth?"

"Later." He was lazily thrusting into her hand. "I want to make you come first."

"I don't have a problem with that." She ached to feel his mouth on her. She was soaked at the very thought of his tongue creeping into her secret places. She spread her legs wider in anticipation.

He slid backwards over her body, grazing her flesh with his buttocks. Stopping to tease her. Expertly plucking at an erect nipple with his teeth. Suckling it until she felt the dull ache right through to her shoulder blade.

He traced a path down her trembling stomach, took a left at her hip and nibbled his way back up the inside of her also now trembling thigh. Parting her soaked lips with his tongue, he lapped at her. She lay her head back on the bench and couldn't help arching her back, pushing herself into his expert mouth.

He consumed her. She wanted to grind herself into his face, grip his head and force him into her as deep as she could.

Fingers explored her wetness, twisting and probing, adding to the pleasure - the appetizer for the main event. She wanted him inside her, wanted to feel his length impale her. His touch and the incessant way his tongue was lapping at her clit took her to the edge she sought. Bucking into him, she let herself fall, the thrill of release coursing through her taut body.

Tamsen lay quivering, barely able to catch her breath. The flush of orgasm had scarcely cooled on her flesh when through the froth in her mind she heard his voice, strong and demanding.

"I want you on your hands and knees on the floor."

She shivered. If only she could get her exhausted muscles to co-operate.

Enjoying her apparent struggle, he helped her limp body up. Matt paused for a moment to suckle a nipple, so hard she moaned in response to the deep pain. The sound came from a pit he'd penetrated, primeval emotions coursed through her. She felt wanton - deranged even.

Half out of her mind, she allowed him to drop her to all fours in front of him, then lowered herself onto her forearms, spreading her fingers wide on the cool parquet floor. She spread her legs, knowing she was giving him a full view of herself.

She closed her eyes, breathed deep and willed him with every ounce of her being to connect with her. Matt was on her in an instant, and in her in a single movement. The subliminal call had done its job. She felt him slide home and abandoned herself to the powerful, physical and spiritual being behind her.

He grasped her by the hips, his fingers burrowing into the soft flesh of her abdomen. She pushed herself back onto him again and again with solid strokes, each punctuated with a grunt she barely recognized as her own. Her arms slid on the floor and she scrambled to push herself back harder. She wanted to feel him deeper inside. It was almost as if he were splitting her in two, but all she cared about was him. His scent, his musky sharp maleness filled her, every thrust bringing him closer to her core.

Her nostrils flared, every muscle in her body tensed, and her lips pulled back baring her teeth. Her desire to have him come escalated. She wanted to suck every single last drop of his essence with her body. Needed him to explode in a cacophony of lust and desire. Needed to know she'd driven him to the edge, that she could push him over and make him lose control - the same way he'd shattered her own.

Bucking and moaning against him, her temperature soaring, she was filled not only with him, but with an energy - a connection to life she barely understood. He drew her roughly to him one last agonizing time and bellowed out loud as he came.

She felt the rush of her own primordial orgasm, that split second of absolute loss - an out-of-body experience as she soared with him. He held her tight, not letting her go. She didn't want him to let go; she wanted to stay connected while she waited for the shattered remains of her world to come back together.

He eased the balance of her body and himself slowly to the floor, where they lay spoon-like in a hot and sweaty mass on the cool parquet. She could feel his heart beating furiously against her back. Her own was fluttering in her chest.

As the pleasurable sensations receded, Tamsen became aware of her body's other needs. "Don't suppose you have any energy drinks stashed round here, do you? I'm parched."

Matt continued to pant into the back of her neck. "Anyone would think you'd been working out or something." He kissed her and she could feel the sweat on his face.

She wriggled out from the soggy hold he had on her and they both flopped onto their backs.

"I don't know if I've ever sweat this much down here," he said. "You've obviously a bad influence."

"Go on, you love what I do to you." She noticed a bead of sweat running down from his hairline and couldn't resist lapping it up, the salty tang reminding her that she hadn't eaten lunch.

"Oh, God, you're not wrong." He hunkered up onto his elbows. "I can't believe you've just let me shag you on the floor."

"What's wrong with the floor?"

"Nothing, I suppose." He looked a little puzzled. "It's just...well..."

"You've never shagged anyone on the floor before?" She laughed. "I find that hard to believe."

"It's true." A flash of embarrassment crossed his face. "You're not like anyone I've ever been with before."

She didn't take her eyes of him, enjoying making him squirm.

"I don't mean like..."

"I know. You mean it in the nicest possible way." She couldn't resist kissing him in the middle of his chest, right over his heart. "You don't have to apologize - I gave up trying to be ladylike years ago. And besides, there's something about you that makes me want to throw any semblance of ladylike behavior right out the window."

"That would be my raw sex appeal and rugged masculinity, right?"

She wasn't sure by the tone of his voice whether he was being sarcastic or whether she should agree with him, so decided a kiss was the best response.

He smelt of her and she liked that. Liked that her scent and his were mingled together. But they'd not only had a physical exchange - she felt a spiritual and emotional encounter had taken place too.

He smacked her on the bottom. Oddly, she liked the sound of it as much as the feel of it.

"Come on, you." He struggled to his feet and pulled her up after him. "You're not the only thirsty one, and there's not a drop to drink down here."

He picked up his business shirt and, to her delight, shimmied her into it. "Let's go upstairs, get showered and then I'll throw some lunch together."

"Sounds delish." Her stomach was rumbling; sex always kicked other appetites into action for her. "But what about your mother?"

He pulled her to him, collected her hair in a bundle between his hands and tipped her head back so she was looking directly up into his eyes. "I'm over worrying about what Mother thinks."

He kissed her on the forehead. "If I want to bring a beautiful woman home, shag her senseless and then parade her around the house for my viewing pleasure, then that's just what I'll do."

He plucked his Calvin Kleins out of his trousers and pulled them on. "Now, get that smelly body upstairs for washing."

Freshly showered and feeling more relaxed than he had in a long time, Matt busied himself throwing pasta into a pot of boiling water. Then he needed to locate the pesto he thought must be hiding in the fridge and pray it wasn't past it's use-by date - otherwise he'd have to leg it downstairs again and see what he could chip out of the freezer.

"There's something really sexy about a man cooking you lunch, especially after you've just had mind-blowing sex."

Tamsen was untangling her wet hair with her fingers; he loved the way she carefully separated each strand. Wet, her hair looked incredibly dark, almost orange. They were barely dry after their shower and already he felt a stirring in his trousers again.

He told her, "God, it's such a turn on when you do that."

"When I do what?" Her puzzled expression made her look pure, almost innocent. That thought amused him, considering the hot sex they'd just had.

"Play with your hair like that."

"I'm not playing." She tossed her head coyly, water spraying across the room. "I'm preening."

"There's a difference?"

She shook her head. "Uh-huh. Preening's about grooming and that's all about me."

"And playing?" he enquired.

"Playing's about driving you crazy."

"I see." She drove him crazy all right, no doubt about that.

The timer pinged on the stove. "Be a good girl and get a couple of bowls out of that cupboard over there, would you?"

He drained the pasta and tossed the located pesto quickly through it, before dropping large dollops in the bowls she'd brought over.

"Where did you learn how to cook?"

"It was either cook or starve when I was going through law school." He pulled out a chair for her. "I decided starvation wasn't an option."

She kissed him lightly on the cheek before she sat down. A simple gesture, but he was touched by it. "Much better to be a girl, starvation's preferable, keeps you thin."

"And that's your excuse for not learning to cook?"

"I can cook. It's just that everything takes me ages. I don't seem to be able to organize it so everything's ready at the same time."

"That's why God invented microwaves."

She laughed. "I see." Stabbing at the pasta tubes with her fork, she held a couple up at eye level. "Problem is, though, you couldn't microwave this - it'd turn into mush."

"You're probably right." He watched her pop the pasta into her mouth, visions of his cock sliding between those very lips racing through his mind. "You've got the sexiest mouth."

"Stop it and eat some lunch."

"But you have." He watched her lick some pesto from the fork with the tip of her tongue and felt a shiver run up his spine. "It's erotic just watching you eat."

"Well, shelve your lustful thoughts. Mom could walk through that door at any moment."

"Aw, I keep forgetting about her."

"How long is she going to be here?"

He thrust a forkful of pasta into his mouth, hunching his shoulders at the same time. The universal sign for who knows and who really cares. "She can be hell on wheels. I suppose she'll be here for as long as it takes."

"As long as what takes?"

"For me to concede defeat and live my life the way she wants me to."

Tamsen looked thoughtful. She had a cute way of running a piece of her hair over her top lip when she was thinking. He found it endearing.

"Why don't you tell her what she wants to hear," Tamsen suggested, "and then run your life the way you want to?"

"That's rather dishonest, don't you think?"

She shrugged. "I suppose. But, you can have rather dishonest with her out of your hair, or honest and her here driving you insane for the next who knows how long."

"Hmm. Maybe. But I don't want to talk about her anymore." He wanted to talk about Gina, but didn't know how to bring it up.

"What do you want to talk about?"

"How about what's going on in your life?"

Tamsen smiled. "You are quite dishonest, you know."

"How d'you mean?" He was insulted.

"You want to talk about Gina. You're just putting out fishhooks, hoping I might pick up on the bait. It's an underhand way to direct a conversation."

"And since when were you as pure as the driven snow, Miss Tell-Mother-What-She-Wants-To-Hear?"

It disturbed him how well she read him. He'd spent his life making sure no one got too close, carefully doling himself out in small slivers - a slice here, a portion there. But this woman, this beautiful enigma, seemed to be scrambling all his defenses. Taking the sum of his parts and - far too quickly - putting it all together.

"Okay." He put his fork down; the conversation had come to the point he'd been dreading. "You've got me. I've been terrified of how you were going to react over the whole fiasco. So how's it been at your end?"

"Terrible."

His stomach lurched; it was as bad as he'd thought it would be. "Like, on a scale of one to ten."

"Hmm." She rolled her eyes at him. "Twenty-four."

"Oh, shit. You must hate me."

"Absolutely, that's why I was happy to have your dick in my mouth less than an hour ago."

"Tamsen, I'm being serious."

"So am I." She reached across the table and took his hand in hers. The gesture settled some of the butterflies careering around in his stomach. "Gina's a disaster that's been looking for a place to happen for a long time. It's just unfortunate that it had to happen in your office at the same time I met you."

"You say the nicest things."

"It's a fact. If it's any consolation, I've been rescuing her from herself for years and I've had enough. She can just stew in her own juices for a while. It might bring her to her senses."

"Wow. Tough woman."

"I try to kid myself. But really, it's crippling our friendship."

He thought he saw a tear escaping from the corner of her eye. "Oh babe." He was at her side in an instant, on his knees beside her.

She wrapped her arms around him, laid her head on his shoulder. He could feel the rapid beat of her heart and hear muffled sniffling on his neck.

He didn't know what to say, so he just held her. For a man who worked with words he was lost. Even though she'd said he wasn't responsible, he certainly felt as if he was.

"You know what the worst thing is?" Tamsen lifted her head off his shoulder, her eyes glassy with tears.

"No, tell me." He stroked her hair, smoothing the still-damp strands down her back.

"We were supposed to be going on holiday together." She sniffed again. "And Gina said she won't go unless I throw you over."

The pain in his gut was sudden. He felt as if he'd been hit. The possibility that Gina was a threat had become very real.

He worked hard to sound composed and calm. "So what did you tell her?" He wasn't sure if he wanted an answer, but the question begged to be asked.

"I've told her I won't be blackmailed." She kissed him on the nose and he felt as if he wanted to burst into tears.

He laughed nervously. "You could always just throw me over. I mean - " he took a deep breath; he wanted to sound jovial and secure " - you girlies have to stick together, don't you? Aren't we men a dime a dozen?"

She smiled, and even through his own angst and pain her smile plucked at his heart. "No. Not all the time. Sometimes us girlies have to stick with you boys." She reached out, trailing a finger down the side of his jaw. "Especially when you boys are as gorgeous as you."

He couldn't help smiling. "Does that mean we get to have rampant sex again?"

She laughed. He loved the sound; it filled the air. "No. We get to load the dishwasher and then you get to help me work out what the hell I'm going to do about my insane room mate and what I'm going to do about my trip away."

"Easy."

"Who - me or the room mate?"

"Both." He couldn't help himself. She was wide open for the broadside and it was one of the things he loved about her - the ability she had to poke the borax at herself and at him.

"Steady on, pal." She gave him a light cuff around the ear. "You'll be beginning to think you're God's gift to the poor working girl soon."

"What do you mean? Beginning."

"Now look here. Just because my room mate hunted you down like some sort of prize animal in the kitchen-"

"And you happen to be shagging my brains out." Bless her, he thought, she had the temerity to blush.

"That still doesn't give you a license to think you're a stud."

"I don't. But I hope that maybe you might."

"Hmm. Jury's out on that one at the moment, counselor. You may have to present a little more evidence."

"Is that right? And how much evidence, exactly, would I have to present?"

"I haven't decided." She smiled at him from where she was, he suddenly realized, cleaning up his kitchen.

"Hell. I'm supposed to be doing that."

"You cooked, so I can at least clean up. Wouldn't want your mother arriving home and finding the place looking like a pigsty, now would we?" She tipped her head sideways in that cocky way she had. "She might think you were spending time with a woman waaaaay below your station."

"Tams, stop it." He'd be having words with Marguerite. She wasn't about to drive Tamsen out of his life. "Tell me about your trip away."

"More like lack thereof."

"Well, lack thereof. Maybe I should come with you."

There, he'd said it. He'd been mulling the idea round in his head since she'd mentioned Gina pulling out. Now he wished he hadn't. She'd probably think he was moving too fast and run a mile. But the more time he spent with Tamsen, the more time he wanted to spend with her.

She hadn't moved a muscle. He could hear his own heart beating in his temples. He should've kept his mouth shut.

"Could you get time off work?"

Could he get time off work? Hell, yes!

"Maybe." Now he sounded like a complete asshole. "When were you looking at going?"

She grinned. "Don't you want to know where we were going?"

Shit, they could be going to the ass end of the country for all he cared. As long as he was going with Tamsen.

"You mentioned where you were going." Did she? He couldn't remember. Why would he even consider lying to her? He felt like a complete dick.

"Yeah, well. We'd talked about going down on the train - you know, sort of make it a girls' own adventure."

He nodded knowingly. A train. Where the hell would you be able to get to on a train?

"But then we thought that flying would be so much quicker. Though I'm not that keen on planes and the thought of landing in all that wind in between all those houses..." She shuddered.

Wellington. They were going to Wellington; nowhere else in the country had wind and an airport landing strip between houses. He'd hoped for somewhere like...at least Melbourne. But, he figured, if he was going with Tamsen he could stand Wellington.

"So what's in Wellington then?" He felt like a total schmuck for deceiving her.

"A trade show." She finished loading the dishwasher and closed the door.

Turning to face him, she trapped her hands against the bench behind her back. The pose was hideously sexy and he felt his desire for her soar again. A trip away with her was just what he needed - a chance to get to know her inside and out, without the pressures of other people.

A chance for him to work out exactly what it was he wanted from his life

CHAPTER THIRTEEN

"Matty, darling. Where are you?"

Tamsen felt every inch of her body go rigid. There could be only one owner of that voice.

"In the kitchen, Mother." Matt cast his eyes to heaven and Tamsen's stomach lurched.

The urge to vomit was strong. Maybe she'd eaten far too much lunch - she couldn't blame motion sickness or, God forbid, pregnancy. Where had that thought come from? Terror at the prospect of finally meeting his mother?

She found herself hurriedly checking her hair. She had no make-up on. The last vestiges that hadn't been smeared across Matt's floor had been washed off in his shower. She shivered, feeling sure she must have "You just missed me sucking your son's cock" running across her forehead for the entire world to see.

Matt held his hand out and she took it gratefully as the owner of the upper-class drawl came into sight. His firm grip supplied much-needed reassurance.

"Tamsen, this is my mother, Marguerite Solomon. Mother, I'd like you to meet a special friend of mine. Miss Tamsen Parsons."

"A special friend. I see." Marguerite looked Tamsen over as if she were something the local tabby would drag in.

Tamsen resisted the urge to crawl away into a corner and wait for an acute case of dengue fever to hit, releasing her from her torment. Instead, she proffered a hand and a smile in welcome. She'd always been taught you didn't have to lower yourself to someone else's level.

"I'm delighted to meet you, Marguerite. Matt's told me so much about you."

Tamsen resisted the temptation to squeeze Marguerite's scrawny sparrow-like fingers together in a show of feminine dominance. Instead she concentrated on making sure the filigree around the whopping great ruby the woman wore on her ring finger didn't tear the flesh from Tamsen's thumb. It was a possibility, given the velocity with which Marguerite retrieved her hand from Tamsen's grasp.

"All good, I hope?" Marguerite enquired.

The challenge was more than Tamsen could bear. "No, not all good." She smiled sweetly. "But I expect you're used to that."

Matt looked as if he'd been poleaxed. The color running from his face, he opened his mouth to speak, took one look at his mortified mother's face and closed it again. He reminded Tamsen of one of her fish.

"Why don't I go and wait for you in the car, Matt?" This seemed a good time to make her exit.

"Er, yes. That would be a good idea." Matt found his voice at last.

He looked sheepishly back and forth from his mother to her. If she wasn't so totally pissed off with the arrogant attitude his mother had taken she could almost have felt a little sympathy for the man. But she remained blinded by fury. How a woman could be so obnoxious and even revel in her own unpleasantness?

"Right. Well, I'll be going then." She couldn't resist turning her attention to the off-putting creature before her. "I don't expect we'll be seeing much of each other, having gotten off to such a great start." She plastered a saccharine smile on her face. "Goodbye."

And Tamsen walked out, leaving the two of them gaping in her wake.

"Matthew, that woman is atrocious. What in the world do you think you're doing with her?"

"Mother, be quiet. Tamsen's only out in the car - she'll hear you."

She was shrieking now. "Hear me! I don't care if that excuse for a lab-rat hears me. Didn't you hear how she spoke to me? She's got absolutely no respect for me at all."

He was tired of fighting. "And you think you showed any respect for her? It was pretty obvious you weren't prepared to give her a chance so you can hardly be upset at the way that she spoke to you." His voice rose an octave, anger constricting his throat. "You looked like you wanted to disinfect your hand after she touched you."

He turned and stormed out of the room, worried sick about how Tamsen would be and desperate to get out of the toxic waste dump his home had become since his mother's arrival. *His home*, he reminded himself as he ran away yet again.

What was it he'd read somewhere? Taking the same action and expecting a different result is the definition of insanity. He might not be insane, but at moments like this he felt fairly close.

Climbing into the driver's seat, he noticed Tamsen staring straight ahead - into nothing it seemed. He sat beside her with no idea what to say, prepared to wait forever for her to say something. Anything. He was tired of his mother getting in the way of the good things in his life, and for the first time was prepared to fight for something that meant a lot to him.

"I'm sorry."

He looked at her in amazement. "*You're* sorry? Tamsen - " he was finding it hard to keep a conversational tone; he wanted to scream like a lunatic " - there is absolutely no reason for you to be sorry." He could feel his rage stalking him and there wasn't a thing he could do about it. "If anyone should be sorry it's me."

She turned to look at him. Were those tears collecting in her eyes? They had a glassy, liquid look, turning them an iridescent green. "You haven't done anything wrong."

"Other than expose you to my mother." He slapped himself on the forehead. "The woman drives me nuts. I really don't know what I've done to deserve her."

"Maybe you were evil in a former life?"

Her impious grin was infectious. "Maybe I've just been wicked in this one."

She leaned over, planted her lips on his and forced them apart with her probing tongue. In a moment he was hard, all his frustration and emotion concentrated in an immediate, lustful desire to take her again.

She pulled away, smiling. "You have no idea how much you turn me on."

He switched on the ignition and the engine roared into life. "Baby, I think I'd better get you out of here before you have the chance to find out just how much you turn me on."

As they drove back into town, Matt realized later, the silence that fell between them wasn't a difficult one, but a comfortable one. A silence suggesting an intimacy and trust he'd never experienced with a woman.

The scene with his mother had been unsettling, but even more unsettling was Tamsen's reaction. He'd not been witness before to anyone who had the courage to take his mother on at her own game, never mind come out on top. He'd sorely underestimated this girl. Here he was believing he'd be the big man while she was out there slaying dragons.

"So. Are you serious about coming to Wellington with me?"

The question took him by surprise and he nearly drove into the barrier arm of the car park building. "No, not really."

He looked across at her; she was biting her lip, a look of bitter disappointment on her face. He could have kicked himself for toying with her in this way. It was a habit he'd developed to punish Angie, an automatic reaction to feeling vulnerable.

"What I meant to say was I'd rather take you to Melbourne for a holiday. I need a break and I think you'd love it."

A smile lit her face in immediate response. "Do you? Really?"

"Yes, I do, really." He couldn't resist popping a quick kiss on her glowing face. "I quite fancy catching a show at The Globe. It's terribly civilized and it'll be great taking you shopping. My treat."

"I'm not taking handouts." She got that obdurate look he'd begun to love.

"You'll take what you're given, my girl." He felt sinful. "And enjoy it too."

He saw a shiver dance up her spine and her obstinacy give way to a look of anticipation.

"When shall we go?"

He shut down the engine, having carefully maneuvered them into his car park. The way she'd said "we" touched him.

"I don't know. How soon can you get away? It's reasonably easy for me to block a couple of days out of my schedule. But your fish - don't you have to do regular rounds or something?"

She tipped her head sideways in that delicious way and he could almost hear her thought patterns.

"Hmm. I'll have to check my diary, but I'd blocked time out in a fortnight to go away with Gina - " a wave of despair crossed her face, gone as soon as it arrived, a passing cloud almost " - so I'm sure I can just rearrange a few things if you want to go. Not this weekend, but next?"

"Sounds perfect to me. Why don't I check my diary and give you a ring tonight? We can compare notes and then I can get the whole thing booked."

"You'll get the whole thing booked, huh?" That you think you can push me around look was back on her face.

"I will." He couldn't resist the challenge. "Have a problem with that, do we?"

"We might." She ran a perfectly manicured fingernail up the inside of his thigh. Even through the material the touch disturbed him. "But we might not too." Her tone was playful and any misgivings he had about her - or the trip - vanished into the ether.

He picked up the hand that was still idling on his thigh and clamped his teeth around the firm, fleshy part of her thumb. She squealed and vainly tried to wrench it from his mouth, all the time playing tag with his tongue.

"I love it when you play rough." He smiled, still not releasing her.

"You've no idea where that thumb's been."

"I know exactly where it's been and I'm already planning where it's going."

"And on that smutty note, I'm on my way." She opened the door and he got a clear view down her top as she reached back into the car to collect her purse off the floor. He could hardly wait to get her on the plane.

This is the second Tuesday night Gina's refused to have our usual dinner. Tamsen's despondency increased as she wrote the words in her morning pages. Nothing's been the same since she stormed out of Matt's office and I'm at my wits end.

The ocean was an iridescent shade of aqua blue. Fresh salt-laden air filled her lungs as Tamsen pondered the prospect of two more days of work and then four away with Matt. Anticipation hung on the horizon, a jewel tantalizingly close, hers for the taking. She could barely contain her excitement; it was like waiting for Christmas to come, only better.

"Suppose you're writing more lovey-dovey shit about that anal wanker you're going away with?" From the tone of Gina's voice it was obvious she was hung over - again.

"You didn't come home for dinner. That's two Tuesdays in a row. Do you want to talk about it?"

Gina planted herself in the chair opposite. Tamsen decided her flatmate's eyeballs looked like a map of France, trails of mascara and kohl rimming them like an oil slick.

"Are you still going away with that prick?"

"Yes."

Gina took a drag on her cigarette; it seemed to be all she had for breakfast these days. "Then there's nothing to talk about, is there?"

"Gina, I really miss you." Compassion was about the only thing left to feel. She was way past being angry and it didn't seem to help. "I can't believe how fast you've gone downhill since you quit your job. Look at yourself. You're a mess."

"Well, whose fault would that be?" Defiance flashed in Gina's eyes.

"Yours."

"I said there was nothing to talk about." Gina stubbed out the rest of the cigarette and stared insolently out to sea.

"There's the matter of the rent. Your share hasn't gone into the account this month."

"I'll get it in today."

"For God's sake, Gina, how? You haven't worked-"

"It's my problem. I'll get it solved." She stood up, her beady-eyed stare making Tamsen feel as if she were something revolting stuck to her room flatmate's shoe. "Besides, you've made it patently clear that you're no longer going to help me solve my problems - that I'm on my own."

Gina turned and stalked off in the direction of the bathroom.

With a sigh, Tamsen turned her attention again to her diary.

The thud of a bucket landing at her feet made Tamsen jump.

"What's this?" She looked up at Gina, wondering again who the stranger was standing in front of her.

"Call it a peace-offering."

A small forest of aquatic plants swayed in the water, inside a bright yellow bucket.

"Where..." Did she really want to know?

"Don't ask - " Gina almost smiled " - just say thank you."

CHAPTER FOURTEEN

Reaching again for the half-drunk coffee on the smoked-glass table in front of her, Tamsen hoped it would wake her up after the flight. She sank back into the soft leather armchair and took a moment to take in the awe-inspiring surroundings of Melbourne's Grand Hyatt.

The atrium windows, crossed with...what? She didn't know, but it reminded her of masking tape used on glass during old war movies. The glass seemed to climb for two or three floors and she had ridiculous thoughts about how the poor sucker must feel who had to clean them.

"You'd think they could hurry it up, wouldn't you?" Matt's irritation that their booking had been mislaid washed off him in waves, like the slow, destructive movement of lava. She'd only witnessed his temper a couple of times, but the thought of him exploding in such beautiful surrounds behoved her to act.

She decided to try agreeing with him. "You'd think with five hundred-odd rooms they'd be able to rustle one up for us now, wouldn't you?" It might work until she could work out a way to jolly him.

"You would." His foot was jiggling against the small glass table.

She put one hand on his quivering knee. "Suppose I go and suggest that I shower in the fountain in the foyer. You think that might get them moving?"

It worked. He broke out a broad smile. "Dunno, but it might relieve some of the tedious boredom I'm feeling at the moment. Sex in the fountain." An evil glint appeared in his eyes. "Now there's a cool concept."

"I never said anything about sex."

"I wouldn't be able to look at your nakedness without thinking about sex."

"Who said anything about being naked?" She winked at him and got up, heading toward the flustered looking blonde on the reception desk. "You've got a mind like a sewer, Mr Solomon."

Ensconced in their room at last, Matt felt so much better. "What did you say to the concierge to get us in here so quick, or shouldn't I ask?"

Tamsen shrugged. "Just told her we'd had the day from hell and that you were threatening gratuitous sexual activity in their fountain."

He was mortified. "You did not!"

"You'll never know now, will you?"

"You are such a tart."

She giggled. "But a scheming, lovely one."

He threw himself on the bed. "That's my problem. Come here." He patted the silky coverlet next to him. It reminded him of the soft caress of her skin.

He ached to touch her and he hadn't realized how much until a stirring in his loins reminded him they were alone, finally. "Come here, you. I won't ask again." He was acutely aware of the length of time he'd been in close proximity to her, but unable to touch.

She looked at him, desire registering in her eyes. Certainly she was one of the most alluring souls he'd ever known. If he had his way, he thought, she could very likely be the last alluring soul he would ever know.

"And if I don't come over there?" The question hung provocatively between them.

"Then I'm afraid I'll have to be firm with you."

Her smile broadened. "I quite like it when you're firm with me. I have a particular fondness for firmness in a man."

A rush of heat took him by surprise. He continued to be amazed at his body's reaction to the slightest suggestion from her that she found him desirable.

"Get your body over here now, you trollop."

"Or what?"

"Or you'll be sorry."

She smiled. It was enough to light the touch paper of his desire; it had been smoldering - now he was on fire.

"How can a girl resist an order like that?" She walked toward him, deliberately slow and seductive. He'd been trying to find words to describe the way she moved. She had a particular rhythm about her. She'd have made a great snake charmer, he thought, parts of his anatomy behaving as if they were hypnotized by her erotic grace.

Halfway across the room she stopped and shimmied out of her skirt. He loved the way the fabric billowed around her; she looked like an elf stepping off a mushroom cloud.

In what appeared to be a single step, she covered the rest of the space between them and was on top of him, her turquoise G-string begging for attention from his eager mouth.

"You have no idea how sexy you look."

"Tell me. I want to hear." She gyrated that small scrap of material over his sternum and it was all he could do to stop himself exploding in his pants. Catching the odd waft of her muskiness, he was painfully aware of how sensitive he was to everything about her.

"Take your top off." He desperately wanted to see her nipples.

She obliged, teasing him, cupping her ample breasts in her hands, palms over the nipples he so longed to see.

"You just love tormenting me, don't you?"

She rolled her nipples through her fingers, allowing him a teasing glance at them. "Just want to make sure I'm at my best for you. I know how visually stimulated men are."

"And you like the idea of stimulating me visually, do you?" Obscene thoughts about her doing a striptease for him came crashing into his consciousness.

"What do you think?" She continued to twist her nipples savagely.

It was too much. He wanted - no, needed - to taste her.

"Come here." Grabbing her wrists, he pulled her down and latched leech-like onto the nearest breast, rolling its tip with his mouth and tongue. The hardened nub grated against his teeth and he clamped on tight as she wriggled against him. Her moans were music to his ears and again his groin begged for some much-needed attention.

The phone rang.

Tamsen registered it, reaching for the receiver. He wanted to yell for her to ignore it, but that would mean releasing the delicate morsel in his mouth.

"He-hello."

He suckled harder. An evil part of him wanted to distract her from the phone call, see how much she could stand. She stared imploringly at him but he just smiled around the flesh trapped between his teeth and continued, adding to her discomfort by tucking a thumb inside the edge of her G-string. He was pleased to discover that she was warm and wet.

"Gina!" There was a look of dismay and panic on her face.

What the hell did that nutcase want? He released Tamsen's nipple and mouthed Get rid of her. Christ, the hellcat's timing was atrocious.

"You haven't wanted to speak to me for weeks, so why do you have to wait until I'm away to decide you want to talk?"

He pulled a face again, but Tamsen seemed to be ignoring him. He wasn't impressed. She looked distracted and maybe a little bit in pain. His feelings of resentment over *telephonus-interruptus* surfaced in a flurry.

He tried the universal sawing finger across the neck, a last-ditch attempt to have Tamsen terminate the call before his flagging libido went completely south on him. She just held her hand palm up in resignation and rolled her eyes sideways. All was obviously lost.

Utter despair had Tamsen in its vice-like grip. Matt continued to pace the room at a frantic speed, as he'd been doing since she put down the phone from Gina.

"Matt, please, honey. Just come and sit down."

"The woman's a freak. You did the right thing. She can't expect you to drop everything and jump on a plane just because she says she's depressed."

"But she didn't sound right."

"The mad cow's never sounded right." The look on his face - how could she describe it? Revulsion? She wasn't sure, but she knew she didn't like it one iota. It all added to the overbearing claustrophobia that threatened to crush her.

"You can't say that." She knew he could, even as she spat the words out. How had a great holiday come to be so hideous? She quelled a crushing urge to escape and instead felt her soul flee. It was sick of this and taking a much-needed break without the rest of her.

His features softened. "Babe, look at you. She wears you out." He crossed the room in two easy strides, the warmth of his hand as he took hers alerting her to how cold she'd become. Physically as well as emotionally.

"I know." She sighed. "But it doesn't make it any easier. You should have heard the way she was begging for me to come home. She's never been like this before. I'm scared for her."

"She'll be okay." He kissed Tamsen on the forehead, the sweet, simple gesture soothing her ragged conscience. "People like her are survivors, emotional vampires that suck the life out of lovelies like you." His smile was warm and genuine; the touch of his full lips on hers reignited the bonfire of desire that burned in her for him.

He was right. Gina would be okay - she always was. Surrendering to his probing lips and tongue, she allowed herself to be seduced away from the worrying thoughts. A small speck of doubt and fear lingered, but she closed her consciousness to it. She was living in the moment, and this one belonged to her and Matt.

"You wouldn't really have shagged me in the fountain in the foyer, would you?" Tamsen stretched, cat-like, enjoying feeling her senses on alert, almost heightened, and the wonderful afterglow of glorious sexual connection. Her mind, body and soul all sat in perfect alignment.

"I'd like to. I've always fancied being arrested for indecent exposure." He flashed her a wicked grin. "But it's not the done thing when you're climbing the legal ladder."

"Maybe you're not cut out for legal-ladder climbing."

He lifted his head up off the tangle of pillows and she watched with fascination as the peak of his Adams apple was reabsorbed into his neck. "The thought's entered my head on a couple of occasions."

"And?"

"I dismissed it." He was starting to look uncomfortable.

"Why?"

"Do you always ask so many questions?"

"Yup. Stop trying to turn the conversation around to me. We're talking about you."

"Are we now?" He idly circled her nipple with his finger and she was surprised it peaked at his touch.

"Yes, we are. And you can't distract me by playing with my bits."

"I can try." He suckled her and a shot of pain - or was it pleasure; she could never be sure - racked her exhausted body.

"So you have thought about giving up law. You just don't want to talk about it."

He let her nipple go, the rush of cool air adding to the pain/pleasure. "How do you get to be so smart?"

She shrugged. "Dunno. Just observing people, I suppose. You really don't want to talk about it?"

"No." He grinned. "But I suppose you're not about to let me off the hook."

"You got it, pal."

"All my life I was told I was going to be a solicitor. I honestly had no choice." He turned over onto his side, nearly in the fetal position, clutching one of the abandoned pillows to his stomach. "I cruised through law school, top honors, and never really thought about anything else, to be honest - it was just expected that I would follow the path set for me. I didn't want any sort of trouble."

He grimaced. "I mean, you've met Mother. Would you like to try and explain why whatever she decided was best for her golden boy might not be best for him?"

Tamsen could see his point; the thought of crossing that demonic woman made her skin crawl. "But lately?" Yes, she was leading him, but she felt a powerful urge to keep pulling.

"I don't know. I'm beginning to wonder if I've done the right thing. I just don't seem to fit in. You know, the day I first saw you - when you were floating a fish around in that plastic bag, talking to it - I felt something I don't understand. Up until that moment I'd thought I was the only person on the planet who talked to goldfish." He smiled sheepishly.

She felt an unexpected rush of compassion for him; he was as trapped as that fish had been in its little plastic bubble. She'd been there to release that little fish, could she do the same for Matt? "Everyone talks to goldfish."

"Not everyone I know. And that's my point. I'm a fish out of water, and it's taken you walking into my life to show me just how out of place I really am."

"Hey, less of the me-walking-into-your-life speak. As I recall you dragged me in kicking and screaming."

He pulled her closer to him, abandoning the pillow he was cuddling in favor of her. "Kicking and screaming? Hmm." He ran a hand expertly down her buttocks, reaching for her most sensitive spots. "Screaming orgasms, more like." He dug deeper.

"Get out of there, you horror show." That appetite was most certainly whetted, but she was aware that lunch had been a very long time ago and her stomach was in desperate negotiation with her brain. "Isn't it about time we ate? I dunno know about you, but I can't live on love alone."

"Hello. We're up to love now? A minute ago you were talking about being dragged kicking and screaming into the relationship."

Tamsen smashed a pillow over his naked body. "Stop being a solicitor and get that grubby body of yours into the shower. I'm starved."

They skipped the restaurants in the hotel, deciding instead on a small café-style eatery along a side street by the cathedral. Matt was determined to spend some time in there while he was in town. He had no idea how Tamsen would cope; most of the women he'd attempted to share his spiritual beliefs with had completely shut down on him. But he had a strange feeling Tamsen would be different. Either way, he found himself happy to take the risk.

Maybe it had something to do with her ability to see inside him. For someone who seemed outwardly so disconnected from the material world she had a surprising knack of being able to hone in exactly on what was bothering him. He hadn't been faced with himself for a long time, so maybe that was why God had brought her into his life.

"Gawd, I'm stuffed." She wiped a droplet of sauce from her chin with a starched linen napkin. "That venison was out of this world."

"I still can't believe you ate Bambi," he said. Tamsen had a healthy appetite for food that he'd not seen in a long time.

"Get over it, pal."

"But aren't you spiritual-plane types supposed to abhor eating meat and live on lentils?"

"I tried that but it didn't work. I got really anemic and couldn't concentrate on anything. Ended up obsessing about hamburgers to the point I couldn't function."

"Sounds scary."

"It was, believe me."

"So you eat meat all the time now?"

"No, I wouldn't say that. I still struggle with the suffering of mass food production - or any kind of food production really. I can never look at a dead animal without wondering if its last remaining moments were in terror.

"Yeah, but I suppose everything suffers one way or another. Even your beloved fish. I'm sure they'd much rather be out swimming around in a huge lake than stuck in a little glass prison in the foyer of my office."

"You're sure it's just the fish that are stuck in your office?"

"Don't start on that little hobby-horse again, Tams, or you might just pay for it later."

She looked at him slyly. "Is that a threat or a promise, Mr Solomon?"

Strolling hand in hand through near deserted streets, Matt found himself comforted by her presence. He was aware of the scents of the city - the oily smell of tar drifting from the road, and exotic spices mingling with the unmistakable smell of deep-frying escaping from restaurants. Gusts of used air spilled from vents, powered by overtaxed air-conditioning units whose constant dripping nourished small weed seedlings in the cracked concrete beneath.

This was the only world he really knew. The world he functioned well in, his place in the scheme of things. So why was he beginning to feel so disturbed and trapped by it all?

He gazed at the unselfish woman holding his hand. She'd changed the way he looked at his life, yet the scary thing was he didn't even think she'd been trying to change him at all. She reminded him of a butterfly, the layers of her lime-chiffon dress moving gracefully with her.

"You're beautiful, do you know that?"

She smiled. It lit up her face and he couldn't help smiling back.

"If you keep telling me, I might just start believing it."

"Well, you should, because you are." It felt good to see her happy and knowing he had a part in causing that joy. A feeling of love and attachment welled up inside him, a tide of intense, fuzzy heat rolling up his body.

"What do you want to do with the rest of the night?" she asked, the twinkle in her eye warning of pleasures he didn't dare to try and envisage.

"I want to take you back to our room and ravish you, sleep it off, and then repeat the whole procedure until the sun comes up." He allowed his imagination to run riot – a new experience. "Then I want to order dessert for breakfast and sit in bed eating it - with strong coffee, you and a morning paper."

"You might get newsprint on the sheets."

He laughed. "I'm sure newsprint on the sheets will be the least of our worries."

She looked thoughtful. "Sounds decadent enough for a holiday. Lead the way, Mr Solomon.".

CHAPTER FIFTEEN

Tamsen was barely in the door before she felt his iron grip. Spinning her round, he kicked the door shut behind them, the sudden assault on her body and senses making her jump.

"A little on edge tonight, are we, sweetness?" His tone and the look in his eyes screamed lust.

"Shaking with desire for you, actually." It was the truth. The ride up in the lift had seemed an eternity. All she wanted to do was devour him.

"I can help with that." He picked her up in one swift movement, and the gesture unhinged the hunger she'd been trying to contain. She reached out with her tongue to that soft, secret place behind his ear and tasted him.

He squeezed her closer as they moved toward the center of the room. The bed had been turned down and a chocolate wrapped in gold paper lay on each pillow.

"I love it when they do the chocolate thing. It's so indulgent, don't you think?"

He dropped her on the bed and lay on top of her. "I can think of far more debauched things about a bed than chocolate."

She leaned up and licked his throat, his Adam's apple vibrating under her tongue. "And things that taste better?" she teased.

"Come here and let me taste you then." His tone was urgent, sparking longing inside her. Even through his aloofness he had the strange ability to draw her closer with his every word.

His scent and nearness fueled her aching need for him. "Let me get these clothes off." The words came out as a near whine. "I need to feel your skin on me."

He was off her in a moment, strong hands tearing the jade material from her flesh. She felt like a butterfly being freed from its cocoon.

"I love your body, your skin...so smooth." His words whispered across her breasts between warm, sensual kisses.

Desire to touch him overwhelmed her. Dealing to his buttons with efficiency, ripping his shirt from his body, she delighted in flinging it across the bed in a dramatic fashion. Around him she felt dramatic, inspired, playful - a whole horde of mixed emotions.

She'd always felt inhibited about sex, but she didn't feel this with Matt. She wanted him to look at her. She didn't care that her boobs might sag, or that she had stretch marks on her thighs from her constant teenage yo-yo dieting. Under his gaze she was aware of nothing except the fact that he wanted her - adored her - and she liked that.

She struggled with his belt. What was it about the immediacy of lust that turned you into a fumbling idiot, she wondered.

"Here, let me help." Matt brushed her hands away and deftly saw to the bothersome piece of leather. "There, that's better." She was assaulted by his hard cock, its heat offset by cool silk boxers.

She moaned with pleasure. "I don't know which I adore more - the feel of the silk on my skin, or knowing that you want me so much."

He moved over her again, pressing his hardness into her tummy, forcing her legs wide apart, the rough stitching of his jeans cutting into her soft inner thighs and only arousing her more.

She ached to feel him inside her and vainly pushed her pubis skyward, moaning in frustration when there was nothing to grind it against.

"God, I want you," he whispered, his tongue finding the warmth of her mouth.

Her pubic bone hit pay dirt and she was rewarded with the feel of cock thrusting against her. He eased his mouth away from hers; she could feel his hot breath on her neck. He teased her with the tip of his tongue, tracing patterns around her ear.

"Get rid of those clothes. I want you in me."

"Patience, baby cakes. We've got all night and I intend to use every last minute of it."

She shuddered, her body responding to his promise.

Abruptly he lifted himself up off her, almost as if he was intent on proving he was a man of his word and would make her wait. He set to removing his shoes and socks and she set to releasing his cock from its silken prison.

There was something wonderful about feeling the head of a man's cock on her lips and face.

"Who taught you how to do that?" Matt's words were interspersed between moans. Powerful urges ran the length of her body, a sense of universal energy fueling her every movement. She felt alive, vital and in control.

"I can't stand much more of that." Matt pulled himself from her glistening lips. "I've something else I want to put in that gorgeous mouth of yours."

Reaching over her, his lean, muscular body further inflaming her need, he produced one of the small golden chocolates and began slowly unwrapping it, a look of mischief in his eyes.

"I'd rather have you than chocolate." It was the truth.

"Well, I want to sweeten you up." He held the star-shaped treat just short of her lips and she couldn't resist reaching for it with the tip of her tongue, adding to the overall feeling of decadence.

He waggled a finger at her. "Naughty, naughty, you're in such a rush. I want to make this last."

"You want to make everything last tonight." She moved onto her hands and knees, enjoying the illusion of begging.

He licked a point on the star, a streak of chocolate running across his tongue like lava over a mountainside. "Now, no biting." He looked menacing. "Or I'll have to bite you."

His tone did nothing to quell the rising tide of lust and she offered herself to him unconditionally.

The fine point of chocolate began to melt as he ran it over her lips, the smooth, creamy texture coating them. It reminded her of honey drizzling over hot pancakes.

"Lick it off."

That feeling of decadence returned as she tasted the sweet treat. "Hmm. It's mint. You want some more?" The idea of returning the favor appealed.

He handed her the chocolate; it was slippery in her fingers. May as well be bold, she thought, pushing her tongue out between her lips. He rewarded her with a flicker of acknowledgement in his eyes and his sweet chocolate-coated fingers on her outstretched tongue.

"You're getting the hang of this, aren't you?" he asked. She'd never have believed eating a chocolate could be so sexy.

The shrill ringing of the phone startled her and she dropped the chocolate. "Shit. Now there's going to be chocolate all over the bedding."

"Don't worry about it. I'm sure they've seen worse." He still had a glint of guilty pleasure in his eye. God, she wanted him.

The phone continued to ring. She needed to ignore it, but an uneasy feeling settled in the pit of her stomach. She looked at Matt.

"Leave it. It's not important," he said.

"How do you know?"

"Because no one knows we're here."

"Except Gina." She couldn't hide the urgency in her voice.

"She's a fruit-loop, Tams. Just leave it."

His tone was so abrupt. She didn't know what to do. Everything screamed to answer the damn phone.

Tamsen made a move toward it.

"I said leave it!" He grabbed her arm.

"You're hurting me."

"I'm sorry." He relaxed his grip just as the shrill ringing from the phone ceased. An uncomfortable silence fell over the room. Sexual tension and escalating pleasure replaced by painful quiet and budding resentment.

The flashing light on the phone dial, testament to a message left, pulled at her gut. But the dejected look on Matt's face hurt even more.

Matt removed the almost melted chocolate from the cream linen, a hideous tan smear testament to the heat of their now chilled arousal.

"Chocolate's supposed to activate the same sensors in the brain that love does." It was a ridiculous thing to say. Why didn't she just keep her mouth shut?

"Is that so?" He couldn't hide the sarcasm in his voice. "I'm tired and I'm going to have a shower."

"Would you like me to come scrub your back?"

"That would depend." He threw her a challenging look.

"On what?" She wasn't going to back down.

She'd kill Gina when she got home; this really was the last straw. A fortnight of no talkies and then, as soon as Tamsen was out of the country, plaintive, whining phone calls making all sorts of ridiculous demands. A bucket of aquatic weed, probably stolen from somewhere, did not a friendship mend. The more Tamsen thought about it the angrier she became.

"On you leaving the phone alone for the rest of the night," Matt said, "I'd like to have your undivided attention, if that's at all possible."

Tamsen smiled. "I'm all yours. You know, the more I think about it, the more I can see where you're coming from about Gina."

"Good." His face softened. "I knew you were a smart girl and would see reason eventually."

As much as she hated herself, Tamsen bloomed under his approval. "So does that mean the back scrub's on then?"

"It does." He slapped her hard on the backside. "Now, get thee to the bathroom, wench, and get that shower started."

Leaping off the bed, Tamsen worried that she might have found the slap far too arousing.

Sweet pastries and the morning newspaper - there was nothing more a man could wish for, Matt thought as he unfolded *The Age*. It didn't matter where he woke, as long as there was a local newspaper he could avail himself of he was in heaven. Nothing like being informed. Why, only last week he'd blown one of his colleagues' clients away with his opinion on the pros and cons of leaving sheep at high altitudes unshorn.

"That wouldn't be coffee I can smell, would it?" Tamsen's voice was thick with sleep; if at all possible, she sounded even sexier than usual.

"It sure is. Would you like some?"

"Hmm. Yes, please." She had the tousled look of someone who'd been indulging in passionate sex all night. Which of course, he reminded himself, she had.

His own perkiness amazed him, but waking up beside Tamsen was a real thrill. On a high for the day already, he barely needed the coffee. Pouring the fragrant liquid into an espresso cup, he stopped mid-pour.

"Hey, you don't drink coffee. Only that herbal muck."

His train of thought went right off the rails when she stretched unselfconsciously, the bed linen falling away from her pert nipples and pooling at her ample hips. Squeezable hips they were - not the sort that would slip through a man's hands, but the variety you could get a good hold of. He loved them, even if she didn't.

"Coffee's good in the morning when I've had next to no sleep." She grinned, scratching a shoulder blade. He was sure she knew exactly what she was doing to him.

"You could have gone to sleep any time you wanted to."

"Like there was any chance I could have said no to you during the night."

He finished pouring the coffee. "What flavor?"

"Coffee flavor." He could hear the confusion in her voice.

"No - milk? Sugar?"

"Black with one."

"One what?" He so loved teasing her.

"Don't be a dick."

"I'm not putting that in there."

"I should hope not. Hell, you never know where it's been." Even half asleep she was gorgeous, desirable and smart. What more could a man ask for?

Setting the pastries and newspapers out picnic style on the bed, he joined her for a bizarre breakfast. He couldn't remember the last time he'd read the paper in bed. Tamsen was fun and she brought out the best in him.

They browsed the paper and grazed on breakfast, tentatively feeding each other pastries between bouts of laughter and gulps of coffee.

"So, what do you want to do today?" He'd been indulging her and he wanted to continue doing so.

"I thought I might go to church."

"What?" He nearly choked on his coffee. "Won't the roof fall in or something?"

"What are you talking about?"

He tugged on the silver pentacle at her throat. "Witches going to church? Surely it's not the done thing?"

"Nothing wrong with it at all."

"Don't you have covens to go to or something like that?"

"Only if you belong to one. I'm a solitary practitioner."

He looked puzzled. "You can do that? Just decide you're going to be a witch and, hey presto, before you can wiggle your nose you are one?"

"Don't be facetious."

"I wasn't. I'm just wondering how the hell one becomes a witch. You can't just decide, surely?"

"Well...I suppose, yes. You can."

"That's ridiculous." He couldn't hide his contempt. "Doesn't it run in families or something?"

He watched as she wrinkled her nose in that delicate way she had when she was thinking hard. "You might be talking about family teachings. You know, handing down information from generation to generation."

"What did you do - go to witches school?" The thought made him laugh – until he saw the look on her face.

"You can do, if that's what you want."

"You're pulling my leg, right?"

Though maybe not, he thought. At this rate, there was a good chance he'd be hopping out of here after she turned him into a toad. "Okay, I'll be quiet and serious. Tell me about your faith."

Tamsen's demeanor softened. "What makes you call it my faith?"

"Because that's what it must be. A power greater than yourself, right?"

She nodded.

"So it has to be a faith."

"I'm sorry, Matt. Most people are just so dumbfounded by Wicca - they expect me to be some Buffy type, or make fun of me. You know, asking whether or not I dance naked on the full moons, or have a Whitelighter who arrives out of nowhere."

"Well, do you?"

"Have a Whitelighter?"

"Dance naked under the full moon."

She blushed. "Sometimes."

"Would you do it for me?" He was enjoying flirting with her, gauging the reaction. It was like lighting a candle and watching the flame splutter into life.

"I might." She grinned. "But only if you did too."

"I doubt there'd be much dancing if I got naked with you. I don't recall doing the foxtrot last night." He pulled the sheet away from her stomach, exposing the milky flesh.

She arched her back in response. "Hungry for some more, are you?"

"I am." He launched himself at her nakedness, undoing his toweling robe in a flash, the sensation of flesh-to-flesh contact causing an immediate arousal in him.

"What about our discussion on faith?" she sputtered from under the rain of kisses he was showering on her face.

"That can wait. I've far more important and pressing matters to deal with."

"So. Are you going to tell me where we're off to on this mission of yours?"

Tamsen noted the slight irritation in Matt's voice and made a mental note. He liked to be in control.

"No." She smiled sweetly. "I told you, it's a surprise."

"And I told you I don't like surprises."

"You're just going to have to trust me." She linked her arm through his and started walking down the steps of the hotel toward the street.

"Hey." He stopped and she nearly lost her footing. She'd been careful to put low heels on, it being a reasonable walk to St Patrick's, but she hadn't wanted to compromise sensuality too much. Running shoes were out of the question with her princess-line dress. "We're taking the Boxter, right?"

"No, Matt, we're walking. Now come on."

She pulled him on down the steps and he begrudgingly came with her, muttering under his breath.

"What's the use of hiring a bloody Porsche if we don't use the damn thing? I don't enjoy walking, you know."

"Rubbish - you must spend hours on that nasty jogging contraption in your basement. But there's nothing like the real thing."

She threw him a beaming smile. He still looked determined to have a lousy time whatever she did. "Besides, you didn't mind walking to the restaurant last night."

"That was different."

"How?"

"We were going to get something to eat."

"Ah. So it's different if there's nourishment involved."

"I suppose." He sounded defensive.

"Well, just think of this as nourishment for the soul."

"You're nuts. You know that, don't you?"

"If you say so." His attitude wasn't going to ruin her morning.

She'd been looking forward to this for ages. The cathedral was one of the first places she'd discovered on the internet when she found out they were going to Melbourne. She had a passion for all places of worship and then she read about the Pilgrim Path and ever since had itched to walk it.

Ten minutes later, with Collins Street at their backs and Macarthur Street stretching before them, Tamsen was glad to leave the hustle and bustle of the inner city behind. St Patrick's sat proudly at the top of the street, the sight of its triple spires stirring her excitement.

"Come on, Matt, it's not too far - just up the hill."

"I thought we were going to a church? This is the way to the cathedral."

"Yeah?" She was puzzled.

"But you said we were going to a church."

"It is a church." What was he going on about?

"No. A church is a building with a cross on the roof. This is a cathedral."

She'd done it again. She had no idea how she did, but she'd managed to find herself another Catholic. She must have "Heathen in need of saving" tattooed across her forehead or something.

"You're a Catholic and yet you didn't run screaming for the hills when you found out I practiced witchcraft. How come?"

"How do you know I'm Catholic?"

She grinned. "You've got that shed with a cross on it thing happening. The one true religion. My soul needs saving. I could go on."

"Please don't." He looked unimpressed and she wished she'd kept her mouth shut.

"Sorry," she said meekly.

"Don't apologize. I haven't been a practicing Catholic for years."

They narrowly dodged being collected by a taxi, its driver oblivious to them as they negotiated the roadway.

"Maybe God's suggesting that you might like to take another look at that decision." She couldn't help herself; the opportunity was just too good to miss.

"That's why he'd have me here, in the middle of Melbourne, on the arm of a mad witch whose sole objective at the moment, when she's not trying to have me run over by the locals, is to get me into a Cathedral." He rubbed the back of his neck. "It's all too weird."

"No. I'm sure it's exactly how it's supposed to be." She kissed him on the cheek. "Now come, my little altar boy - there's a Pilgrim Path up here

I'd like to walk with you."

With no real religious instruction in Tamsen's home she'd had a difficult journey trying to channel some sort of spiritual faith for herself. Many religions and a number of self-help gurus later she'd finally settled on the Wiccan way, a culmination of so many aspects of the belief systems she'd studied - a neat package predominantly surrounded by a love and respect for all living things.

However despite having rejected Catholicism along with a number of other religions, she'd never been able to shake her affection for it - as much for the pomp and ceremony as for the beautiful cathedrals she loved visiting.

St Patrick's Pilgrim Path was more beautiful than Tamsen had hoped it would be.

Matt stood, almost in awe, gazing at the grey stone of the building. Tamsen thought it really wasn't a surprise that she was attracted to him. Even if he was lapsed, as he described himself – not that she believed there was such a thing - his faith simply leaked out of him.

He caught her watching him and smiled. "Why are you looking at me when there's something as beautiful as this in front of you?" He thrust his arm toward the cathedral.

"I was wondering what karmic lesson you've been sent to teach me." She couldn't help running her fingers along his strong jaw. "Besides the obvious."

"The deadly sin of lust." His tone was calculating.

She slapped him on the backside, catching the stud from his jeans pocket on the tip of her finger. "Ouch."

"That'll teach you." He looked skyward. "Thanks, Hughie. Keep her in line, will you?"

She sucked her finger; a nasty mark was developing on it. "When was the last time you went to confession?"

"None of your business - and besides, they don't call it that anymore."

"They don't?" She wondered when that had changed and why she hadn't heard about it.

"No." His pleased look was beginning to annoy her. "It's reconciliation now."

"Sounds like marriage guidance counseling."

"I can assure you it's not."

"Anyway, getting back to why we're here..."

Patience replaced his amused look. She knew he was just indulging her.

"Yes, please. Remind me again why we are here."

She pulled a small, folded piece of paper from her purse. "Hey, no peeking." She flattened her set of internet instructions against her chest, ignoring his feigned looks of being hurt. "Now, according to this we have to approach the Pilgrim's Path from the south." She looked at him expectantly. "Any idea where that is?"

"We've come from the south."

"I knew I brought you for a reason."

"I was beginning to wonder."

Stopping to read the path's first inscription, a quote from the Australian poet *James McAuley*, Tamsen was taken by the symmetry of the inclined pathway, cut by cascading water. An immediate sense of calm overtook her, the soothing sounds of water washing away the nervous tensions accumulated on their excursion.

Matt had ventured ahead, walking the other side of the concrete bank. She hadn't even noticed his departure, she'd been so engrossed in the challenging message before her.

The words she read evoked fiery images of desperate and repentant men in her mind's eye. She shuddered, remembering why she oftentimes fiercely disliked organized religion.

Hurrying up her side of the path to catch Matt, she stopped for a moment to ponder St John the Baptist's words, a much more comforting message.

Matt continued his steady ascent and it occurred to her she was the one who'd wanted to be here. Why then was she hurrying through the experience to catch up with him? She should take her time and enjoy the precious moments. She didn't need Matt to hold her hand, physically or metaphorically.

The revelation startled her. How long had she been dependent on another person's approval? Was that what she was doing with the fish business? Granted, she enjoyed it - but her dream, as Gina so often reminded her, was to get sponsorship for a retreat.

Gina. Oh, shit! She suddenly remembered the previous night's phone call that Matt's rising tide of disapproval had persuaded her to ignore. Dammit, she should have checked the answerphone this morning, but despite the little red light had flashing all night she'd completely forgotten about it. How could she have done that?

Redoubling her resolve not to chase up the path and catch Matt, she took advantage of a strategically placed seat to rest a while and ponder on the last few days. He could bloody well wait for her, or even turn around and come back.

What she couldn't understand, however, was why Gina had taken it into her head to ring the hotel. Twice. Surely it was just more head games? Life at home had been horrendous since Gina quit work. Not another job in sight and the drinking had gotten horribly out of control.

Tamsen gazed at the craggy stonework of the cathedral; its exterior fairly oozed peace and serenity, in total contrast to the turmoil she felt inside.

She was at a loss as to what to do for Gina. Maybe Matt was right. Maybe she should just wipe her and get on with her own life, but that seemed somewhat drastic. Even for someone who pretended to be as callous as Matt.

He was further up the path, studying a bronze bowl that was the origin of the water trickling down the concourse at her feet. As angry as she was with herself for giving in to him and forgetting to call Gina back, she couldn't help admiring his physique. He was truly beautiful. She got up and walked to him.

"You didn't wait for me?" Her anger had dissipated; it was as if the water, pouring out of the copper basin, had washed it all away.

"I figured you'd want some time alone." He smiled. "You know, to take it all in. It's just magic, isn't it?"

She felt like an idiot. Why did she listen to the garbage that went on in her head? "It is magic - of the most spiritual kind."

"Any idea who the saints are?" Matt gestured to two striking statues whose presence appeared to be supporting them as they looked back down across the open space.

"Catherine and Francis."

"You have done your research, haven't you?"

"Always." She slipped her arm through his. "You're not the only one who can investigate a subject, counselor."

He squeezed her arm in a gesture of support. "It appears I'm not."

Tamsen couldn't help but be touched by the dramatic freshness of

Louis Lauman's saints, whom he'd identified with the suffering of Jesus - Francis bearing the wounds of stigmata and Catherine the crown of thorns. A shudder ran down Tamsen's back; the thought of such pain and torment being inflicted on any living creature was appalling.

"Do you want to go inside?" Matt asked.

A light breeze had come up - or was it just the thought of so much suffering that made her shudder.

Matt took her hand in his and renewed warmth spread through her body. It was amazing the effect a simple touch had on her nervous system – but then who wouldn't feel calm and serene in this spiritual place, despite the reminders of Jesus' suffering?

CHAPTER SIXTEEN

They entered the cathedral through the main doors, its ascetic façade giving little hint of the ethereal beauty cloistered within. Matt touched the tips of his fingers into the small vessel of water at the door and crossed himself.

"Don't you just love the way these places smell?" Tamsen's hushed tone startled Matt. He'd been held captive in a world of his own making for most of the morning.

"Hmm. Takes me back to my childhood." His voice was as quiet as hers. He'd never been able to bring himself to talk naturally in the awe-inspiring catacomb-like interior of a cathedral. It seemed disrespectful.

Tamsen stood motionless in front of a large ornate crucifix that dominated his view; it reminded him of center stage in a production. They were dwarfed by the majesty of the surroundings and he felt an insane urge to cry. Working hard to swallow the raw emotion, he felt beads of sweat erupt on his temples.

In an effort to distract himself he bent to whisper in Tamsen's ear, close enough to feel tendrils of her hair on his lips; the feeling was almost decadent, especially in this holy place.

"You look like an angel." Every word caught in his throat, as shafts of soft light fell through the stained-glass windows, muting the harsh Australian sunlight and bathing them in a cosmic glow. "What's going on in that beautiful head of yours?"

There wasn't a moment of hesitation before her reply. "Jesus - on the cross like that. It's always fascinated me."

"Why?" He was still whispering into her ear, drinking in her subtle scent, a hint of citrus - or was it musk?

"I just like the image. The aesthetics. Visual beauty, yet the underlying suffering and pain isn't lost. A perfect balance."

He was losing himself in her - the melody of her voice, her scent - and he was mortified to discover that he was becoming aroused. In this of all places. Cascading emotion crashed through him; he was caught between desire and despair.

How was this happening? He was in the most safe and secure space he had ever known, yet he was feeling emotions here, with Tamsen, that he would never have expected. Where was the lust coming from? He was in a cathedral, for crying out loud.

"Don't you find it a real turn-on?"

"What?" He felt the instant need to slap his own face, or maybe hers. Instead, he cast his eyes skyward and whispered, "Straight aim Hughie, she's the one you have to hit, not me," acutely aware of the growing strain in his groin. "I need to sit down."

Feeling almost faint, he led Tamsen to the nearest pew. Caramel-colored wood carried the sheen of wear, attesting to thousands of hours of worship.

"Are you okay?"

He was touched to see concern etched between her brows, and a bizarre desire to run crashed his confused mind.

"I'm not sure, to be honest." Rubbing his sweaty palms on his stone-washed jeans, he realized that at least he no longer had to worry about being caught with a hard-on in church. "I'm not sure talking about how the Son of God turns you on is a good thing here."

"Why not?" Her concern had turned to bewilderment.

"I just don't think it's appropriate."

"Matt, if you can't talk about your feelings honestly in a church in front of God, where can you?"

She had a point, though he didn't like feeling on the back foot. "But it's disrespectful. This is a place of worship."

Her ears were turning pink, a sure sign she was worked up. "Matt, darling, everywhere's a place of worship. You don't think God can only hear you when you're in church, do you?"

"Well, no." Now he really was squirming. "But it just doesn't feel right to be talking about lustful thoughts here."

"You didn't have any problem acting on lustful thoughts in my bedroom."

"No, but - "

"My room is where I commune with my God."

Outrage rushed through him like a flash flood. "That's not the same."

"Why not?"

Damn. She'd well and truly sucked him in here. "Because it's not."

Her eyes seemed to expand in her face as he looked at her. "You don't think mine's a real religion - is that what you're saying to me, Matt?"

In that moment he felt connected to her in a way he'd never felt connected to anyone before. Fear clawed at him and he wasn't sure why.

The silence hung heavy between them. She reached over and held his hand, said nothing but just sat there next to him, serene and composed, apparently meditating, an unblinking vision of calm and beauty.

How did she do it? He, on the other hand, was unable to stop obsessing about the deterioration in their relationship since they'd arrived in Melbourne. The supposed fun trip away - a real chance to get to know each other without any distractions - had become a shambles. If anything, there were more distractions from home, courtesy of the spinner room mate. The lack of logic disturbed him nearly as much as the circumstances.

Obsessive thoughts ran on fast forward through his head in an unrelenting fashion, like one of those lousy old eight-tracks that just kept going around and around.

The trip's only highlight so far had been coming here this morning - well, apart from the mind-blowing sex over breakfast. Why did he keeping think about sex in church?

"You haven't spent a lot of time in churches since you were a boy?"

The question jolted Matt out of the tortuous scenarios being played out in his head.

"No. If I'm honest, I had a crisis of faith." She was asking far too many probing questions. Maybe that was why he wasn't having such a great time.

She looked around the cavernous interior of the cathedral again and sighed. "I don't know how anyone could possibly have a crisis of faith in these surroundings."

"You're probably right." He was so used to giving everyone else advice yet was unable to look at himself.

"Come on." Agitation set in again and he knew he needed to keep moving - almost as if his thoughts and emotions were chasing him, and if he never stopped then he'd never have to turn and face them. "I've had quite enough of this place. You ready to leave, or should I wait for you outside?"

"Why don't you wait for me? There's a lot I want to look at." A fleeting look of despair crossed her features. Maybe she felt the strain too, or was that his own paranoia? "You don't mind do you?"

"No, of course not." He felt uncomfortable, desperate to get out. "Once you've seen one cathedral you've seen them all." Now he felt stupid.

She pecked him on the cheek. "I won't be long. Promise."

"No, no, take as much time as you like. If I get bored listening to the babbling brook I'll just make my way back to the hotel." Nausea and panic building within, he wasn't sure if it was the surroundings or his guilt for spoiling her morning. "You really wanted to be here. Enjoy it. I'll be fine. Honestly, take your time."

Bless her, if she didn't have the decency to look relieved. He turned and almost sprinted out of the building, all the time unable to pinpoint what was going on. She had the most absurd effect on his emotions.

Cool air hit him as he left the ecclesiastical building. Storm clouds were brewing - not just in his mind, but on the horizon. There wasn't going to be any great chance of him spending time on a bench contemplating his navel. "Bloody Melbourne weather," he muttered to no one in particular.

Feeling dejected and forlorn, and not wishing to risk a soaking, he headed for the nearest taxi rank - unable even to take in the loveliness of the park-like grounds he'd so appreciated not more than an hour ago.

"Where to, mate?" The Australian drawl coming out of the Italian-looking tax driver's mouth caused Matt's teeth to ache and he struggled to be polite.

"Grand Hyatt."

"Not a problem."

The man's voice tore at his nerves. Matt hadn't felt this claustrophobic since his Brett Masters locked him in the linen chest when he was seven. He still found it hard being in anything that even resembled a small, dark place.

"On holiday, are ya?"

The peasant wasn't going to let up. Maybe if he ignored him he'd simply shut up. The cab had that nauseating spurious citrus scent that seemed to permeate all manner of public transport. The one you knew hid an infinite number of repulsive reminders of past inhabitants. The suit who, after over-zealous drinks at work, vomited his greasy fries and milkshake through the synthetic carpet, or the grubby youth who, after due ministrations by his adoring girlfriend, in a fit of adolescent lust left more than the scent of his aftershave on the seat.

Matt closed his eyes and tried to pretend he was somewhere else. Why did Tamsen stir him up? He hadn't felt this conflicted around a woman ever - well, except for his mother, but she didn't count. Yet Tamsen ate away at his very soul and he couldn't fathom how.

The driver continued to babble away. Matt closed his eyes and allowed the motion of the cab to calm his frazzled nerves. He hated being driven; it brought up all his inadequacies around taking direction. He'd spent far too long being pushed around by his father. The man of the house always drives - that had been drilled into him since before he could remember.

"Grand Hyatt."

Opening his eyes, Matt was relieved to see the hotel entrance. "Thanks. How much do I owe you?"

"Why don't we just call it six bucks?"

Matt dug for his wallet and noticed the meter read $5.40. Typical. Hairs bristled on the back of his neck but he couldn't be bothered suggesting they call it five, and handed over the cash.

"Thanks a lot, cobber."

He was so not this man's cobber.

A crimson-clad doorman - maybe the same one who'd met them yesterday - opened the hotel door, a smile pasted on that Matt thought must be held in place by some sort of hidden prosthetic device. What a job. Spending your day smiling at arrogant bastards like himself who couldn't even find it in their souls to smile back. Matt decided he needed a nap.

The first thing he noticed when he walked into their room was the flashing light on the phone. They'd not cleared the message from the night before. He knew it would have to be that poisonous bitch - no one else knew they were here. He was tempted to just delete the message and hope she'd go away, but conscience got the better of him. Besides, Tamsen would suspect he cleared it intentionally. At least he could check the call first, and then he'd know the current state of Gina's lunacy.

Venomous, drunken wailing, just as he'd suspected. He could hardly bring himself to keep the receiver to his ear; the sound of her voice repulsed him. His desire to delete the message burned with a vengeance bordering on mania.

Trembling, he put the phone down. "For fuck's sake, Matt. Pull yourself together."

The apparition speaking to him from the gilt-edged mirror hung on the wall above the phone barely resembled the man he knew himself to be. He made his way to the bathroom, running cooling water into the marble basin and splashing some over his reddened face with shaky hands. Under the glare of the fluorescent lighting he was even more afraid of the man who peered back at him. What the hell had the power to stir up these unwholesome emotions in him?

Tamsen's determination not to let Matt's sudden departure stop her enjoying the experience she'd looked forward to for so long prevailed. But she decided to walk the busy streets back to the hotel, needing time to compose herself. Difficult as it had been burying her resentment over being abandoned in church, it amused her - the thought of a witch being deserted by a Catholic on his home territory.

Surely, she reasoned, Matt should have been comforted by the surroundings. Instead he'd appeared to grow more and more aggravated the longer they were there. He couldn't have been worried she would be struck down, could he? She'd heard him whisper, 'Straight aim Hughie, she's the one you have to hit, not me.' He must have been joking.

The wind whipped her skirt around her legs as it pushed her down the hill toward the thickening mass of humanity accumulated in the concrete-and-glass labyrinth of the city. She shivered, wrapping her now inadequate crochet shawl around her shoulders, not sure if it was the wind-chill or her abhorrence of the city's vulgar display of wealth that was causing her discomfort.

The climate-controlled atmosphere of their hotel room was a welcome sanctuary, much as the cathedral had been. Tiptoeing around the spacious interior, thankful for plush carpeting as she tried not to wake the slumbering Matt, Tamsen collected her diary and settled herself on the luxurious couch in front of the window.

Panoramic views of the river winding its way into the distance settled the nagging, insecure feeling that had been on the rise. More calming water for her frazzled psyche. Mouthing a small prayer of thanks to the Goddess, she opened the pages to write.

Gina's name caught her eye and she remembered the phone. A quick check and she noticed the small light no longer blinked. Creeping across the room, Tamsen perched precariously on the edge of the large bed. Matt's quiet, rhythmic snoring brought a smile to her face. There was something special about studying someone you love while they made their tiny sleeping sounds. His lips twitched as she watched him, almost as if he were trying to whisper something to her; she felt connected to him in an extraordinary way when he lay defenseless like this.

All loving instincts bolted in a wave of anger as she heard Gina's voice on the line.

"Tamshen. Yoof jush got to come home."

How much and how long, was all Tamsen could think.

"I know weef had our differenshes." It was painful listening to the drunken drawl. "But I really mish you and want you to come home."

The blathering was broken by sobbing and pleading. Sorely tempted to hang up and pretend the call never happened, Tamsen stayed on the line.

"Pleash, pleash, jush call, Tamsh. I can't belief you've stayed away with that prick from the offish. Afta he sacked me and everything. I should have been on holiday wiv you. I jush don't know what to do without you here. I feel like shit and - " more sobbing and loud nose blowing " - you jush always know what to do. I can't go on. Not like thish." The message deteriorated into incoherent sobbing and babble.

Tamsen deleted the message, feeling more sick than usual. This was how it always happened after bad binging. First snubbed, and then the gifts and then when things got bad Gina came crawling back, expecting to be forgiven and that all would just be how it had always been. Maybe the answer lay in a different approach. Nothing would change if nothing changed. Surely it was time to cut the umbilical cord and force Gina to sort out her own life.

Matt stirred and opened one eye. "Hey, gorgeous girl. When did you get back?" His voice was sexy and deep with sleep, the drawling tone music to her ears.

Overcome with desire to lick him, she found herself devouring his prostrate form with her eyes. "A while ago. I didn't want to disturb you, but I'm glad you've woken up."

Her reward: the sexiest grin. A small surge of delight grew inside her. Much the same way a tiny spark starts a forest fire - and did she ever want to be burned by the solid and sexy man before her.

"That sounds promising." He lifted himself out of the cocoon of covers. "I'd like to continue that inappropriate discussion we were having in church."

"That wouldn't be the one that caused you to scurry away like a startled rabbit, now would it?"

He cocked an eyebrow. "I do believe that's the discussion I had in mind."

He brushed the linen aside, enough for her to take in the plane of his stomach but not quite enough to judge the state of his arousal. There was no doubt that she was interested, even if he was being coy about how interested he might be.

He suggested, "Why don't you let me give you a little demonstration of why I thought the topic was so inappropriate?"

She couldn't help herself. "Only a little demonstration?"

His laugh was slow and rumbled from deep within. Right at this moment she wanted him like she'd never wanted another man in her life. It didn't matter that Gina was causing problems, or that the morning she'd planned hadn't gone the way she wanted it to. What mattered was here, this instant in time.

A deep and primal urge overtook her; all conscience, worry and trepidation flew from her mind. "I want you to do what I say." Her voice sounded husky and the overwhelming desire to touch him drove her, but she wanted to make it last, to extract every single ounce of pleasure from the moment.

He nodded, his eyes never leaving hers as he settled back against the pillows, propping his hands behind his head, exposing the dark, downy hair under his arms. She longed to run her fingernails through it, scratch the soft flesh of his underarms until he moaned and begged her to stop.

Instead she walked to the door, hung the "Do not disturb" sign on the outside and clicked the deadlock into place. The air was thick with anticipation. "Don't want to be disturbed now, do we?" she purred.

"Better take the phone off the hook too then."

"Don't worry, baby. I was getting there."

"There was a message - " his face took on a worried look " - from your...friend." The last word came out as a strangled sound.

"I've listened to it and I don't want to talk about it. Not right now, anyway." She knew instantly from his relieved expression she'd said the right thing.

"What do you want now?" The look in his eye was wanton.

"You." She crawled up the bed, navigating her way around the tangle of legs and linen, planting a kiss in the cleave of his chest, drinking in the scent of him. "Mr Sex-on-a-stick."

"Tell me more," he almost moaned.

"I won't tell you..." She licked her way around a nipple, then changed her mind and upping the stakes, giving it a savage bite. "But I'll show you."

He sucked in a short breath that whistled through his teeth. "Show me what?"

"What I do when I think about you and you're not there."

Kicking the covers off him, she was no longer under any illusion as to the state of his arousal. She caught her breath. If ever such a thing as a perfectly proportioned dick existed, she thought, there it was sitting right in front of her.

"Show and tell. Does that mean you talk dirty too?"

"No. But you can." She felt suddenly depraved. "Tell me what you'd like to do to me."

"But no touching, right?"

She smiled; his hand was weaving its way down to his nether regions and he wasn't even aware of it. "No touching me."

"You're deliciously evil - you know that, don't you?"

"Hmm."

Lounging on the end of the bed, she made herself comfortable, visions of all the things she was going to do with him after her little show running through her mind. The prospect of slowly torturing him played through her mind.

Returning again to the moment, she concentrated on the horizontal figure before her. One strong hand lay half open across the peak of his hipbone, as if he'd somehow become aware he'd been going to pleasure himself but was holding back, waiting to see where she would take him.

The thought of his hand on himself, his thumb gliding up his shaft, sent tingles of heat down her spine. She wanted to touch herself for him. Show him how she liked to be touched. It was too embarrassing to tell him, but showing him seemed, saucy and scandalous almost; it turned her on in the most delicious way.

"Are you going to be long?" He was beginning to sound impatient.

She felt the blush rise from her chest and was powerless to control it. "I'll be as long as it takes."

Feeling on display to the universe, not just one man, she closed her eyes and took a calming deep breath. She was at once aware of the sickly-sweet scent of lilies; she'd not noticed them before. "I smell flowers." Tamsen said as she opened her eyes.

"I had housekeeping bring them when they serviced the room."

"I didn't know you liked flowers."

"There're lots of things you don't know about me, but I get the feeling you're willing to learn."

He smiled at her, the kind of smile that clambers over your nose and erupts in your eyes. Not returning it would have been a sin.

"I'm very willing."

"Good. I'm willing you to take your dress off. I want to see what you do to yourself when I'm not around."

She'd often fantasized about displaying herself in front of a man, but now the opportunity was here she felt unnaturally shy. The burning surge of lust that had kick-started this trip had spluttered out. There wasn't much option other than to get on with it and hope for the best.

Laying her modesty aside with her dress, she found solace in the fact that she'd had the good sense to put some pretty pale blue underwear on this morning. Nothing like a budding romance and a holiday to float the best bra-and-knicker sets to the front of the underwear drawer.

The blue lace couldn't hide her arousal. Familiar dampness began to form between her legs and she took delight in running her fingers down her belly and sliding them into the wetness. A growing sense of security from her own familiar touch eased her jangling nerves. Matt's eager attention and the fact he was expertly massaging pre-come over the head of his raging hard-on spurred her on.

"Taste yourself for me."

An overwhelming desire to please him surged through her and Tamsen found herself suckling her own juices from her fingers. A rush of excitement exploded from some dark place inside, sending tendrils of warmth across her body.

She removed her underwear with haste, finding it impossible to figure out a way to look sexy while doing so. Kneeling up over him again, beginning to enjoy the power, she played her fingers down her breasts, stopping to squeeze her now rigid nipples, even aware of the tiny buds on her areola.

"I want you to touch me too." Matt's words were more of a moan.

"Soon. I promise." She ran her finger down to her clit, picking up a little lubrication and circling the sensitive node of flesh. The look on Matt's face, his frantic squirming beneath her and the familiar sensation of her fingers was all too much. "Oh, God, I'm going to come for you, Matt - would you like that?"

He nodded, frantic, and let go of his cock, both hands clutching at the linen. She noticed the white of his knuckles before she lost herself in a sea of feeling.

Rubbing against his perfect cock, she came, fast and hard and with an openness she'd not experienced before. Panting and breathless, she collapsed on top of a sweating and squirming Matt.

"Don't you dare." She felt his words on the side of her damp neck more than heard them. "Don't think you can display yourself to me like that, turn me on and then just lie there."

He lifted her limp form and thrust his hard cock inside her in a single, piercing motion. A moan escaped Tamsen's lips as she felt him bottom out deep within.

"Look at me!" If his cock hadn't already snapped her back into the present moment his voice would have. "I want you to watch <u>me</u> come now - in you."

He started lifting her up and down - slowly at first, then building to what she could only hope would be a quick finish. Yet despite herself and her exhausted state, as she felt the tension in his body building beneath her she couldn't resist matching him stroke for stroke. Repositioning herself on the balls of her feet, without him missing a beat, she took control. She liked dominating him; there was a sense of wonder at the ability she had to turn an intelligent, competent, powerful man into a begging, gibbering wreck.

"Come on, come for me then." She couldn't help verbalizing her thoughts. Surely that would tip him over the edge? She was barely hanging on, so he couldn't be far away.

She leaned down and whispered into his ear, "I want you to come in me, right now."

That was all it took. A violent shudder beneath her, and then she couldn't work out who the moans were coming from - him or her.

CHAPTER SEVENTEEN

The next three days passed in a blur of food, sex and sightseeing, not necessarily in that order.

Tamsen couldn't believe how picturesque were some of the out-of-the-way places they visited. Matt seemed to drop his omnipresent guard; the wide open spaces and harsh Australian scenery dug at his core, exposing a beautiful vein, clearly as precious as the gold mined from the very territory they visited.

He astounded her with his hunger for the arts - galleries, theaters, and even an evening with the Melbourne Symphony Orchestra at the Town Hall. To her surprise she lost herself in Tchaikovsky's *Pathétique* Symphony, the combination of music and historic surroundings causing every cell in her being to scream in pure unadulterated delight at being alive.

She'd bored Matt senseless with her fervor for fine detail - especially on their visit, at his insistence, to the Botanic Gardens where Tamsen fell in love with a tiny, pre-fabricated cottage that had been brought out in pieces from England in 1839. As she regaled him with its history Matt seemed alternately amused and frustrated by her passion for diligent and thorough research.

The familiar *toi toi* sculptures before the harbor bridge signaled home to Tamsen, as did the pukeko strutting along the median strip, oblivious their passing vehicle, playing some sort of native game of chicken. But home meant Gina, and Tamsen realized her hands were tingly and sweaty with fear – though fear about what, or whom?

How she wished she could return to that safe place of oblivion her time away with Matt had been. A wonderful fantasy she hadn't wanted to end but now reality beckoning with a firm hand. As Matt slowed down for the entrance to her apartment block she shuddered involuntarily.

"Are you cold, sweets?" Matt looked concerned.

Despair gripped her and she fought not to cry. "No. I'm just not looking forward to being back. Things have been so bad between me and Gina." She sighed. "And I've had such a lovely time away with you."

"The harsh reality of living with the spinner from hell."

"She's not that bad, really." Even as the words fell from her mouth Tamsen knew he was right. Maybe it was time to think about moving on, giving Gina notice.

"Just throw the mad tart out." He had that look of disgust on his face, the one that screamed if things didn't quite fit Mr Solomon's view on the world they needed to be gone. And Gina had never fitted. It was an impossible state of affairs - her lover versus her best friend. Tamsen felt trapped.

As Matt pulled into the visitors' park she noted Gina's yellow VW parked in its usual spot.

"She's home, then." Matt stated the obvious, his voice sounding as flat as she felt.

"That appears to be the case." Climbing out of the Audi, Tamsen wished for the first time in an age that she hadn't given up smoking. "Oh, God!"

"What's the matter now?" Matt was busy unloading her case from the boot.

"I've just remembered. That phone call we had a couple of days ago - the drunken, abusive one."

"They've all been drunken and abusive for quite some time." Tamsen didn't miss the venom in his voice.

"I never called her back." She felt the wail rising in her voice. "Gina'll hate me."

Matt brushed the hair out of her eyes, tipped her chin with his finger and almost looked straight through her. "She was so drunk she probably won't even remember making the call. Don't worry, it's all going to be okay."

"Do you think so?"

"I think so. Now stop upsetting yourself and let's go and get this over with. I mean, really - how much trouble can a mad, drunken woman be?"

It hit her as soon as she opened the door. A foul stench that hung in the air, reminding Tamsen of the stink that comes from public toilets. She shuddered.

"Fuck. What's that smell?" Matt's mood wasn't getting any better.

"I have no idea." She spoke the truth. What the hell could Gina have gotten up to? Five days away and the world fell apart.

"I'll open the French doors and see if that helps." Matt headed off toward the lounge and Tamsen started for her room. No doubt her irresponsible friend would be sleeping off another hangover.

Partway down the corridor she called back to Matt, "I don't know if the windows will help - it seems to be getting worse the further down the hall I'm getting."

He brought her suitcase down to her bedroom. "You don't think the cat's gotten trapped somewhere and died, do you?"

"Oh, gross." Tamsen shuddered. "Don't say that, Matt. Azzie's pretty clever - and besides, there's not really anywhere he can get trapped." She added, "And besides I had Janice on the third floor keep an eye on him. I didn't think Gina could be trusted to make sure he got fed every night."

"Good thinking. What about the mad woman's room, could he be stuck in there with her?"

"Well...I don't know."

"Seems to smell worse up that end of the hallway." Matt screwed up his nose. It only added to his charm.

"It smells foul everywhere." She hunted around in her drawer for some vanilla incense; that helped with most things.

"Why don't I go and check Gina's room anyway?"

"Not a good idea. If she's in there, you're the last person she'd want to see."

He grumbled, "She's not exactly top of my hit parade either, but don't you think we should do something about this smell? It's disgusting."

"Here..." Tamsen held up a packet of incense sticks. The frankincense scent reminded her of church, but they were the only ones available for the moment. "Light some of these and pop them in the holders around the house - it'll help with the smell."

"Finding the source would help more."

"Maybe darling Gina can help us with that." Tamsen couldn't help the sarcastic tone, it almost matched his.

It wasn't on, she thought, coming home to this mess. She could feel months of frustration building, ready to explode. She'd made so many concessions for Gina's atrocious behavior - constantly repairing ailing friendships, smoothing over ruffled family members, dealing with despairing employers, not to mention the chaos the woman was causing with Matthew. Enough was enough. It was time to admit this just wasn't working.

Tamsen knocked on the door and waited. The smell was definitely worse near Gina's room. *Could* Azriel have gotten trapped there? Her stomach knotted, the tension ratcheting up another notch. Confrontations were just the pits, but at least she had Matt here with her for support. He'd need to stay well out of the firing line, Gina could likely detonate, but then at least he'd be here for Tamsen afterward, a huge help with the post-explosive fallout. Her own little bomb shelter.

"Gina, are you in here?" Tamsen opened the door and was assaulted by an almost solid wall of the smell; she could damn near taste it, choking on it at the back of her throat. The room was dark and warm and it took a few seconds for her eyes to adjust to the dim light; Gina never opened the blinds even though Tamsen always told her it was unhealthy.

She turned on the light and felt her knees go weak. She'd found the source. Overcome by nausea, she gripped the doorframe for support.

"Matt!"

"What is it now, babe?"

She had no words. Opened her mouth, but nothing came out. Gaping, she thought of her fish.

"Oh fuck!" His words rang in her ears.

She felt his arms around her and then her knees did give way. With Matt still holding her, the two of them slumped to the floor as if their bones had turned to rubber, unable to hold the weight of their flesh. She didn't know if she wanted to laugh hysterically or cry. Maybe screaming would be the best option, but she had the absurd thought that seemed melodramatic.

There. In the middle of the room, suspended over one of her hard-won wrought-iron dining chairs that had been kicked out from under her, was Gina.

She was so obviously dead, all the life seemed to suck itself out of Tamsen too.

"She's hung herself." An unemotional bald statement of fact.

"I know." Matt's voice was a whisper. She felt the words on the side of her neck.

"I suppose we know what the smell is now." A little giggle escaped from her throat. She couldn't stop it. Somehow it didn't feel inappropriate.

"We do." Rocking her gently backwards and forwards, he made her feel safe and she didn't want him to stop.

She couldn't stop staring either. She'd never seen a dead person; an urge to avert her eyes was competing with a need to gawk. A need to work out what the hell had gone through Gina's mind to get her to this final place.

Tamsen didn't think Gina would mind her staring. She looked sort of serene, as if all her cares had been released - which in a way, she supposed, they had.

Yet as peaceful as she looked now – despite bulging eyes and her tongue poking out sideways from swollen lips - Tamsen could tell Gina had struggled. Not just in life, she thought ruefully, but in death too.

Was it panic, or a sudden will to live after she'd kicked the chair away - or fear of being damned to an eternity shoveling sulfur in hell? And what could have been so bad as to provoke her best friend to take her life in the first place?

Tamsen stumbled to her feet. The weakness was subsiding, replaced by a feeling of utter and total acceptance. Moving toward the body of her friend, she felt Matt's hand on her shoulder.

She turned toward him. His face was quite white - no mean feat with his complexion.

"You mustn't touch her, Tams. We have to call the police. There's a procedure for these things. I'm sorry..."

His voice trailed off and he cast a glance over her shoulder to the body behind.

"I know - " her voice was barely a whisper " - but I need to say goodbye...sorry ..something..." She felt tears welling up. "I should have been here."

"Don't start blaming yourself. This wasn't sudden - it'll be something that's been brewing for a long time. It's not your fault."

Why didn't she believe him?

"You go and call the police. I'll be okay." Would she, she wondered. Tears were streaming down her hot face; there was no way of stopping them and she wasn't even going to try. Her soul was weeping for her dead friend, but she, Tamsen, felt nothing except a comforting numbness.

"You're sure you'll be okay?" He looked at her and she saw real fear in his eyes. What was it about death that frightened people?

"I'll be fine." She gave a hysterical laugh. "She's less trouble strung up there than she ever was alive."

Matt looked pained and she thought she'd better be quiet before she said anything else he might find offensive.

"Please, just don't touch anything. Okay?"

"You can take the lawyer out of-"

"Tamsen!"

"Okay, okay." She held her hands up in surrender and backed away from him. "I promise, I won't touch a thing. It's okay to talk to her, right?" His training had kicked in and he was being a lawyer.

"Of course. I won't be long."

"Take all the time you need, pal. We ain't going nowhere." She looked up at Gina again. "Are we, girlfriend?"

The appeal of hanging had definitely evaporated at some stage, judging from the welts and scratches Tamsen could see around Gina's neck. She'd lost a couple of fingernails, clawing at her neck and the rope; congealed blood sat in globules on the ends of her fingers where her nails should have been. It reminded Tamsen of making toffee, the way it set in tiny, hard balls in a saucer of cold water when you checked to see if it was cooked.

There were rope burns too, on her palms and fingertips, as if she'd tried to climb back up the thick rope. God only knew how long it had taken for her to die, or how terrified she'd been. Tamsen felt an intense ache in the middle of her stomach, the work 'gutted' didn't come close to the physical pain.

Desperate to touch her friend, all she could do was stand there. Her beautiful, beautiful girl, scratched, broken and so bruised. Blood, no longer circulating through her body, had gathered in her chin and at the ends of her limbs, giving her a strange two-toned look. It was as if all her essential energy was trying to find a way to return to the earth.

"Why?" Tamsen addressed the question to her friend. Feeling the futility of life and the crushing finality of death, she wept - for every unsaid word, for every missed moment and for every lost chance. "Baby girl, why?"

"Yes, that's right." Matt was over trying to explain what he'd seen in the bedroom. He knew he wasn't ever going to forget it. "I should go. My friend's in another room and I think it would be best if I get back to her. You're sending someone right away?"

He only half listened to the telephonist assuring him they would have a squad car around there as soon as they could. God help anyone who had an intruder in the house and was really in trouble, he thought - not for the first time.

"Okay. Fine. Thank you."

He hung up the phone, and realized he was unsure what to do next. Unnatural death they called it. He wondered if there was such a thing as natural death anymore. This was the type of situation he read about in the morning newspaper. Two inches of words, that's usually all it took up. How could something that only took up two inches in the daily newspaper have such a devastating effect?

Now he'd dealt with the phone call and the formalities, the things he was trained to deal with, he was left with Tamsen, the body and his feelings. He wasn't sure he was ready to deal with any of them.

Christ. The woman had damn near been an alcoholic; surely there must be something around the place that could take the edge off? Food, drink - wasn't that what you did in these sorts of situations? He'd read somewhere once about a woman who, when delivered the news of her husband's death during the war, invited the man who'd delivered it inside for a cup of tea. Upon enquiring why she could possibly want a cup of tea when she had just been advised her husband was dead, she'd replied that her father taught her to just do whatever she had planned to do when she got bad news.

Matt found next to no food in the pantry - no surprise there - but there was an abundance of dry mixers, and two huge bottles of ouzo. That didn't appeal - he'd nearly choked to death on an aniseed sweet as a child and had never been able to get past the gasping feeling whenever he smelt ouzo.

Thoughts of choking brought back vivid images of Gina hanging in the bedroom. He shuddered and opened the fridge – and was immediately assaulted by the smell of rot. It was all he could do not to dry-retch on the spot.

He'd lived in some pretty hostile flats when he was at varsity, but the fridges in those places had nothing on this one. It was almost as if someone carefully selected from all of the food groups, calculated how long it would take for each item to perish, then placed them abstractly on a clear glass and waited for them to spread, puddle-like into each other. How the hell Tamsen, with her sensitive nature, had managed to live with this slob for as long as she had was beyond him. He had a sick thought that maybe they were all going to be better off.

At least there were cans of brandy, safely stored in the door, and he grabbed a couple. Now to check on Tamsen. As much as he didn't like the idea of going back into that room - Gina was as loathsome a sight dead as she had been alive - he was cautious about leaving Tamsen there on her own for too long.

The long walk down the hallway gave Matt time to think about the pleading, drunken phone calls while they were in Melbourne. Christ. What if the police pinned the timing of this back to the call he'd talked Tamsen out of returning?

A wave of nausea hit him, terror holding a vice-like grip on his internal organs as securely as the rope that grasped Gina's neck.

Tamsen had barely moved since he'd left, leaning up against the door frame and just staring. He couldn't tell if she was staring directly into space, not really seeing anything, or whether she was participating in some kind of morbid voyeurism.

When he cracked a can of brandy open Tamsen jumped as if she'd been slapped. She took the can he passed her, and suddenly looked aware of her surrounds.

"Matt, I know I had nothing to do with this and there's not a lot I can do now, but I can be here for all the official stuff. I wasn't there for her when she needed me."

A vertical line ran down her usually smooth forehead and her nose was scrunched up. She looked like she'd just bitten a lemon. "That call I didn't return, it's been driving me insane thinking about it. Why did I listen to you?" Her voice had risen steadily. He could see the well of frustration and hurt erupting. "I made the fatal mistake of not being true to myself."

She was getting hysterical. Pounding on her heart as if she were performing some sort of maniac pulmonary resuscitation. "And now Gina's paid the price!"

Matthew was scared, really scared. He looked from the woman he'd grown to love, to the cadaver and back again. Tamsen had collapsed again in a crumpled heap on the floor, brandy can in hand, looking almost as if she were worshiping the corpse hanging awkwardly above her.

The place gave him the creeps. He'd gotten used to the stench – though, hell, he might never get it out of his clothes. In fact, burning them once he got home would be the most sensible thing to do. But getting her out of this godforsaken room was the most pressing thing on his mind.

"Come on, babe." His voice was soft, gentle; he wanted to tempt her from the bedroom. "Let's go and wait for the police in the lounge. They can't be too far away."

He hoped not. The sooner they got the body out of the apartment the better. There was something inherently evil about the taking of your own life. You could take the boy out of Church, but religious principles ran too deep.

"I just don't know if I can leave her again." The look in Tamsen's eyes and the quiver in her voice was more than Matt could stand. If he spent another moment in this room he knew he'd break down and that was the last thing they needed.

He bent and picked Tamsen up off the floor. A rag doll in his arms, she offered not an ounce of resistance. He struggled to maneuver them both out of the room without putting down his brandy - the thought of having to come back for it left him nearly as cold as the suspended stiff.

In the lounge, Tamsen sobbed in his arms, her tears creating a damp patch on his chest. He tried to soothe her, burying his face in the sweet smell of her hair, whispering comforting platitudes. He drew in the scent of her hair; it reminded him of crisp green apples.

The buzzing of the intercom intruded.

"That'll be the police." Matt rose from the couch to unlock the doors and let them enter, his feelings of inadequacy dispersed, fallen leaves blown away on an autumn wind.

"You don't have to stay, you know. I can deal with them myself." Tamsen's voice was as cold as a southerly gale and it cut straight through him.

"I think they would like me to be here. They will want to ask questions."

"Well, just as long as you understand that it's not me who's asking you to stay." She took a long drink from the copper can in her hand and he felt his insides wither a little.

"I know." She'd cast him aside. Gina, damn her had played the masterstroke and won.

CHAPTER EIGHTEEN

Sergeant McKean had been sympathetic and businesslike though he looked far too young to deal with the horror in her back bedroom. Even measuring in at a staggering six foot four inches, he still had the boy-child air about him many clear skinned blond men carried.

It must be a hell of a job, Tamsen thought, arriving to collect a body, survey a scene; take notes from witnesses, discuss the state of mind of the deceased. Though how could she possibly imagine what had been going through Gina's mind when she'd strung herself up like a prize marlin?

Tamsen coped with the interview process, the constable taking pictures, and even discussing the pleading phone calls in Melbourne. What she hadn't steeled herself for was the sight of her best friend leaving the apartment in a body bag.

Blue canvas, suspended between two officers struggling with the awkward cargo. A life reduced to some sort of bizarre taking out of blue trash. She was certain the straps would give out and Gina would crash to the floor in the middle of the hallway. The last time anyone had crashed to the floor in the hallway it had been her and Matt, making mad, passionate love. How the hell had it all come to this?

"Oh, Matt. No." She clung to him.

She'd spent the afternoon clinging to him, one way or another, vacillating between that and wanting to beat the living daylights out of him. She'd been riding an emotional roller-coaster since they walked into the apartment, and now exhaustion crept in to take her, the same way the police took Gina. Numb and beyond feeling anymore.

"Babe, it's okay. You've got to let her go now," Matt whispered. He understood that it seemed somehow disrespectful not to whisper.

"Will you be okay, Mr Solomon?" Sergeant McKean's baritone voice broke into their quiet intimacy. "Someone from Victim Support will be in touch with you both." He flicked through his notes again. "They can get you at this address." It was a statement, not a question.

"I'm taking Miss Parsons to stay at my home for a few days. You can get us both there."

The sergeant made further notes in his pad and shook Matt's hand. "Don't worry about seeing us out, Mr Solomon. We'll be fine."

He looked directly at Tamsen, who was starting to feel nauseous. "Thank you for your assistance, Miss Parsons. We'll be in touch if we have any more questions."

She couldn't imagine what other questions they could possibly have - she'd told them everything she knew, short of what Gina usually ate for breakfast.

"Come on, you." Matt's tone gentle and loving. She wished he'd just yell and scream. She would if she could, but she didn't have the energy. "It's a good job you didn't start unpacking - we can just put your case back in the car and get the hell out of here."

Past caring, she sat glumly on the couch and watched Matt retrieve her cases from the bedroom and put them at the front door. She didn't have the strength to fight with him anymore and knew she couldn’t stay the night in the stinking apartment. The place felt cold, death, destruction and darkness filling the void created by the universe when someone died. She knew she'd have to come back and not only physically clean up the mess in Gina's room, but also spiritually cleanse the area too. She figured it couldn't do any more harm to leave the bleak emotional and spiritual energy swarming around in the meantime.

"I'll just get these down to the car and then be back up for you - okay?" Matt opened the front door and a bundle of black fluff shot between his legs. "Christ. What was that?"

"Azzie, baby." Tamsen's spirit lifted a little above that of a bottom-dwelling catfish. Azriel never failed to lift her mood.

The cat leapt into her lap and began rigorously scenting her chin. Tamsen couldn't help giggling and her furry friend purred in response.

"Have you missed me, Azzie, hmm?"

Azriel's purr sent reassuring shivers through to her earlobes. She nuzzled into his furry head, the cold, fine skin on the top of his ears stroking her hot cheeks. Cooling the emotional fallout, helping her find some sense of calm. "We've gotten through a lot together haven't we, Azz, and we'll get through this too, won't we?"

Kissing the top of his fluffy head, she tucked him under her arm. "We can't leave you here all by yourself, can we, Azzie? I need you. Now, where's your cage, hmm?" Big yellow eyes peered inquisitively at her, but he made no move to break free from her grip.

She found the golden cage on top of the utility cupboard. A newspaper from nearly eighteen months ago lined the bottom, confirming her suspicions it had been quite some time since Azriel had been anywhere.

"Your shots must be overdue. We'll have to get you to the vets, my little friend."

Either he understood every word she was saying or - more likely - the sight of the cage brought back terrifying memories. He struggled in her arms, almost making a break for freedom before the lid came down firmly, holding him prisoner.

"Don't fret. We're just going to stay at Matt's for a couple of days. You'll be fine." Azriel sat hunched, fur standing on end, clearly not fine.

They stopped by the kitchen to collect cat food. Even rattling the dried food box, which usually prompted a positive response, didn't work. At the front door they ran into Matt, literally.

"What the hell?" He looked stunned. "You're not bringing that cat."

"He comes or I stay." She was non-negotiable. Enough had happened today and she wouldn't be leaving another friend behind.

"He's a cat. I live in an area with endangered bird life."

"Fine. We'll stay home then."

"Do you know how difficult you can be sometimes?" Matt raked his hand through his hair; he looked as exhausted as she felt.

But she was adamant, she and Azzie were a package deal. "I won't leave him Matt. I couldn't stand it if he ran away - it's enough trauma just dealing with..." The sense of loss hit her again, a full frontal blow. She might as well have been punched.

"Okay, okay." He held his hands up, looking solemnly at the cat in the cage. "I know when I'm beaten."

He slipped an arm around her waist, and Tamsen allowed herself to lean into his solid bulk. He felt safe and she needed safe.

"I suppose we can always lock your little beast up in the house." Matt's expression changed to one of concern. "It is house-trained, right?"

She smiled. "Of course." And directing her speech to Azriel: "You're an apartment dweller, aren't you, boy?"

"A tomcat. Great." Matt picked up the dried food and cast his eyes to heaven.

"He's been done so he behaves himself - unlike some of the men in my life."

"I'm too tired to argue with you, Tamsen. Come on, let's get you both out of here before anything else happens."

Two on a scale of one to ten, with ten being eventful - that's how Matt's day should have been. What it had become, however, was another matter entirely. Macabre and maudlin thoughts filled his mind as he drove the familiar motorway and winding tree-lined roads back home, feeling disconnected from himself, his environment and Tamsen.

Dusk light fell over the landscape. Cerulean blue sky meeting the dark shapes of the trees. Tension and terror rose inside him as those same trees rose to meet the sliver of a new moon hanging perilously on its back. It looked almost as vulnerable and small as he felt.

Azriel's pitiful yowling filled the car and Matt's sense of doom deepened. "Isn't there anything you can do to shut that animal up?" Matt couldn't hide the irritation in his voice. He was intolerant at the best of times; these were not the best of times.

"He hates car trips." Tamsen's voice sounded flat.

"Great." Matt flicked on the radio, hoping to drown out the noise. The cat's loathsome wailing just increased an octave.

"Does he never shut up?"

"He'll calm down as soon as we stop. It's not far, and considering what we've been through today he's the least of our worries."

"You're not wrong there." All hell was about to break loose. The thought of Tamsen, his Mother and the shrieking cat were more than Matt's frazzled nerves were able to deal with. He'd tried to talk Marguerite into accompanying him to the airport five days ago and heading home, but she wouldn't hear of it.

"Looks like your landscape people have finished." Tamsen cut short his morose musing.

He barely recognized the entranceway to the house off the bush-clad right of way. "If I'd known going away would speed the process, I'd have gone weeks ago." At least he wouldn't have to unload Tamsen and her precious feline at the top of the drive and have them all risk life and limb on some sort of suburban assault course - he could deliver them right to the front door, a convenience he hadn't even realized he'd missed until this moment.

The engine died and the feline wailing came to an accompanying halt.

"Oh, thank you, God." Matt clasped his hands together in appreciative prayer, gazing at the ceiling of the vehicle. "I don't know what I've done to piss you off lately, but whatever it is, surely I've done my penance."

"Maybe you just need to talk to him more." Tamsen's matter-of-fact tone caused a flood of Catholic guilt. Her straightforward approach to spirituality often caught him off guard.

"Come on. Let's get you and the demon cat settled in."

"Don't listen to him, Azzie. He's just upset 'cos God's punishing him."

"I'm not being punished!" He relieved her of the cat cage so she could get out of the car. The cat eyeballed him through the bars and he had an unnerving feeling they just weren't going to be friends. Some people were cat people and some people were dog people; unfortunately, he was the latter and Azriel seemed to have worked that out already.

"If you give me the front door key, I can get him inside and then come and help you with the rest of the bags."

Matt popped the boot before obediently passing over keys and cat, glad to be relieved of the furball from hell. "It's the biggest silver key," he told her, all too aware that, the way things were going, this might well be the one and only time she put a key into his front door.

Foreboding feelings manifested in the far reaches of his mind. He tried to brush them away but they stubbornly remained. He could almost feel them taking root, like the moss and lichen that crept up the cold, southern corner of the house.

Shuddering, he turned his mind back to the task at hand. He was determined they should have some time to sort this mess out, and wanted her to stay until at least after the funeral. She needed somewhere safe to grieve. He'd witnessed first-hand what suppressed grief could do to a person: it made them bitter and cold. Tamsen was too lovely and vibrant a person for that.

Gina's life had affected her almost on a daily basis, now he worried that the fallout from her death could destroy the woman he'd grown to love.

Tamsen struggled in the door with the cat cage in one hand, Matt's keys in the other and the box of cat biscuits, which she'd absentmindedly picked up off the floor of the car, tucked under her arm. She kicked the door closed behind her and then remembered Matt was following with the bags.

"Damn!" She put Azzie down and attempted to open the front door. To her dismay it wouldn't budge.

"You need to put the key in again - it's a deadlock."

Tamsen screamed in shock. Spinning around, she dropped the dried food, the lid popping off the box and light brown and yellow circles and crosses spilling all over the polished wooden floor. It looked like midgets were playing some obscure game of noughts and crosses.

"I didn't know Matthew had a cat?" The look on Marguerite's face advertised in no uncertain terms she wasn't a cat-lover.

"He doesn't, he's mine." She unlocked the deadlock and opened the door, to find Matt materialized on the doorstep. Thank God, she thought, he could save her from a fate worse than death - his mother.

"Mother."

"Matthew."

Tamsen didn't understand the apparent lack of love between them. Why did Matt have her here if they so obviously disliked each other?

Marguerite almost looked through Tamsen. "And why, pray tell, has she brought an animal with her?" Marguerite had an enviable, upper-class way of sounding spiteful while still managing to keep a pleasant expression.

"Tamsen's staying for a few days." Matt sounded tired and Tamsen felt unexpectedly sorry for him.

"She simply can't. I'm in the guest room." Marguerite sucked in a breath and puffed out her chest, a superior smiled pasted on her face.

Tamsen lost patience with the up-herself social climber. "Not a worry." She picked up Azriel and strode past the unpleasant woman. "I'm in Matt's room with him."

"I'll be along with the bags in a minute, babe." From the pain in Matt's voice Tamsen knew it would be a long few days.

"Mother, why are you still here?" Matt was exhausted. The last thing he needed was a confrontation, but it looked as if he was going to have one anyway.

"I told you before you went to Melbourne with that...that..."

"Tamsen. Mother. Her name is Tamsen." Anger boiled in his gut, a long, slow boil; it had been simmering all day and so far he'd kept it capped. If his mother wasn't careful she'd would wear the lot.

"It's not worth me making the effort to remember that woman's name, Matthew. She's not you. Now, Angie, she's your type. I've spent a lot of time with her while I've been here and I think she's prepared to forgive you and come back."

"Mother..." He was trying hard to be civil, but all he wanted to do was shake her. "I've had the day from hell. I'm going to order in a pizza and then go to bed with my girlfriend. My girlfriend, Tamsen!"

He was so close to Marguerite as he spat out his words she jumped. "I suggest you forget Angie ever existed and make arrangements to be on the first flight back to Sydney tomorrow or - " he lowered his tone to menacing "- I can't be held responsible for some of the things I might say or do."

It had all become clear to Matt. His crisis of faith at the Cathedral in Melbourne. Finding Gina strung up in Tamsen's flat. Life was short. He needed to make some changes and the first of them was standing up to his mother.

He moved to within an inch of Marguerite's face, so close he could see where her translucent face powder collected in the small vertical creases between her eyes. "I have no desire to destroy what's left of our relationship, Mother, but if you continue to meddle in my life then I will." Her eyes were wide with shock. "Are. We. Very. Clear. On. This?"

Marguerite inched slowly away from him, eyes like saucers, never leaving his. "We'll talk about it in the morning, Matthew." She turned and bid a hasty retreat, he assumed to the guest room.

He'd have to suction her out.

Azriel lay stretched out and purring at Tamsen's feet. He'd circumnavigated the room, satisfied himself there was no way out, and eventually settled next to her prostrate form. Matt, poor exhausted soul, didn't object when the litter tray went into his adjoining bathroom. He'd even been so kind as to bring her little furry friend a saucer of milk to wash down his dinner.

Tamsen figured Matt must be too beat from the scene with his mother. She shuddered, thinking about the woman. The words vile and wretched came to mind.

A nightmarish day and now hunger had set in with a vengeance. However the gentle vibration of her companion's purring went a little way to soothe her spent soul.

"A la carte dining, mademoiselle." Matt swung a pizza box into the bedroom, bowing lavishly and placing it, complete with garlic bread and potato wedges, on the duvet. Azriel lifted his head, sniffed the cardboard suspiciously, gave Tamsen an I-wouldn't-eat-that-if-it-was-the-last-morsel-on-earth look and returned to his slumber.

She giggled. "He's not impressed with your cooking, but I'm past caring."

"Well, I'm not trying to impress him." Matt leaned over placed a gentle kiss on her forehead. "It's nice to hear you laugh."

"I'm so over crying. I'm sure there are no tears left. I've cried myself dry."

Matt opened the pizza box and the room filled with the delicious aroma of spicy meats and melted cheese. "Aw shit." He looked mortified.

"What's the matter?" Aside from her salivating like Pavlov's dog, what else could possibly have gone wrong now, she wondered.

"I forgot you don't eat meat and this is full of the damn stuff."

"Spare me. It's not a moral decision; it's a liver function decision. I ate Bambi last week, remember?"

"Oh, yeah, I forgot."

"Now hand me a piece before I have to resort to violence."

Matt grinned and took great delight making a big deal of extracting a piece of pizza, collecting the stretchy strands of mozzarella cheese and twisting them into a tidy bundle. He then placed the whole arrangement on a red-and-white checkered paper napkin - the kind that doesn't manage to keep the grease from the cheese off anything, but looks good. It reminded her of Matt's mother: pretty, tastefully designed and packaged, but not much use for anything at all.

"How'd it go with Mother?" She couldn't help stressing the r so it came out as a low growl, and was amused when Azriel's ears went back and his tail frizzed, as if he understood.

"I told her she's got to go back to Sydney."

Tamsen took another bite of the delicious pizza. "You told her that before we went to Melbourne and she's still here." She wiped some cheese fat from her chin with the inadequate red napkin.

"I am aware of that." Matt took a huge bite of garlic bread, then howled with pain, his hand flying to his mouth. "Aw, fuck. Now I've bitten my tongue."

"Sorry, I didn't mean to wind you up."

"For a change, this time it's not you." He chewed gingerly, his hand still hovering under his chin. "The woman won't see I want to live my own life. Thinks she can bowl over here and tell me what to do, and if that doesn't work, simply sit it out until I do what she wants me to do anyway."

"You're a lawyer. You could always take out a non-molestation order."

"I wish." He looked in real pain and Tamsen was sure it wasn't just his mouth.

Matt rearranged himself and the food on the bed, in the process being the recipient of a disgusted look from Azriel.

"Does he always behave like this?"

"Like what?" Tamsen tucked into the garlic bread; no reason for her to have to suffer garlic breath all night.

"Like he owns the joint."

"He's a cat. They don't have owners, they have slaves."

"It's eerie. It's as if he's looking out for you."

"He probably is. I wouldn't leave him because we've got a special bond."

"I got that impression."

"You don't mind him sleeping here with us?" Tamsen knew he did mind, but was hoping that under the circumstances he'd lie.

"Yes. There's only one pussy I want to share my bed with."

Tamsen laughed. "Well, looks like you're in for a treat, 'cos tonight you've got two.

CHAPTER NINETEEN

"Oh, for fuck's sake." Matt's howl of anguish from the bathroom woke Tamsen from a dreamless sleep.

"What's the matter?" She stretched her legs and found Azriel perched between them. Scratching him behind the ears, she met Matt's hostile gaze.

He was wearing nothing but a cobalt towel, the contrasting color setting off his black hair, damp and darker looking than usual. A bolt of lust snaked through her and she ran her fingers over Azzie's cool, smooth ears, the sensation similar to running her fingers over the velvet tip of a penis though she wanted the real thing.

"There's cat litter all over the bathroom floor and I've just had a shower."

"Don't worry, it'll be clean." It was neither here nor there, she thought - by the time she was finished with him this morning he was going to need another shower anyhow.

"How do you know that?" Matt's face looked grim; he almost pouted. She so wanted to taste his lips with hers.

"Trust me, you don't have to worry. I'll clean it up."

"I do bloody worry - about everything. That's my problem."

"Come here." She patted the bed beside her, and on impulse picked Azzie up and dropped him on the floor. "I want to touch you."

Matt eyed her suspiciously. "You mean, like sex?"

"No, you prat! I mean like I stroke the cat!" For an intelligent man he could be so stupid sometimes.

"But your best friend's dead."

"I'm well aware of that fact, Matthew."

"Well..." He looked perplexed, but made advances toward the bed, even if they were at a snail's pace.

She said, "Someone's died, so I'm not supposed to get horny when a gorgeous man walks in the room half naked?"

"Something like that."

"Death always makes me horny."

"You are so weird."

"No, I'm not. I bet most people are at it like knives after funerals."

"You think so?"

He had at least made it to the bed now and she could smell the fresh scent of soap on his skin. She asked curiously, "What do you think about after you've been to a funeral?"

"I haven't been to many." He eyed her with suspicion. "You're not a funeral groupie, are you?"

"No." She ran her fingertips along the edge of the towel, just hooking her nails under the bound edge near his knee, making promises he knew she'd keep. "But didn't you come away sort of energized, full of life in a way you didn't understand? Somehow determined to change at least some area of your life, live in a better way - maybe be a bit more reckless? Because you realized that at any moment it could all be snatched away from you?"

"Er, not really, not that I remember." He watched her fingers toying with his towel.

She could see stirring under the toweling. "See, even talking about it's turning you on."

"I can assure you that talking about death is not turning me on. The very alive feeling of your fingers on my inner thigh is doing it for me, though."

Tamsen ran her entire hand up under his towel, her efforts rewarded when she struck his solid shaft. She brushed his towel aside in one swift movement and feasted her eyes on his nakedness. Such a thrill, knowing she turned him on so much. She wanted him, wanted him badly, and nothing would to stand in the way of her having him.

Licking her lips in anticipation, she lunged for that soft, sacred space between his legs.

Tonguing his sack, she felt him shiver in response. She suckled one ball into her mouth and ran her fingernails up the underside of his dick, hearing him moan and feeling the balance of his body physically relax under her hands and mouth.

"Too good, Tams," he whispered. Matt caressed the top of her head, stroking her hair, the way she'd stroked Azriel. She'd purr too if she didn't have a mouth full of his balls.

Matt leaned back against the crumpled bedding, as she continued her suckling. "Aw fuck!"

His surprised scream brought Tamsen to a sudden halt; he was lucky she didn't clamp down with her teeth and do permanent damage. At the same time a yowl came from Azriel and a black streak of fur shot toward the bathroom.

"Fucking animal." Matt was furious. "It was lying nearly under me on purpose, I'm sure of it. Do you know how disconcerting it is to lie on something furry?"

Tamsen couldn't help laughing.

That seemed to incense him more. "I'm serious. The frigging cat hates me."

"Don't be silly. He does not."

"I am not being silly." Rage began to cloud his eyes. "I'm sick of the time we have together being interrupted by..."

"By what, Matt?" Tamsen's anger rose to meet his, pent-up frustration and hurt welling to the surface.

He scowled, his beautiful lips set in a harsh line. "Don't push me, Tamsen. I might say something I'll live to regret and I don't want to do that."

Fury spilled from her gut. "What, something like if we'd stopped the last time the phone rang and I'd talked to Gina she might not have hung herself? Something like that, Matt?"

"Stop it, Tamsen!"

"Why?" No chance of her holding back the torrent now - the dam had burst. "The truth hurt, does it, Matthew?"

She could see the veins bulging up his arms as he gripped the duvet, the tightness in his jaw as he ground his teeth together. She wanted to rip at his skin, tear at his throat with her nails and see his skin ripped and bleeding the way Gina's had been when she clawed at the rope in her death throes.

She spat, "You may as well have tied the rope and kicked the chair out from underneath her."

"Tamsen, that's enough!"

"You're just so fucking composed, aren't you?" She moved her face to within inches of his, close enough to see the perspiration forming on his top lip. "Mommy's got you so well trained you aren't even in touch with what you're feeling. How long did it take, Matt, to squash those horrible feelings, bury them and pretend they didn't exist?"

His eyes started to bulge as he continued to fight with himself. Tamsen wanted him to fight with her; she wanted to hurt him as much as she hurt - as much as Gina must have been hurting when they both ignored her.

"Don't bring my mother into this." He could barely sputter the words out.

"Why, Matt? She's so firmly ensconced in your life I'm surprised you didn't invite her in here this morning to watch."

"That's enough. I don't have to listen to this crap. I'm out of here."

She laughed, an almost hysterical laugh. She could feel her control slipping away. "Don't even think about walking away from me, Matt."

He looked at her then - not really at her, more through her. "If I stay in this room one minute longer, woman, you are going to get hurt - " he stood up and made a movement toward his walk-in-wardrobe " - and you've been hurt enough."

"Big fucking man. Walking away. What a hero." The voice didn't even sound like hers anymore. "I told you, no one walks away from me."

She grabbed him by the arm, swinging him around to face her. He opened his mouth to say something else, but the words were lost in the resounding sound of her stinging slap. She caught him square across the left cheekbone and his face started to redden, even before she registered the pain in her right hand.

They both stood looking at each other, Matt dumbstruck, Tamsen feeling immediate release from pain and torment. She lifted her hand to hit him again.

"You fucking bitch. You're as psycho as..." He stopped, as if he were hearing himself for the first time.

He intercepted the next blow, grabbing her wrist before her hand found its target. The impediment enraged her further and she clawed at his chest and neck with her free hand. He made short work of pinning her arms to her sides.

"What are you trying to do?" His tone had softened, a look of pity and confusion on his face.

"I want to hurt you."

"You need to stop. I don't want to hurt you."

She hesitated, looked down at the small space between their bare feet, "Maybe I just want to hurt myself."

"Why would you want to hurt yourself?" The puzzled tone in his voice matched her own.

She shrugged. "It's hard to explain. If I hurt myself I think I'll feel better."

"That's insane. It doesn't make any sense."

"I know. But I think I'm prepared to try anything at the moment."

He let go of her hand and slapped her, hard, on the buttock.

She jumped. "That hurt."

"That was the idea." He had a strange look in his eye.

The sting from the slap ate away her anger and frustration. "Do it again."

He obliged, slapping her even harder on the same spot. Calmness overcame her, the sting radiating outward and upward, its energy devouring her frustration and despair.

Matt released her other hand. She noticed the red finger marks on his cheek and a wave of remorse flushed through her. She reached up with her face, standing on her tiptoes, willing him to lower his cheek to her so she could brush the marks with her lips and kiss the hurt away.

She said, "I want you to hit me again." Her voice was low, raspy and full of desire.

He didn't look confused anymore. "You mean, like spank you?" His tone was matter-of-fact.

"Er, I'm pretty sure that's what I mean." She felt a flush of embarrassment run up her breasts.

"I could really hurt you, you know?" As if he needed her to be aware of how much, he viciously twisted her nipples.

Her breath caught in her throat and she became immediately wet in response to his cruel touch. "I know. I want you to."

Matt released her tortured nipples and a fresh rush of pain ran through her breasts. Nausea and excitement fought for control. Excitement overcame any resistance.

Sitting down on the edge of the bed, he pulled her toward him. She knelt between his knees and he cupped her face in his hands, lowering his full ripe lips to hers. He suckled her bottom lip and she moaned, the sound vacuumed from her mouth by his.

"You sure about this?" He sounded calm in a detached sort of way.

She nodded. She needed something - anything - to take the pain away. She'd discovered a long time ago that physical pain gave her relief and needed Matt to understand. As an adolescent she'd scorched herself with hot water. A sensible way, at the time, to deal with the pain of growing. Huge water blisters forming on her inner thighs. They'd taken weeks to heal and years for the scars to fade.

Matt found himself lost and appalled at Tamsen's request. But on some perverted level that he didn't understand he wanted to do this for her. He loved her enough to understand her pain while still not comprehending how beating the crap out of her ass could bring relief. Was willing to trust and let her take him there - a huge step for both of them.

She had crawled up into his lap. Her breasts were draped warm and snug over his left thigh; her bare ass, with its one pink and tender looking cheek, hung over his left. The sight of her like that, submissive and waiting, was more of a turn-on than he'd ever imagined it would be. He could feel the blood rushing to his cock and was embarrassed.

She pointed out, "You're enjoying this, despite yourself."

"I think you should shut up before I lose my nerve."

She wriggled over his growing erection, the movement making him even harder.

He pawed and stroked her buttocks. She had a fine ass and he'd loved it from the first moment he'd seen it. "You've done this before?" he asked, hoping she might have.

"No. Now would you hurry up before *I* lose my nerve."

The first stinging slap hurt his hand. The force vibrated through her body and he felt it, almost as if he'd hit himself. Warming to the task, he slapped the other cheek, enjoying the sound as much as the sensation.

Another slap on each cheek and his hand began to ache. He could only imagine what Tamsen must have been feeling. Circling the warmed mounds of flesh with his fingers, he couldn't resist dipping a finger down lower, just to see if she was as turned on as he was.

"Nice," Tamsen moaned. "You have no idea how good you're making me feel."

His finger hit her slickness and his cock immediately responded by throbbing. "I have an idea. You're soaking."

Deciding a second round was in order, he rained stinging slaps on her backside until he could barely feel the force of each. She moaned every time he slapped her, gripping his ankle with her hands. The harder and faster he slapped, the tighter she gripped. Fingernails dug into his skin, yet he couldn't - didn't want to - stop. Her backside reminded him of a pre-dawn sky, bright pink with small slivers of purple bruising forming.

"God, Matt! Enough! Please stop." Her protests brought him out of his frenzy. He was panting, small beads of perspiration gathering on his upper lip. His hand seriously ached now.

Tamsen struggled to lift herself up off his knee. He still had a raging hard-on. She clambered up into his lap, her face flushed, enough to set off another stream of longing and desire in him.

"I so want to fuck you." No use denying the last few minutes turned him on immensely. He was still unsure about that, but not enough to kill the desire to be inside her.

"Fuck me." Wild eyes and a face streaked with tears were no deterrent. "I want you to come in me."

Positioning her hips over his hard cock, he lunged inside. Her hot buttocks slammed into his thighs as she tipped her head back, moaning in pure delight.

The sight of her being gripped by an approaching orgasm was more than he could stand. Driving her down onto himself over and over, he merged with her and the wonder of the moment.

"Matt, I'm coming. Come with me - *please*."

He didn't need asking twice.

"Danni!"

Where could she be? It was the second time he'd called for her. Matt scratched the back of his neck; his collar and tie just seemed too damn tight since his return, adding to the claustrophobic feel of the entire office. Undoing his top button and loosening his tie, again he wondered how Gina had managed to hang herself. He couldn't erase the vision of her corpse from the theatre of his mind and it disturbed him more than he was willing to admit.

"Dan-"

"Calm down, Matt." Danni strode into the room, looking nearly as flustered as he felt.

"Where the hell have you been?" He couldn't hide the impatience in his voice.

"Helping the new receptionist."

"Well, get someone else to help her."

"There is no one else, and the feeling around here is that since you were responsible for the last one walking out it gets to be my problem to train the new one." She glared at him.

"It wasn't my fault."

"What? That she walked out or that she hung herself?"

Danni had voiced the question he'd been hiding from for over a week.

He'd managed to get through the clean-up of the apartment, steadfastly refusing to let Tamsen do it. Bringing in commercial cleaners, though he was certain the goddamn, awful urine smell would never come out of the carpet. Even prepared to have the entire apartment recarpeted if it came to that.

He'd managed through the funeral. Been the great boyfriend. Held Tamsen's hand while she sobbed. Helped her cope when the circus passing for humanity - aka Gina's friends - wept and wailed. Succeeded in putting that question out of his mind while they lowered the casket into the cool, dark earth. Even managed not to think about an eternity of hell and damnation for someone who'd committed the cardinal sin.

Now, two days after the funeral, when life should be trickling back to normal, the question had been asked. Only this time he hadn't done the asking.

"How's Tamsen doing anyway?" Danni asked, a hint of shame haunting her face.

"Getting by." He was sick of fielding calls about Tamsen. What about how *he was doing?* His life looked much the way his desk did - drowning in a sea of crap and most of it not even his.

"Jeff Sinclair wants to come in at two o'clock to go over the franchise agreement he couriered to you yesterday."

"What agreement?" Matt surveyed the manila folders piled high on his desk and realized he hadn't a clue what terror lurked between their covers.

His gaze drifted past Danni and her fervent search through the mass, to the view of the harbor beyond.

Hundreds of times he'd surveyed the view in his years sitting at this desk, but today it looked different. Inviting. Fresh. Today he saw an ocean vista as if for the first time, through new eyes. His mind wandered to happy memories of the family bach, up at the Island. He'd not thought about going there for years.

"Here it is." Danni put a garish plastic courier pack in front of him. Obviously she'd received and opened it though he was certain he'd never seen it - or its undoubtedly toxic contents.

"Haven't looked at it. Tell him what you like, but I'm going home." He stood up and went to the back of his door to collect his suit jacket.

"Matt, please. You can't keep doing this to me." Danni burst into tears.

"What is it now?" He'd done nothing but deal with weeping females for days. His mother - crocodile tears, but still tears. Tamsen, tears of grief and anger. And now Danni. He felt all cried out.

"I don't know how to deal with you anymore. It used to be easy." She collapsed in a little businesslike heap in his chair. Even her emotional outbursts were competent and organized.

He searched his pants pocket for the perfectly ironed handkerchief he knew would be there. Too many years of an overbearing mother who'd insisted no son of hers would leave the house incorrectly dressed - handkerchiefs being an essential item for the properly groomed man – combined with his own anal inability to let go of the archaic practice.

He passed the handkerchief to her. "Come on, Danni, I can't have you fall apart on me too. You're my rock."

"Well - " she snuffled, wiping foundation off her nose and leaving a brown trail across the fresh linen " - if I'm your rock, I'm a crumbly one at the moment."

"Let's both get out of here. I'll take you for a coffee downstairs and we can talk."

She brightened a little. Tears gleamed in her eyes, reminding him of the sun shining off the ocean below. "What about Jeff?"

"You can ring him when we're done." He gave her a quick hug. "I don't know. You're having a breakdown and still worrying about my clients. What would I do without you?"

Danni snuffled again into his handkerchief and sent him a half smile. "Survive. You always will, Matt."

He was beginning to wonder about that.

The new receptionist eyed Matt suspiciously when he told her he'd be gone for the rest of the day and that Danni would be out for at least an hour.

He stopped at the aquarium on his way out. "I can only see four fish." He searched thoroughly, making sure none were hiding in the long weed. "What's happened to the rest of them?"

Danni went pale. "They keep dying."

"Of what?"

"I have no idea and we didn't want to bother Tamsen, what with everything she's been through."

Matt checked the fish again and, sure enough, one of the surviving four had a disconcerting horizontal lean.

Danni pointed the tilter out. "That one looks like it's on its last legs too."

"Well, considering fish don't have legs that's quite a problem, don't you think?" He didn't try to disguise his sarcasm, then immediately felt guilty. Danni looked ready to cry again.

"I'm the only one who hauls them out of there when they die," she snapped. "It's not in my job description and I don't think it's funny."

"I'm sorry." He hated himself sometimes. "Come on, let’s get out of here and find some coffee."

"Shoo!" Marguerite waved a Harrods tea-towel viciously in front of Tamsen, chasing Azriel from his warm sunny spot on the oak dining room table. "It's just disgusting, that flea-ridden animal sitting on the table. I can't imagine what Matthew was thinking when he allowed a feline on the premises. He knows I don't like cats."

Tamsen leapt to Azriel's defense, as she'd been doing from the moment they walked in the door a week ago. "He's not flea-ridden and I expect Matt thought you'd have pushed off home by now."

"I'll thank you not to take that attitude with me, young lady."

"I can take any attitude I like with anyone." Tamsen picked up Azriel, who instantly began purring. "At least I'm a welcome guest."

"And you're suggesting I'm not?" Marguerite looked appalled. She had a nasty way of sucking in her nostrils when angry, an expression Tamsen had become accustomed to over the last few days.

"I'm not suggesting anything. Think what you like."

"What I think, young lady -" Marguerite's eyes narrowed and gave her face an even more pinched look " - is that you are a scheming, gold-digging harlot who is getting in the way of my son's reconciliation with his fiancée."

"Get over yourself, Mom. If he wants to be with Angie he's more than welcome." Tamsen, feeling on the upper, pressed her point home. "What you don't seem to get - " she moved closer to the older woman, a sense of the young cat dominating the aging queen " - is it's his choice, not yours. The sooner you accept that relationship's as dead as my best friend, the sooner you can go home and leave Matt to live his own life."

"What you don't understand, young lady, is that I am home." Marguerite let out an almost hysterical laugh, the sound taking Tamsen by surprise. Azzie leapt out of her arms, inflating to full fluff-ball status before his feet hit the polished kauri floor.

Marguerite gestured. "Look around you. You don't think Matthew could afford all this on the meager amount he earns in that ridiculous second-rate law firm, do you?"

Tamsen hadn't even thought about it.

"Costings on the week he spent with you in Melbourne alone would have killed at least three months' salary. The Grand Hyatt doesn't come cheap, my girl. And I don't believe my son would skimp on anything. Only the best will do for Matthew."

Marguerite was right. They'd wanted for nothing while they were away. Top of the line everything. It hadn't occurred to her at what cost.

"But...he's got investments." She thought about the night Gina had accused her of stalking him. He owned property.

"Gifts from the family," Marguerite sneered, walking toward the front door, "and I can take those away as quickly as I gave them to him. All I have to do is say the word and my trust will call in every loan and advance and Matthew will be penniless."

Tamsen couldn't believe what she heard. It seemed absurd. But a small part of her brain registered. Everything probably in family trusts. Matthew would own nothing. He, like she, was at the mercy of manipulating family members.

"So you see," Marguerite continued, "he's going to do what I want him to do in the end. Otherwise all of this - " she cast her arms wide " - will disappear in a puff of smoke."

She opened the front door wide. "So I strongly suggest you and your lice-infested feline pack up and be on your way, because you are not welcome here."

Tamsen, lost for words, stood there feeling...what? Twice in a week her world had crumbled, her reality well and truly fucked over. The universe seemed to be constantly shitting on her and she had no idea why.

"Shut the door, please." Her voice was barely a whisper. "Azzie will get outside."

"That monster should be outside anyway." Marguerite waved the tea-towel over Azriel again, and he hissed and bolted for the open door.

Tamsen screamed, "No!"

CHAPTER TWENTY

Their first date, two months ago, in this very courtyard, Matt mused. It seemed such a long time ago.

Danni cut into his thoughts. "You haven't heard a single word I've been saying, have you?" A look of despair crossed her perfect features.

Women would sell their souls to have even features like hers, he was sure of it. "I'm sorry, Danni. I just don't seem to be able to stay with it at the moment."

"You want to talk about it?" She sipped her coffee.

It was refreshing, he thought, to have someone order something as easy as a flat white. No soy this, or decaf that, just simple coffee. His Danni, plain and predictable.

"I assume this won't go any further?" He looked up from the empty caramel-colored sugar wrapper he'd been twisting around his pinkie finger. "I really don't need to add to water-cooler gossip."

She crossed her heart and smiled. "Promise. You can tell me your secrets - I'm an expert with professional privilege."

Matt dragged his gaze from the line of lace hugging her breasts; he hadn't noticed the fine scallop pattern until she'd drawn his eye there by crossing herself. Somehow it felt disrespectful to Tamsen, his eyes having almost a mind of their own.

He said, "It's nice to know something I taught you has come in useful."

She smiled again and he felt immediately at ease. "So what's up, boss?"

He shrugged. "Don't know, really. Except I haven't wanted to work for ages and that's not me."

"You've been through a lot in the last week. Not many people I know find a former employee hanging in their girlfriend's apartment and expect to walk away from the whole ordeal without some emotional scars."

"That's what I don't understand, Danni. Why should it bother me? I mean, I can understand Tamsen falling apart, but me? It doesn't make any sense. The woman was nothing to me."

"Maybe you feel guilty?" She cocked her head, looking up into his eyes - searching, he thought, to see if she'd hit a nerve.

She had, but he wasn't going to let her know that. "What do I have to feel guilty about?"

"I don't know. You tell me."

He felt as if he were in a poker match. Any slight twitch or movement would alert her to his thoughts. "You know how bad it got with Gina at work?"

"Don't remind me, I was the village idiot constantly running around after her, tidying up the messes she made, remember?" Danni rolled her eyes.

"Well, things were as bad for Tamsen at home. I don't want to go into the sordid details, but it even got to the stage where I felt terrified to be alone in the same room with the mad cow."

"In what way?" Danni leaned closer and his eyes again drawn to the lace at her breasts.

He coughed, averting his gaze and concentrating on the uglier recent scenes he'd had with Gina. "When she got drunk she was really aggressive."

Danni looked confused, and he felt he needed to elaborate. "Like, sexually aggressive."

"Oh, I get it." She laughed. "Like trying-to-get-into-your-pants aggressive?"

He felt himself flush. "Yes."

"That's no shock."

"What do you mean?"

"Matt, for a smart man you can be so naive sometimes." Danni giggled, tipping her head forward, her hair falling over one eye. She looked up at him from under her hairline, almost embarrassed. "You've got no concept of how attractive you are. Gina wasn't alone thinking like that."

"The woman hated me. I could see it in her eyes."

"She hated that you were with Tamsen." Danni waited a beat for the information to sink in. "She wanted to be with Tamsen."

He shook his head in dismay. "Wow, how could I have missed that?"

"If it's any consolation, I don't think you were looking."

"So Gina was jealous? That's what all the attention seeking was about? All the phone calls when we were in Melbourne, all the tantrums at the apartment?"

"I'm not suggesting just jealousy - the girl had a pretty heinous drinking problem. You could still smell it on her from the night before, some mornings. And she often arrived at work looking as if she'd just come from a party, or at least slept in her clothes."

"Pretty shoddy state of affairs, really, wasn't it?"

"It was."

"I could be forgiven for giving her that written warning."

"Matt, is this what this is really about?"

"Maybe." He felt uncomfortable, thinking back to the day Gina quit. He'd felt relief at the time. It saved him having to go through the whole rigmarole of more meetings and warnings before he could fire her.

"You didn't set her up, Matt. You've always been genuine about helping your staff. You've got nothing to feel guilty about."

"I just can't help thinking I contributed to the whole sordid mess somehow."

"You were involved, of course - you were sleeping with her friend and you were her boss. Only you can judge where the ethical lines were drawn. But as far as the firm's concerned you acted in everyone's best interests. No one could possibly have known how sick she was. She even managed to hide it from Tamsen, for crying out loud."

"I suppose you're right." He shrugged. "It's a waste of time and energy doing the 'what ifs' but sometimes I just can't help it."

"Matt. Honestly. I don't think you'd be human if you didn't."

"You're probably right. Thanks, Danni. You've been a rock through all of this."

"That's what I'm for boss. PR, Personal Rock."

"I'll give you rocks. You best get back to the pit face and see if you can stave off the impending disasters on my desk. I'll be in tomorrow morning - I can't face it today. There're a couple of pressing problems at home to be sorted."

He thought of his mother and Tamsen, and a pending sense of doom wrapped itself around him, almost like a comforting quilt.

"Azzie. Here, Azzie." Tamsen's attempts to track Azriel through the newly landscaped garden resembled a reconnaissance mission gone decidedly wrong. She was becoming more distraught by the moment. No, she thought, sidestepping yet another hebe, not just distraught - very bloody angry. So angry she could string Matt's mother up, and Matt too for that matter.

Hebe "Champagne" according to the yellow horticultural label still attached to the small bush. More references to alcohol.

Fuming, she seated herself on a ponga log. The earth smelt damp, the kanuka trees alive with a small flock of wax-eyes fluttering from branch to branch, their tiny wings and erratic flight disturbing the insects they were feasting on. Tamsen felt sure Azzie would be in the area, especially with this many small birds to hunt.

What to do? Azriel would reappear eventually - hunger if nothing else driving him back to the house - and she could pack them both up and go home.

Home. She hadn't even thought about going back there. The tedious matter of finding another room mate loomed ahead. What to tell prospective tenants? "Actually, the last girl hung herself right in this very room. Not superstitious or concerned about ghosts, are you?" She'd have to ensure a thorough energy cleanse had been completed.

A shiver played down her spine; the afternoon sun still hung reasonably high in the sky, but the huge trees on the property cast forlorn shadows over the area she occupied. Matt would be home soon. What to do about him? She'd never felt so alone and betrayed in her life - Gina gone, Matt effectively taken away, and Azzie run off. Could anything else go wrong?

Sighing, Tamsen picked herself up off the log and trudged back toward the house. The sunshine cutting through the tall trees highlighted the small turret window forming part of Matt's bedroom on the third floor. A shadow caught her eye passing across the window. It could only be Marguerite.

Struck by another bolt of fury, Tamsen struggled to prevent herself tearing up there and cutting the smug bitch's throat. No more, she and Azzie were on their way as soon as she'd caught him. Spending another night under the same roof as such a conniving piece of work repulsed her.

Tamsen stopped dead in her tracks. There in front of her - and how she hadn't noticed it on the way down she wasn't sure - was a yellow box. A Timms trap, she knew, from her days of petitioning councils to abolish gin traps. The most humane available - if killing anything could be considered humane.

Shuddering, she remembered Matt mentioning trapping around the property for possums. A few were devouring the new seedling trees.

At least the action was quick. A sharp pin through the underside of the animal's head. Death, pretty much instantaneous. Nothing like the frantic chewing she knew went on with poor creatures trapped by the leg in gin traps.

And this one had been disturbed, she noticed - it was sitting on a slight angle.

A startled cry of pain broke the quiet stillness of the afternoon. A few moments passed before Tamsen realized the sound had come from her. For the second time in just over a week she found herself viewing the body of a dear, departed friend.

No mistaking the prostrate form of Azriel. She knew every white mark and speckle on his coat.

Tamsen collapsed to the ground, anguish and tears coming in a deluge. For the last couple of days she'd somehow been sitting in the calm eye of an emotional cyclone. The winds of grief, visiting again, blew strong and she buried her face in the familiar fur, the familiar scent of Azriel. Trying to lock him in place in her heart.

And she wept. Wept for herself. Wept for Gina. Wept for Matt. Wept for Azriel. For all their losses.

For the injustice of it all.

"What do you mean, she's not here?" Matt was losing patience with his mother. He'd come looking for Tamsen, but she and her bloody cat were nowhere to be seen while Marguerite was making even less sense than usual. "And what the hell were you doing in my bedroom going through Tamsen's things?"

"I wasn't going through her things, Matthew." The revulsion on his mother's face could well have been hiding remorse at being caught snooping. It brought home how little he really knew of the woman.

"Cut the bullshit, Mother. What's going on here?"

"Not a thing, Matthew. I was returning some of Tamsen's clothing from the laundry. She's packing up and going home, and I didn't want her to leave it behind, that's all.

"Read, you've made her life here a living hell when I've not been around."

"I'm insulted, Matty. I have done no such thing."

"Where is she then?"

"Outside, looking for that mangy animal she brought with her."

"How the hell did the cat get out?"

"I chased the parasite-ridden creature out. It was sitting on the dining room table." Marguerite pulled a face. "Disgusting."

Matt felt the blood drain from his face. "Jesus, Mother. If she loses that cat..."

"The cat's the least of your worries, Matthew. That girl is the real problem, and the sooner she's out of your house the better."

"The sooner you're out of my house the better." He hung his suit jacket on the rimu hanger in his walk in closet. "And you can start by removing yourself from my room. I'm going to get changed and then look for Tamsen."

"You don't need to go very far. I'm here." Tamsen walked into the room, cradling Azriel like a baby to the breast.

"Oh, fuck!" All Matt could see was blood seeping into her pale blue shirt. "Is he okay, babe?" He was certain the cat was not, but felt obliged to ask.

"Does he look fucking okay to you, dickhead?"

No escaping the venom in the attack. This was not good, he thought.

"There's no use for foul language and abuse, young lady." Marguerite couldn't keep quiet.

Matt was tempted to clobber her with one of the spare coat hangers in the wardrobe. "Would you stay out of this please, Mother?"

"Would you stay out of this please, Mother?" Tamsen swung her head from side to side like some deranged five-year-old. "The woman won't stay out of anything, Matt - haven't you worked that out yet?"

Tamsen pushed the bloody body in front of Marguerite's face. "Look what you've done!"

As Tamsen moved closer Marguerite backed away, attempting to keep a civilized distance between them. It was like watching some sort of absurd line dance, Matt thought.

Tamsen snarled, "If you hadn't chased him out of the house this wouldn't have happened."

The insane and bloody line dance continued. They were moving into the bathroom, and short of climbing in the shower and closing the door Marguerite would soon be trapped.

"Matty! Do something!"

Tamsen turned on Matt, a deranged look in her eye - the one he'd expected when she found Gina, but which had been surprisingly absent. "That's it, Matthew - Mommy's calling. You dance to her tune because she holds the purse strings. *Don't you, Matty*?"

What the hell was she on about now? The situation had gotten way out of control. What to do?

He tried stalling for time. "Mother, get the fuck out of my room. Now!"

Not another word passed his mother's lips as she slid, snake-like, around the tiled walls of the bathroom and made a hasty exit. That left him and Tamsen. The unhinged look hadn't left her and he wondered if maybe he'd sent the wrong person out.

"Tams..." He spoke quietly in what he hoped was a reassuring tone. He'd not seen her this close to the edge before and was terrified of what she might do next. "Come and sit down with me." He held his hand out - tentatively, as you would trying to make the acquaintance of a vicious dog.

She stood gazing at him, as if she didn't recognize where she was or who she was looking at. He'd seen the look before, when she sat gazing at Gina's body in the bedroom. She seemed to be someplace else.

Her voice came to him in a monotone, as if from another planet. "I have to put Azzie in his box and we've got to go home. We can't stay here anymore."

He sat down on the velvet sofa under the turret window and patted the space next to him. Encouraging her away from the bathroom doorway. "Come sit with me, Tams. Bring Azzie too. We need to talk."

Almost in a dream, she walked and sat next to him. Ceaselessly her hand caressed the fur on the cat's back, an unconscious movement he'd witnessed hundreds of times. The simple gesture brought home to him Tamsen's loss.

Despite himself, he began to cry.

Something beautiful had broken today. Been irreparably destroyed. Not just the maimed animal Tamsen rocked in her arms - he had a sense of something larger at work in the cosmos, something dark and evil infiltrating his life. With no idea how to fight it, or what to do, he let the tears flow.

"I want to go home, Matt." Tamsen took great pains laying Azriel out in the cat cage. It was the least she could do. Visions of Gina's body leaving the apartment in that vile blue body bag came rushing back into her mind.

"I really don't think it's a good idea for you to be by yourself, Tams."

"Then you come and stay at my place. But I'm not staying another night here with your mother." Too exhausted to argue, she just wanted to get the hell out of this house.

Matt followed her out to the kitchen. She busied herself collecting all the vitamins and minerals she'd stashed in his pantry.

The look on his face told her there was more chance of Marguerite inviting her to stay in the family home in Sydney than there was of Matt staying the night at her place.

"You're still not over Gina dying in the apartment, are you?"

She watched him blush and then stammer. "Well..."

"Christ, Matt. For a Catholic you've got a real hang- up about death."

"That's not a great combination of words, you know." He sounded really uncomfortable. "Especially under the circumstances." He leaned against the kitchen bench and she had a sudden memory of the two of them, naked on that very spot. It seemed such a long time ago. "It's not so much my faith that's the problem - it's the way my mother indoctrinated it. I worked that much out when we were at the Cathedral." He shifted uncomfortably, "I know I have issued with mother, but if you'd just stay."

Her gut told her he wouldn't be coming, but her head held out anyway. "You won't talk me out of it, Matt. I wouldn't spend another night under the same roof as your mother if you paid me. And you should know she thinks I'm after your money anyway. Not that it appears you actually have any!"

"What do you mean?" He started fiddling with the espresso machine. "Can't we have a coffee and talk about this?"

"I'm not discussing it, Matt. I'm going home. Your mother's practically packed my cases, so if you'd just get your keys we can go."

"I'm not going anywhere until I've had a cup of coffee." He had a thunderous look on his face. "What has my mother been saying to you?"

"Nothing worth talking about."

"Tamsen! Stop avoiding the question and answer me." He added, almost as an afterthought, "Pass me a cup, would you?"

She turned on him, frustration and anger taking hold. She was tired of it all - him, his mother, the arguing, everything. "Sure."

The emerald green cup, complete with blue trim, left her hand and sailed straight over his right shoulder, hurtling missile-style through the glass window beyond. Shards of glass rained on the outdoor table, the cup skipping over its surface like a stone on a pond.

"Your fucking mother deliberately chased my cat outside. There was meat in that trap. She wasn't hunting frigging possums! The woman hates me. Wants me off the scene so you can get back with darling Angie. Well, newsflash - she's won. It's over! Take me home."

Matt's voice rumbled, low and controlled. "You could have just passed the cup."

She threw another one for good measure, taking out another pane of glass.

He seemed unfazed by her aggression. She found that more infuriating. "I won't let her chase you out of my home, Tamsen."

"There won't be much of it left, Matt, if you don't get me out of here. Besides, it's not your fucking home anyway! Is it, *Matty*?"

Plucking a crystal champagne flute from the cupboard, she dropped it on the tiled floor. It chimed musically before crashing into pieces at their feet. "All she has to do is call up your loans and you're out on your ass. Aren't you?"

"She told you that?"

"Are you taking me home yet?"

"There's plenty more crystal, and plenty more we have to talk about."

Tamsen swept her arm across the shelf the shattered flute had called home, its companions tumbling to the floor like little glass lemmings. The sound of smashing Stewart crystal filled the room.

Matt didn't flinch. He simply stepped gingerly across the ruins of his crystal flute collection, unhooked a coffee cup, and opened another couple of cupboard doors to reveal neatly stacked white china.

"There's a Royal Doulton dinner service here that might interest you. About 86 pieces or so. I'm sorry it's not a family heirloom so there won't be the emotional pain of attachment you're looking for, but it is certainly expensive. I hope it makes you feel better. When you've finished I'll be downstairs and we can talk."

He poured a coffee and left her to it. The unmistakable sound of quality china morphing into mosaics followed him down the stairwell.

CHAPTER TWENTY-ONE

Tamsen, still furious, took him at his word and completely destroyed the dinner set. When she finally stopped she felt a strange sort of camaraderie with the fractured glass and china strewn across the floor.

She carried her packed bags down to the car and left them with Azriel by the boot. However short of hot-wiring the car, a skill she'd not learned in this lifetime, she had to converse with Matt.

Sudden brainwave. Flicking through the numbers on her cellphone, she found the local taxi company and ordered a cab. Bugger the cost – she was in no mood to go crawling to him, she'd find the money - no way would she give his mother any opportunity to think she was a gold digger. Marguerite's stinging words came back and Tamsen felt hot tears prickling her eyes. Such a waste. A wonderful man like Matt bound to his mother in such a sick, dependent way.

Determination to never be bound to anyone like that overcame her. Independence was something Tamsen worked hard for. The fish business was going well but Gina had been right, her heart wasn't completely in it. The awful realization dawned. She could end up just like Matt - trapped in a life being run behind the scenes by somebody else. The thought made her physically ill.

A taxi pulled down the long driveway, the driver spotting her bags and clicking opening the boot as he came to a stop in front of her. Best she just got the hell out of Matt's life now, before she became even more attached and wasn't able to leave him.

"You want to put the cat on the backseat with you, miss?"

She couldn't help smiling; the driver clearly hadn't noticed Azzie was dead, not sleeping. "Yes, fine."

Tamsen watched Matt's turret window in the driver's side mirror as it faded from view. Ironic really - Marguerite had managed to kill her cat and her relationship in one afternoon.

Matt heard the door open and his spirit rose. She'd come to talk it out - a good sign. He'd been at a loss how to deal with her and his mother. Lots of loss around here at the moment, he mused.

"That good-for-nothing, gold-digging girl has gone, Matthew." Marguerite's harsh tone made him jump. "So you can stop hiding down here now!"

A searing bolt of hatred and anger roared through him and he rose from the couch, spinning on his heels, iron self-control holding his voice to a bare whisper. "Don't, Mother. Don't even begin to describe her that way."

"Matty, have you seen what she did to your kitchen? She trashed half your china and crystal. In fact, she is trash."

He'd never come so close to hitting a woman in his life. Well, aside from Tamsen the other night, but that was different. His mother should be glad he'd put the couch between them.

"If there's anyone here who is *trash-*" the word came out through clenched teeth "-then it's you. Take a look at yourself. All jewels and finery, yes. Everything perfect on the outside - but the inside? How the hell you have the gall to stand there and tell me the beautiful woman you've just driven out of my home and my life is trash is beyond me. I can't believe the lengths you've gone to in disrupting my life. I'm surprised you didn't just put a knife through the cat and have done with it."

He felt the years of rejection and torment rising from profound depths, spurred on by his frustration at it being Marguerite, not Tamsen, who stood in front of him. "Oh, but just killing Azriel wouldn't have put to use your years of acquired manipulative skills, would it, Mother?"

The color drained from Marguerite's face and she fidgeted with the large opal at her throat. "I was only protecting you, my darling. She was just after our money. You don't really think she loved you, do you? Not really. Not like Angie loves you."

"Angie doesn't love me, Mother. You love the idea of me marrying a diplomat's daughter. Advancing the family name. Love had nothing to do with it."

"But she's such a good match for you, darling." Marguerite inched closer, sensing his growing misery, his exhaustion from battle. As if she could smell blood. "That girl-"

"Tamsen, Mother. Her name is Tamsen."

"*Tamsen* is no good for you. She was just looking for what she could make from you and the family."

"Well, you told her I had no money. That the house belongs to you."

"It's the truth, and you know it's only for our protection, Matty. Your Father, bless his soul, didn't own any property either."

"Spare me the tax evasion lesson." He didn't owe his mother an explanation, but what the hell. "Tamsen doesn't need our money - she comes from a wealthy family. She wouldn't have needed to touch your precious trust funds."

He sank down, anxiety and grief getting the better of him at last. "And since we're into destroying relationships, I thought you should know that I'm resigning from the partnership and giving up law."

Marguerite steadied herself against the side of the couch; it almost looked as if she'd taken a physical blow.

"Matty, if you're trying to punish me, you don't need to do this."

"It's not about punishing you, Mother, I've been unhappy for a long time."

"It's that... that girl. She's put you up to this."

"I haven't breathed a word of this to Tamsen. I was going to tell her soon, but it looks like you've ruined that for me."

Marguerite reached over toward him, then withdrew her hand, thinking the better of it.

Something inside of Matt told him this was how it would be now. There would forever be a distance between them that couldn't be bridged. Relationships lay shattered, like the china and glass smashed on the floor upstairs.

Tamsen closed the apartment door behind her.

The whole place smelt wrong from the commercial cleaners. She checked Gina's room. Empty. No trace whatsoever of her friend, or that she'd killed herself, except for the lousy, heavy, claustrophobic atmosphere.

Tamsen shuddered. Gina's family had made short work of removing her belongings, the gaping space where the dining table and chairs used to be reminding her of their wonderful Tuesday dinners.

Everything about the apartment was tainted with memories of Gina, or Azzie or Matt. How to function here when everywhere she looked were reminders of what she'd lost? She and Matt weren't so different, Tamsen thought, he lived in his mother's home and she lived in her parent's apartment. An overpowering moment of intense, paralyzing despair passed through her body, a palpable ache in her heart.

Jolted out of her melancholy thoughts by the shrill ringing of the phone, she knew it would be him. The answer-phone could pick it up, though then he'd probably try her mobile.

As if one step ahead of her thoughts, her mobile started ringing. A blinking blue broken heart flashed at her with Matthew written underneath. They'd laughed when she loaded his numbers into her phone. He'd said he should have the broken heart icon because he was destined always to have his heart broken by beautiful women. She cried now. It seemed so prophetic.

Not up to conversation, she let the call go to voicemail.

Amidst exhaustion and grief, Tamsen pulled her brass sensor from the Goddess altar, located a small, round brick of charcoal and set to igniting it over the gas hob in the kitchen. It always fascinated her the way each block sparked, its saltpeter igniting, dragging heat and flame through the dense charcoal chunk. A mini Guy Fawkes display, complete with crackling.

She left the block to fully ignite on the sensor and located fresh coffee grounds and her supply of smudge. This was a ritual she performed often, clearing her home of negative energy. The bitter scent of burning coffee permeated every room as she walked with the sensor at arm's length, chanting positive affirmations of peace and love.

Then she retraced her steps with smudge - a mixture of dried lavender flowers, rose petals and rosemary – so the sickly scent filled the vacuum with soft, loving and cleansing smoke. Nature abhorred a vacuum. If she didn't refill it with something beautiful, another nasty would surely take up residence.

Her cleansing ritual complete, she settled into her own bed, a place she'd not been for over ten days. She loved her bed, but tonight it seemed isolating. She wanted to weep, yet just didn't have the energy. So many conflicting emotions had coursed through her in the last few hours; now she was numb and empty - a shallow caricature of her usual self.

She closed her sore eyes, relaxed into the warmth and comfort of her grandmother's bed, and waited for the sweet relief of sleep to take her.

"Danni!" Matt swore under his breath again. He couldn't find the bank documentation for the financing on the Sinclair deal. He'd barely scratched the surface of the franchise documents and was coming to the horrifying realization that financing for the purchase hadn't been completed, yet they were due to settle this afternoon. He was in deep shit.

"Danni! Where the-"

"Matt, please don't shout. I've got a screaming headache."

He gazed up from the mess on his desk. "You look like death." The vision of perfection, his Danni, had gone missing.

"You should try it from this side." She tried for a weak smile but it looked more like a grimace.

"Sit down, girl, before you fall down." He cast his mind back to this morning. She hadn't looked ill when she brought his coffee in, he was certain. "How long have you been feeling like this?"

"Just came on suddenly. I had a headache and an unbearably sore throat when I came in this morning but now I feel as if my entire body's on fire."

She was covered in sweat and he noticed her legs were trembling. With no warning she collapsed, sliding from the chair into a wrinkled heap on the floor, pretty much at his feet.

"Shit.

"Matt - " her voice was barely audible " - I feel real bad."

"Don't worry. I'll get help."

As Matt dialed for an ambulance it occurred to him there weren't many times in a lifetime when you had to call for urgent assistance. This was the second time in less than two weeks.

Matt tried hard not to think about Danni ensconced in isolation or her plaintive request in the ambulance that he confirm her will was up to date. He'd never seen anyone in such excruciating pain.

"There's really nothing else you can do for now, Mr Solomon." The officious looking nurse was, for the second time in less than half an hour, trying to convince him to leave the hospital. "Your employee's husband has been informed and is on his way to the hospital."

The nurse quickly clicked a mouse on a pad that he noticed was emblazoned with the District Health Board's logo. No wonder hospitals didn't run to budget if they were spending money on overprinted mouse pads.

"So I suggest you go back to work. I'm sure you're needed there." She looked up over the top of the latest slim-line monitor and gave him a dismissive look.

"You will inform me if there is any change to her condition?"

"We're not exactly sure what we're dealing with at the moment, Mr Solomon. But I can assure you, her husband will be kept fully up to date with any progress." She gave him another one of those looks that made him feel small. "Him being next-of-kin."

She was right – it was time for him to leave, he decided, before the temptation to shove her mouse where the sun didn't shine overtook him.

Tamsen couldn't understand it at all. Some voodoo curse perhaps? Or maybe she'd inadvertently hexed someone. Lord knows, she'd been tempted with Matt's mother.

She looked with some anguish at the last of the goldfish in the aquarium in Matt's foyer. The poor little guy was struggling to stay upright, swimming for dear life, the way fish do when there's little hope of making it through a few more hours. Her heart lay heavy in her chest.

Tamsen had already been filled in on the sorry aquarium history by Gina's replacement - a tall willowy blonde, heroin chic. The kind who should be traipsing catwalks in Milan, designer clothes hanging off her bones, and the latest electric pink blusher radiating from her high cheekbones. Her perfect teeth and impossibly high fuck-me heels were wasted on today's batch of pensioners sporting orthopedic underwear who lounged in reception.

She was still deciding whether or not to just pluck the poor dying creature from the aquarium and have done with it when Matt arrived. He was all she needed. She'd hoped to get in and out before running into him but the universe continued to crap on her.

"Tamsen. Thank God - a friendly face."

He looked pale, flustered and anxious. Not himself at all. "What's the problem?" Her concern for him, she realized, was genuine. No matter about his mother, her feelings for Matt hadn't changed. He was a victim of circumstances just as much as she. Besides - even after all they'd been through she still felt her heart lift at the sound of his voice.

He pulled her to him, hugging her. Her response to him - the scent and touch of him - was automatic. He said, "It's Danni. She's collapsed. She's in hospital in isolation. They've got no idea what's wrong with her. I don't know how I'm going to cope. I can't take much more, Tams."

"Is someone with her?"

He nodded. "Her husband arrived just before I left. He's going to keep me up to date with what's happening.

"Matt, you really look awful. Maybe you should go home." Although, she thought, with the mother from hell still in residence maybe that wasn't a great idea.

"No, I've got a deal here that's falling apart. But what I do need is coffee. I'll send out for a couple. Would you come down to my office where we can talk?"

She sorely didn't want to spend time with him, but the pleading look on his face and the horrible circumstances he found himself in made her accept. With a heavy heart she followed him down the corridor to his office.

"It's wall to wall paper in here." She couldn't help contrasting the everything-in-it's-place Matt she'd come to know and love with the mess she found herself standing in. "Is it always like this?"

Matt pulled another grim face. "Not normally. I just don't seem to have been able to get to grips with anything lately though Danni's been doing her best." He ran his finger around the neck of his shirt, trying to loosen the firm grip it had on his throat. A sign Tamsen associated with his feeling trapped - which seemed to be happening with monotonous regularity.

The emaciated receptionist arrived with two coffees and just as Matt gestured for her to put them on the desk his cell phone rang. He took the call, barely making more than a couple of grunting sounds.

Tamsen busied herself with the steaming coffee, conscious of her already increased caffeine intake and making a mental note to cut back. No wonder her anxiety levels were up. She sugared Matt's for him, out of habit more than anything else, and felt a small pang of grief tug at her heart.

What might have happened if everyone could have just left them alone to get on with it?

"That was Danni's husband."

Tamsen handed him the coffee and he instinctively reached for the sugar.

"I've sugared it for you."

He looked surprised. "Bless."

An awkwardness surfaced between them, and Tamsen felt the strain of not quite knowing how to behave around him anymore. She asked, "How's Danni?"

"She's in a coma."

"Oh, Matt." Tamsen was shocked. "That's terrible. Do they know what's wrong?"

If it was possible, Matt's features took on an even grimmer look. "I think you should sit down, Tamsen."

"Why?" She felt uneasy. Another life-changing moment bearing down, she just knew it.

Tamsen put her coffee down on a tiny piece of uncluttered desk. No need to compound a lousy situation by spilling coffee everywhere.

"The hospital has done blood tests. Danni's got a streptococcal A infection. Her internal organs are shutting down so they've given her massive doses of powerful antibiotics and put her into a drug-induced coma to give her body a chance to recover. However there's a good chance she might not come out of it."

"Oh, God! Oh, Matt! Why does this stuff keep happening?"

The look on his face was dire. He was nearly as pale as the foreboding piles of paper on his desk. "They think she picked it up from your aquarium, Tams."

"What? That's ridiculous!"

"Is it? Really? She's been pulling dead and dying fish from that aquarium for over a week now." He dropped his head in his hands; he seemed somehow battered, beaten even. "Fuck! It looks like I could be losing Danni as well."

"Matt..." There really wasn't a thing she could say. She didn't have a handle on life anymore. "If there's anything I can do."

"I really think you've done enough!" His angry tone jolted her out of her stupor.

Her own anger blazed, meeting his. "I don't think you can blame this on me!"

"I'm not blaming anyone, Tamsen. I just think you should go home."

"The aquarium?"

"Don't touch it. The health authorities are sending someone to take some samples. I think it's best that you go. Now."

From experience she knew it was useless to argue when he used that tone of voice. "I'll be at home. Just call me when you know something. Would you do that much for me?"

He nodded. "I'll let you know what's going on as soon as I hear."

Collecting her things from by the aquarium, Tamsen couldn't help noticing the little guy who had been struggling had died. Again, the decision had been taken out of her hands.

It wasn't lost on her that this was the fish she'd put in the aquarium the day she met Matthew.

CHAPTER TWENTY-TWO

Matt, in more shit than he cared to admit, was beginning to realize he didn't have a hope of arranging the financing for the Sinclair deal. He would have been pushing it uphill even with Danni on board. He needed time to think, but time was a scarce commodity.

The new girl on reception seemed next to useless, but continued copy-typing forms he'd drafted by hand. He'd forgotten how pedantic banks were about full disclosure information and hadn't drafted a trustee resolution in years. Talk about winging it.

"I can't read this word, Mr Solomon." Emily pointed to the page.

"It's 'insurance', Emily." How the hell had she'd gotten through secretarial college? He could barely keep a civil tone; it must have been the tenth or eleventh time she'd come back into his office over his handwriting. "The same as the one three lines above it."

"Oh. Yes, I see that now."

She scurried back down the hallway and Matt despaired. At this rate there wasn't a chance of him having the documentation in the bank's hands in time to meet settlement. He had barely an hour and needed an alternative plan. The trouble was, there wasn't one.

Tamsen's stomach lurched as she listened to the health official. "I see. You're sure about that now?"

She hadn't lost enough it seemed. A week after Danni's hospital admission she was out of the coma and making progress, but still very ill. Everything seemed surreal.

Tamsen stood in the remains of her flat. Packing cases were everywhere, and now her business being stripped from her too.

The official warbled on about safe and sanitary practice but she only listened out of a sense of duty. Really, it was all over. Packing up and running away. Nothing left here for her now.

"No, that's fine. I'll have someone supervise the closing down of the business. Really. You won't have to worry about it happening again." Her voice sounded like a stranger's, she'd become so disassociated from herself. Like this was all happening in someone else's life. Denial, she thought.

Tamsen sighed. Hopefully this was the last telephone discussion she'd have to have with anyone related to the Department of Health.

Gina's final gift.

Weed.

Weed that harbored a virulent strain of Strep A. Tamsen had felt like a witch faced with the Inquisition when the Department questioned her, expecting them to pull out branding irons or start shaving her head to check for marks of the devil. She shuddered, just thinking about it all.

It's behind you now, she reminded herself and turned her attention to the boxed contents of her life. Neatly stacked, all awaiting the removal men. Everything indexed and labeled for when she wanted to walk back into the trappings of a "normal" existence. Was there such a thing, she wondered. The only normal she knew was a setting on her washing machine.

A buzz from the intercom shattered her thoughts and announced the arrival of the carriers. Pressing the button to open the gate and let them in, she cast a glance again over the stacked boxes. Amazing how a life so out of control could look so organized and orderly when packed. Everything to be tidily stowed in a 12x12 storage shed. A sobering thought.

On the positive side, she felt lightness in her being she hadn't experienced for quite some time. An inner confidence that, stripped of material responsibilities and goods, she could take the time to go and find herself again. She'd spent far too much time looking after everyone around her, and in the process had lost her inner spark and flame. Her soul had gone walkabout.

Now the universe had issued its challenge and she was facing the demons come home to haunt her, squaring for the fight.

Opening the door, her eyes fell upon a young, virile, powerfully built

Maori boy. Obviously a great physique was the upside to humping furniture all day for a living. His deep brown eyes shone, evoking a spirit of youth and hope - of a soul that hadn't yet been bruised and jaded by life.

"Hi. We've come for your stuff." Direct and to the point, she liked that.

She liked even more when something inside of her stretched, as if her soul were warming itself, basking in the heat of adolescence and optimism, and the marvel of living.

Wonder Boy strolled past her - a lolling gait, almost like a puppy who hadn't quite grown into its legs yet. He loaded a couple of boxes on his trolley and flashed her a smile. "Shouldn't be too long," he said as he headed for the front door.

"Not a worry. I'm on my way now. Just close the door behind you when you've got everything."

Wonder Boy looked perplexed. "Youse not going to stay? Check up on us? Make sure none'a the boys take off with anything?"

Tamsen smiled. She'd lost so much; a few trinkets in boxes didn't seem to matter much anymore. "I'm sure you can be trusted."

After one last look at the apartment, she walked out the door, trying hard not to burst into tears. Everything that had ever held her here had gone, but that still didn't make it any easier to walk away.

She stood waiting for the lift, tears streaming down her face, visions flooding her mind of the happy times she'd experienced here. For the past week, every time the lift doors opened she still expected Gina or Azzie to materialize and bounce down the hallway. Stifling another sob, she decided to take the stairs.

Sleeping wasn't an option. No matter how still he lay, no matter how many times he closed his eyes and willed the tormented thoughts running through his head to cease and desist, they didn't. Matt had probably the only bright idea he'd had in ages and he needed to talk to someone.

He'd told Marguerite he was giving up the law, but without any real idea of what he'd do instead. Then it came to him.

The only person he wanted to talk to about his epiphany wouldn't take his calls.

He rummaged through his briefcase for the pre-paid mobile he used occasionally, she wouldn't know the number. Magic.

He dialed Tamsen's number and prayed she would pick up the phone.

"Tamsen speaking."

"Tams, please don't hang up."

"Matt?" She sounded confused. "Where are you calling from? This isn't your number."

Bingo. "Never mind. Please don't hang up - I need to talk to you."

"There's not a lot left to say, Matt."

"Everyone thinks I've done an idiotic thing, but I know you'll understand."

"You've done a lot of idiotic things lately, Matt. Is this a new one, or an old one you're revisiting?"

If he weren't so desperate he'd have tackled her about her tone of voice, but he was tired – and, though he hated to admit it, scared. "I've abandoned my career."

"What? Anything to do with me putting one of your workers in hospital with a life-threatening Strep A infection?"

"Tamsen, don't be trite."

"I'm not being *trite,* Matt - I nearly killed someone."

"It wasn't your fault. We've been over this."

"Try telling her husband that. What's the prognosis? Ahh, wait a minute. At least twelve months recuperating, steroid treatment... For fuck's sake, Matt, she's not even well enough to get out of bed yet and it's been two weeks."

"It wasn't your fault."

"We'll agree to disagree."

He hated the way she sounded, full of despair and self-loathing. If anyone should be feeling like that, he should. "I've given the firm notice. I'm leaving."

"What?"

"You heard."

"You can't do that."

"I did."

"But the law's your life."

"No, it's my mother's life. You're my life, Tamsen, and I want to be with you."

"Oh, fuck, Matt. You idiot."

"That's not what I want to hear. You're supposed to be overjoyed and say you want to spend the rest of your life with me."

The line fell silent. He pulled the phone away from his ear. Yes, the seconds were still ticking away; at least she hadn't hung up the phone on him."

"Can I come and see you?" He desperately wanted her to say yes. "I just want it to be like it was before. You know..."

She sighed. "Yeah. I know."

"So can I?"

"Can you what?"

"Come over and see you."

"No, Matt. Er, I'm not at home."

Oh shit. His heart sank and his stomach lurched up to meet it. He'd just declared his undying love and she'd met someone else.

"Where are you?"

"At the airport."

He didn't know whether to be relieved or angry. Fury won.

"What the fuck are you doing at the airport? Running away, I suppose."

"If you're going to use that tone of voice I'll hang up.

He didn't want her to do that. "Sorry."

"I'm not running away. I just need some time to regroup."

"You could regroup here. I could help."

"You've got enough crap of your own to deal with, and it sounds like you've just added to the load."

She wasn't wrong there. "Tams, please don't go. We've been through so much." He hated begging.

"Everything's in storage. I need to get away." She added, almost as an afterthought, "Not from you, Matt."

His stomach had a moment of respite from the gripping fear.

"From everything. Mum and Dad have gone septic. I've maybe got a chance at last to work out what I want to do with my life but they've cut me off. Told me they won't finance me into anything else if I go. So I'm on my own."

Just as Tamsen had said Marguerite had threatened to do to him. The irony wasn't lost on Matt. "My mother's already told me she'll disown me."

"Do you believe her?"

"No. But it doesn't matter. We've got an old dilapidated beachfront place up north, on an island. Dad put it in Trust for me years ago. Mom hated him going up there. Come with me. We can start again - just you and me.

There was silence on the line again.

A single tear trickled down his face. The best thing that had ever happened to him was slipping through his fingers and there wasn't a damn thing he could do about it.

"I have to go, Matt."

"Promise me you'll come back. You know I love you, Tams."

"I'm not disappearing off the face of the earth. Just going away for a while. It's for the best, Matt - you know that. Deep down, if you look, you'll know."

Now he did weep. Tears running down his face. He wanted to sob, big, like a child under the bedcovers when no one knew.

"If I got in the car and drove to the airport now could I stop you going?"

Her voice softened. "No. I have to do this, Matt. For me."

She paused and he heard her take a deep breath. "I love you, Matt. I love you like I've never loved anyone before. You've mined emotions from me I didn't even know existed. You've brought sunshine into my life, shown me things about myself I would never have seen before. Taught me to think, to stand on my own, fight my own battles. But you've brought dark things into my life too. I feel as if I've been disassembled in the last few weeks. I have to go away and put myself back together. Rebuild and replenish."

"We could do that rebuilding together." It sounded lame even to him.

"No, Matt. This is something I have to do alone and so do you. I love you. Bye."

"Aren't you even going to tell me where you're going?" Now he was desperate.

"I haven't decided. I'll call or email when I get there. Take care of yourself, Matt."

The line went dead and he broke down.

Tamsen closed her eyes. She would not cry. She turned off her cellphone. If he called again her resolve would crumble. Deep breaths. Breathe, dammit. She could breathe through the pain.

It was the downside of loving, the pain that inevitably came - as if God decided the ledger had to be balanced somehow. For all the pleasure Matt had brought her there needed to be an equal measure of pain. No way out but through, her therapist had told her. Though there was no escaping the fact - through sucked.

Digging her fingernails into her palms - the physical pain her great antidote to emotional pain - she looked up at the departure board. Letters tumbled down the wall, clattering in some macabre yellow-and-black fountain, full of promise of exotic places she could escape to.

She couldn't do it. Why would she walk away from the best thing that had happened to her? How could she leave him now? He'd just asked her to live on an island with him. She could almost hear Gina whispering, *'an island for your retreat'*. She'd never told Matt about her dream. Had this been Gina's doing all along?

Groping for her cellphone Tamsen turned it back on and hit reply.

"*Tamsen?*" He sounded stunned. Best be quick, before she lost her nerve.

"I'll do it." Her heart pounded in her chest.

"What?"

"Run away with you to your island."

"Really?"

"Yes," better solidify the deal, "we can make a new life together."

"You really think so?" She heard hope in his voice and it warmed her through.

"Matt. I know so. I've never wanted to be with anyone else the way I want to be with you. But there's something else I need."

"I'll get you a kitten, I promise, I'll even learn to love it."

She laughed. "A kitten would be nice, but that wasn't what I had in mind."

"Children?" Now she could hear the fear in his voice.

"Maybe, one day. But we'd have to get married first."

"Is that a proposal?"

"Might be." She couldn't help teasing him. She loved him. "I never told you, I've always wanted to run a retreat."

"The island's perfect for that." She could hear the palpable relief in his voice. "Well, once we've fixed it up a bit."

"I guess it's settled then. You better get down here and pick me up," she couldn't help adding as an afterthought, "before I change my mind again."

"Sit down. No, don't move. I'm on my way."

Pulling herself up to her full five feet two inches, Tamsen picked up her bag and headed for the nearest exit and the start of their new life, together.

<<<The End >>>

PRIVATE LOVE IN A PUBLIC PLACE

Mags O'Brien lives on the alcohol-soaked, drug-enhanced concert circuit, managing out-of-control rocker Julian MacAvoy. She helps him spread his musical gospel to his adoring followers, despite the fast-spinning turnstile on his bedroom door, and the broken hearts he leaves in his wake.

Mags believes she's immune to Julian's magnetic personality but when controversy hits the tour, she finds herself in danger of falling at his feet, slave to his appetites and her own desire and need.

Julian refuses to be tamed, but the pressure of the ravenous crowds clamps tighter and tighter around him. His chaotic world starts to crumble when he realizes his motivation to continue touring comes from an unobtainable woman. Can he force her to make the agonizing choice between himself and her estranged husband?

An erotic and candid look at life on the road.

Praise for PRIVATE LOVE IN A PUBLIC PLACE:

I'm a huge fan of Rock&Roll love stories.This one rates right up there with Olivia Cunning's "Sinners" & "Sole Regret" and "FitzWilliam Darcy". I can't wait for the 2nd book to come out in April! This story has it all... Heartbreak, Steamy but Very Real love and really tough choices. At one point, I cried like a baby and in the next, I was yelling at my KindleFire. LoL...
Bottom line- Totally worth adding this book to your collection!
(Amazon)

Sexy and gritty, raw and engaging, "Private Love in a Public Place" takes you on a personal behind-the-scenes tour of a rock star's life on the road from the perspective of his manager, a woman who loves the artist as much as she loves the man himself. ... This is a fresh, steamy and surprising love story guaranteed to entertain!
(Amazon)

Mags is open and real, a woman I could relate too in a job many of us would see as glamorous (manager to a rock star or babysitter perhaps) but which she made very real, faults and all. Jules is that mix of arrogant tosser and little boy lost, who you can't help but fall in love with. A rock star who shows us he's human.

If this is Ms. Kenyon's first book, I can't wait to read more of her work.

(Amazon)

THE FAN

Did you enjoy PRIVATE LOVE IN A PUBLIC PLACE? Are you hanging out for Book 2 of the series?

Want to know what really went on between Jules, Barbie and Young Elvis? Pick up THE FAN - a short erotic romp - written for those of you who desperately need to know what happened in *that bathroom*!

RETURN TO ALA MOANA BEACH

Ty Carter's an expert bomb disposal technician who doesn't take anything lying down. But a bullet to the back cuts short his tour in Iraq, returning him to a wife who he believes deserves more than half-a-man as a husband.

Lulu Carter wants nothing more than the man she married to come home. Instead, an injured and disturbed stranger turns life upside down for her and their children.

Only Ty and Lulu can decide if the love they shared is worth fighting for and whether they should stay married after such a traumatic event.

A Personal Message from Toni Kenyon:

I love writing books! But even more than that I love hearing from my readers. If you've enjoyed this book, or any other of my books, please take a moment to email me and introduce yourself - I always respond personally to my readers.

I would also love you to join my book club so you receive notifications about future books, updates and contests. I promise you won't be inundated!

Please visit www.tonikenyon.com and introduce yourself so I can personally thank you for trying my books.

Romance from Toni Kenyon - a fresh look at the world

ABOUT THE AUTHOR

Toni Kenyon lives in Auckland, New Zealand with her husband (and their dog and cat) - the goldfish is just squatting! She writes romance by day, sings in a band by night and in her spare (yeah, right) time, she wrangles difficult heroes into line so they can star in her next novel. Toni loves to hear from readers. Pop on over and say 'Hi' any time, she loves company. When she's procrastinating you'll find her lurking on Facebook.

Links:

Web: www.tonikenyon.com

Facebook: www.facebook.com/Toni.Kenyon.author

Twitter: @Toni_Kenyon

Goodreads: www.goodreads.com/Toni_Kenyon

Instagram: www.instagram.com/toni_kenyon

www.ingramcontent.com/pod-product-compliance
Lightning Source LLC
Chambersburg PA
CBHW072230170626
46813CB00003B/1159

* 9 7 8 0 9 9 2 2 5 1 8 1 9 *